His naked body twitched, suspended high in the air. His arms remained out to the sides, his legs dangling loosely below him. His chin dropped to his chest. For a few long moments, Patty could only hear the animal-like growls of his breathing. He didn't move.

Carl's left leg trembled. A crack of splintering bone suddenly exploded into the silence and Carl's leg snapped backward, the knee joint bending the wrong way. And somehow he laughed and screamed at the same time.

"Oh God..." she whimpered, tugging on a t-shirt, fighting her way into jeans, shoes. Another crack, and then horrible splintering sounds as his right leg shattered.

Carl screamed again, forcing Patty's attention back to him, and she saw claw marks appearing in the middle of his chest, down his stomach. She heard the sound of him coming apart, a wet unzipping of his flesh.

His eyes, cloudy with death, looked through her. And even as he screamed, the thing inside him forced his mouth to move into a smile.

~from *Dominion*

Abominations

Rebecca Brock

This collection is dedicated to my mother, Leah, and my brothers, Matt and Dave, who have always supported me.

I also want to thank Erich and Antoinette Lubatti for their friendship and willingness to read my stuff. Mucho, mucho appreciado, guys.

I wish my dad could have seen this.

http://www.myspace.com/pb_writer
http://www.authorsden.com/rebeccabrock

ISBN-10: 0615164471
ISBN-13: 978-0615164472

Table of Contents

Charlie

Charlie could feel the back of his neck tightening, cooking under the fierce noonday sun. He worked silently—bend over, grab the rock, toss it onto the wheelbarrow, move on—and tried to think of what he wanted to do once the field was cleared out and he'd have the rest of the afternoon to relax. More than anything, he wanted to go swimming up at Poppaw's Creek. He wanted to float around in an inner tube and doze in the sun and pretend that he was anywhere but Kansas.

But first, he had to help Pop clear the field. Last season they'd missed some rocks and busted up the plow, so this year Pop was determined they'd get every last stone, even if it meant crawling through a hundred acres of fields on hands and knees, picking them up one at a time. It was boring, backbreaking work, and every time Charlie tossed another stone into the wheelbarrow, it made him that much more determined that he wasn't going to end up like his Pop, trapped on a farm and getting old before his time.

"Smells like your Momma's frying chicken," Pop said as he straightened up, wiping dirty hands on the seat of his denims. "You about ready to pack it up for today?"

Charlie could already feel the cool water of Poppaw's Creek. "Yes, sir."

"Go on and take that wheelbarrow out to the..." Pop's voice trailed away as he looked over Charlie's shoulder. "What the hell...?"

The look on Pop's face made Charlie's stomach feel suddenly hollow. He turned around to see what had spooked him so badly. A half dozen men and women stood at the edge of the field a few hundred yards away, just watching them.

"What's wrong with them?" Pop put his hand on Charlie's shoulder, squeezing hard. "Good Lord…is that Robert Elkins out there?"

Charlie nodded, stunned into silence. That *was* Robert Elkins, but something very bad had happened to his face. Blood covered his mouth and jaw, soaked the front of his bib overalls. He was hurt bad…so how was he managing to just stand there at the edge of the field?

The others with him were also covered in blood. Even as far away as Charlie stood, he could hear the buzz of flies swarming around the group. An old woman stood beside Robert, swaying unsteadily on her feet. Her bloody robe gaped open in the front, revealing pale, sagging flesh and wisps of gray pubic hair. It took Charlie a minute to recognize that it was Mrs. Olson, who taught Sunday school at First Freewill Baptist and played the organ during revival nights.

So wrong. Everything was suddenly so wrong.

"Maybe they need help…" Pop started to walk towards them, but Charlie grabbed his arm. Pop stopped, suddenly unsure. Charlie knew that everything in his father was telling him to go help those people. They were people he had known for most of his life.

But Charlie had a feeling that if Pop went to them, he wouldn't ever come back. Too much felt wrong.

"I think we need to go," Charlie said softly, pulling his father back a few steps. "Come on, Pop."

Pop allowed himself to be led through the field, never looking away from the people at the edge. That felt wrong to Charlie, too. Any other time, Pop would have argued, would have fought to go help his friends and handed Charlie his ass for daring to tell him what to do. Pop never liked being told what to do by anybody.

But instead, he allowed his sixteen year old son to lead him back through the corn field, like he was the child. And that just wasn't right at all.

The house looked a million miles away. Charlie saw his mother come out on the porch, holding a dishtowel in her hands. She stared out at the edge of the field with the same look of astonishment as Charlie's father.

Charlie couldn't help it. He looked behind them. Now there were a dozen people. And they were moving into the field. Toward the house.

Charlie recognized more of them. Sara Tyler, the homecoming queen at the high school, who now wore a bloody, torn nightgown and stumbled like she had been drinking. Mrs. Thomas, Charlie's sixth grade teacher, who always waddled when she walked. Ned Anderson, Pop's best friend who had served with him in Vietnam. Bobby Carlyle, the smartest guy in Charlie's class, who was planning on going to med school.

All of them stood in the field, covered with blood, moving in slow jerks and hitches.

No way they could be alive. Not with that much blood on them.

Charlie dragged his father up the steps of the front porch, pushing him into the house. They had to get inside. Maybe in the basement. Pop had planned for the end of the world for the last twenty years. He'd fortified the basement against everything but a direct nuclear strike. All they had to do was lock the doors and keep the people out and maybe then they'd be okay until the police could come.

His mother remained at the front steps, watching the slow-moving crowd. Charlie went back to her, touched her shoulder softly. Mom was skittish even in the best of times, so high-strung that sometimes she could only relax if she recited Bible verses under her breath. She'd been raised in the church, and she was firmly convinced that the answer to every problem in life could be found within the pages of the Bible.

Charlie heard her murmuring the Lord's Prayer now, chanting it over and over in a whisper.

"Mom...go inside."

She didn't move. Didn't look away from the shapes in the field. "It's the End Times, Charlie."

Charlie didn't respond. He'd heard the routine before, every time Mom watched the news…or sometimes even the Weather Channel, if she was feeling especially apocalyptic. Every war was a sign out of Revelations. Every tornado or hurricane foretold God's wrath and the Second Coming. After a while, he had managed to tune it out, nodding at the appropriate moments and making respectful sounds of agreement.

Now, though…now he was afraid his crazy mother was finally right.

He pulled her inside and slammed the front door, locking it.

The living room was dim and cool, the smell of fried chicken still hanging in the air. Just a half hour ago, life was normal. Charlie was going to eat chicken and then meet his friends at the creek and spend the rest of the day swimming and drinking whatever beer Eddie Joe could steal from his father's garage fridge.

That wasn't going to happen now. And somehow, Charlie knew in his heart that it would never happen again. Everything had changed.

His mother collapsed on the couch, gathering Charlie's baby sister, Nora, onto her lap. She was only three, too little to understand what was happening, but old enough to sense their fear. She started crying uncontrollably, with such a miserable hopelessness that it was all Charlie could do to not join her.

Charlie's father turned on the television set as Charlie moved to the window. Those people were still out there in the cornfield, moving closer and closer to the house.

"It's the End Times," Mom mumbled over and over again. "Jesus is coming…it's the end of the world…the End Times…"

Nora hid her face against her mother's shoulder, crying quietly now, already exhausted.

"Be quiet, Martha." Charlie's father opened the closet door and began yanking boxes and coats out of his way. Charlie knew what he was looking for. A few seconds later he had the shotgun in his hands, loading it with a few shells he'd found. "Charlie, you go get the extra shells outta my bedroom. Hurry it up, boy."

Charlie moved without hesitation, taking the stairs two at a time. His father kept the shells in his bedroom, in the top drawer of his nightstand. He knew exactly where they were, because his father had threatened to tan his ass if he'd ever touched them. The window on the upstairs landing was open, a hot breeze billowing his Mom's best lace curtain, and Charlie peered out to the fields again. He had to see. He had to be sure.

They were still out there, still standing in the cornfield, still circling the farmhouse. Charlie could still hear his Mom's mutters and prayers and his Pop yelling for her to shut up. Both of them sounded equally crazy. Charlie counted a dozen people out there, with more wandering down the dirt road that led to their driveway. They moved funny, like they'd been drinking for days and couldn't remember how to keep their balance. Some of them were almost naked, like whatever had happened to them happened so quickly, so unexpectedly, that they hadn't even known what had hit them.

Charlie wondered what was happening in town. And he wondered what the people outside would do once they got to the front door.

The thought shook him out of his trance and drove him into his parents' bedroom. He pawed through the nightstand drawer, vaguely surprised to find condoms and a few porno magazines, but he finally found the box of shells.

And it was empty.

Charlie suddenly remembered going quail hunting with his dad a few months before. Just like with all of his father's other hunting expeditions, they hadn't bagged anything, but it had been a good trip. His dad had even let him take a few sips of beer, laughing about how he'd always liked to go drinking and hunting with his own father.

They'd used all the shells. No one had thought to buy more.

"Charlie!" Pop's voice sounded even louder in the quiet of the house. "Forget about them shells and get your ass down here!"

Charlie didn't like what he heard in his father's tone. He sounded scared, and nothing ever scared Pop. He'd fought in Vietnam, survived two years as a POW. He'd told Charlie all the stories and showed him all the scars. He'd even run into a burning house when he was a little kid and saved his two little brothers. Nothing ever scared him. Nothing.

Charlie stopped at the window again before going downstairs. More of them out in the field, moving closer and closer to the house. His stomach flip-flopped, cramping low in his gut as he thought of his father being so scared. His dad couldn't be scared like that. Pop had to be brave so the rest of them could be brave. Otherwise, they were all lost.

He ran back into the living room to see his father standing behind his beat-up recliner, the shotgun hanging loose in his arms. He stared at the television, and the look on his face was that of total defeat. Charlie had seen that look on his own face during football halftimes, when he knew they were going to lose the game and there was nothing he'd be able to do to stop it. His father looked totally defeated, like a man who knew he had no other choice but to give up and surrender. That scared Charlie more than anything else he had seen that day.

Until he looked at the TV. Then he knew why his father looked like he wanted to die.

Somehow, on a spring Saturday with a sky so blue and endless it was like being able to peek into Heaven itself, the world was ending. The President and half the cabinet had died on Air Force One when one of the President's handlers suffered a heart attack and died...and then came back. A reporter had been on board, and every bit of the carnage had been beamed back down to CNN. The guy who had died started attacking everyone within reach. The Secret Service hadn't been able to scoot the President out of there fast enough. His death—

his disembowelment at the hands of one of his most trusted advisors—was caught live on tape.

Charlie watched the footage in silence. The television sound was turned low; all he could hear was the sound of his mother's sobs and his father's labored breathing.

And the moans of the people outside. It sounded like Hell out there.

Charlie couldn't move. He was only dimly aware that his father was pushing a heavy wooden secretary in front of the front door. He couldn't look away from the television. The President's death was triggering a chain reaction of events, each one worse than the last. There were reports of people going crazy, attacking each other, eating each other in every state, in every country. Whatever was happening, it was happening fast. No one wanted to actually come out and say it, but as impossible as it seemed, the dead were coming back to life.

His mother started praying again, louder this time, when the news reported that the Vatican—in fact, the entire Holy City—had been overrun by the dead. One of the last video images coming out of the country had been of the Pope standing unsteadily on his balcony, presiding over a mass of walking corpses in St. Peter's Square. Charlie couldn't tell if he was alive or not. He guessed it probably didn't matter.

"Oh, my God…Reverend Toney's out there." Charlie's father stood to the side of the window, peering out like a Peeping Tom. "Jesus Christ…"

Charlie went to the side window. They were coming from all directions, moving so horribly slowly.

"What do you think they want?" Charlie asked quietly, not really expecting an answer. The muted panic of the news reports was filling in the blanks. The infected people were attacking the living. Killing them. Eating them.

That couldn't happen here, could it? These were people that they knew. Friends. Neighbors. They wouldn't hurt them.

Charlie turned back to face his parents. His father collapsed in his easy chair in front of the TV, dropping as silently and bonelessly as a corpse. He kept watching the frantic footage on TV, his eyes glazing as image after image of bloody violence flickered across the screen. The news out of New York was nightmarish, the entire city under attack with millions already dead. There was perverse footage from a family on vacation at an amusement park in Florida, who videotaped a guy in a blood-stained mouse costume tearing the throat out of a little girl. The film came from everywhere, from everyone.

It was the end of the world.

Charlie closed his eyes, unable to watch anymore. He went back to the picture window, hiding behind the curtains. They were almost to the front porch, scuffling through the dirt patches in the yard. Jenny Flanders, the little girl who lived on the next farm over, blindly bumped into the tire swing hanging from the ancient oak tree in the front yard. Charlie couldn't be sure, but it looked as if her lower jaw was gone.

Whatever was happening in the rest of the world was happening there, too.

His mother's voice sounded like a little girl's as her prayers droned on and on, one long breath of "Our Fathers" and "Hail Marys." Charlie kept staring at the growing crowd in the yard. Their moans were even louder than before. And now he could smell them, like roadkill that had baked in the sun.

They were getting ready to do something. Something awful. Something final. Something that his father's shotgun and his mother's prayers couldn't stop.

"We have to run…" Charlie whispered, throat so dry with terror that each word felt like a razor scratching from the inside. He couldn't look away from the advancing crowd, afraid that if he did, they would somehow rush the house.

"It's no use." His father's voice was hopeless, the voice of a man who knew he was already dead. "You saw the TV. There ain't no running from this."

Charlie let the curtains fall back into place as he turned around again. Pop had that crazy look in his eye, the look he sometimes got when he had nightmares about Vietnam and couldn't come all the way out of them. He stood up and pointed the gun at Charlie's mother, the nose of the shotgun wavering for only a moment.

Mom stopped praying and looked up at him, crushing Nora close to her chest. Charlie crazily realized that she had never looked prettier than she did at that instant, with her eyes shining and blue and her cheeks flushed pink. He saw the horror in her eyes fade away, replaced with a dull acceptance as she gazed up at her husband.

"It's the End Times…" she whispered. "Send me to Heaven, Mitch. Send me to be with Baby Jesus…"

Charlie didn't want to watch it. He knew what was going to happen, knew but couldn't believe his father was actually going to do it. It was a bad dream, a nightmare like nothing he had ever known before. It had to be. It couldn't be happening.

Mom carefully slid Nora off her lap, keeping her eyes on Pop even though Nora screamed to be held again. Charlie watched his mother's face as she silently spoke to his father, twenty years of marriage leading up to this moment.

She nodded, the movement so slight that Charlie almost didn't see it.

Pop pulled the trigger.

Her body managed to stay up for a moment before pitching sideways into the couch, scarlet blood soaking into the blue and white gingham. Pop had aimed for her head, but his hands had been shaking too badly. He hit her square in the chest instead. There was a hole now where her heart had once been.

Nora sat frozen, her wails finally silenced as she stared at Mom's body. Pop reloaded the shotgun, never looking away from

Nora. Charlie wanted to scream, wanted to stop him, but he couldn't move. He couldn't believe what he had just seen, what he was about to see.

His father's eyes were far away, already trapped in an endless hell.

"C'mere, baby…" He held his hand out to Nora. "Come on…Daddy'll take care of you."

Nora clung to her mother's housedress. She started screaming again, breathy high-pitched yelps that sounded like a dying puppy. The sound riled up the people outside, and their moans grew louder, more desperate.

Pop took Nora's hand and led her to an armchair. Nora crawled onto the seat with her usual clumsiness, and somehow seeing that—seeing her struggle to lift herself onto the cushions just the way she always did—snapped Charlie out of his shock.

"Put the pillow over your head, baby," Pop said quietly. "We'll play peek-a-boo, just you and me. Cover your head…"

Nora curled up in a tight little ball, tugging one of Mom's hand-embroidered pillows closer. Charlie could remember watching his mother stitch that pillow when she was pregnant with Nora, remembered how she had wondered if she'd put too many lambs on the green field. Nora whimpered and mewled and pulled it over her head, muffling her cries.

Pop pressed the barrel of the shotgun against Nora's back.

"It's better this way…" he whispered. "I won't go back in the hole…they can't do it to me again…not again…"

He pulled the trigger before Charlie could scream for him to stop.

Nora stopped crying.

Charlie choked, gagging on the sudden bile rising in this throat. Footsteps pounded on the loose boards of the front porch. They were just outside the door now.

He couldn't look at Nora, couldn't look at his father. He heard the click of another shell loaded into the chamber and felt his entire body shaking, jerking, trembling uncontrollably as he fell to his knees and waited for the explosion.

"Do you know what they did to me, back in 'Nam?" Pop's voice was as raw as an open wound. Charlie raised his gaze to him and saw a monstrous stranger. It wasn't the same man who had taught him to throw a football or took him out driving in the pick-up. It wasn't the same man who had dressed up as Santa Claus every Christmas and hid colored eggs every Easter.

"Pop, don't do this..."

"They put me in a pit, a fucking pit, with the guys they'd already killed. I ate bugs for a long time...and then I ran out of bugs and..."

Charlie stared at his father, watching him relive that awful time, and suddenly understood why he had the nightmares, why he went to church, why he never tried to actually kill anything when he went hunting.

"There's nothing we can do." Pop's chest heaved as if he couldn't take a deep breath. He fell to his knees, eyes fixed on the shadows passing just outside the picture window. "What they'll do to us...it'll be worse. You saw the TV. It's over now."

Pop raised the shotgun. Fitted the barrel in the hollow of his own throat. He had to stretch to reach the trigger, but he managed it.

"I've only got one shell left," he said, his eyes finally finding Charlie again. For a moment—a horrible, comforting moment—he saw his father again. "Please forgive me, son...I just can't..."

He blinked, and then his head disappeared in a fine mist of red.

There was a moment of perfect, terrible silence following the explosion. Charlie watched the lump of his father's body thud to the floor, his blood soaking into the antique Persian rug his mother had been so proud of.

Every person he loved was gone. In the space of five minutes, they were just…gone.

A window shattered behind him, followed by a crash of splintering wood.

Charlie turned around just as old Mr. Lohman staggered into the living room, trailing ropy lengths of intestines from the hole in his gut. His cold stare fell on Charlie and he roared, as if calling the others.

Charlie backed away. Another crash of glass from the back door.

They were inside.

Sobbing, Charlie ran to the kitchen, skidding to a stop at the sight of Maryanne Kovis and Jimmy Snider standing in front of the fridge. The last time Charlie had seen them had been at school, making out in the back seat of Jimmy's Mustang. Like every other guy in his class, he'd been envious of Jimmy's luck.

Now, Maryanne's clothes were in shreds, exposing what little remained of her breasts. Charlie saw teeth marks in her gray skin. Jimmy's lips had been torn off his face, taking half his chin and throat as well. Their eyes were clouded, silver-white and flat.

When they saw Charlie, they lunged at him, mouths wide.

Charlie didn't think. He yanked open the cellar door and ducked inside just as Maryanne and Jimmy fell against the door. Pop had been overly paranoid about safety and installed half a dozen locks on the inside, just in case they had to take shelter in the cellar during a tornado or a nuclear attack.

Charlie hit all the locks in less than ten seconds. The door was steel, special-ordered a long time ago. Fireproof. Blastproof. It would stand up to their fists. And unless they remembered how to use tools, the door wouldn't be coming down any time soon.

The cellar was dark but silent. Empty. Pop had bricked up the outside door and all the windows for extra safety. He was sure that one president or another would hit the big red button and bring down the nukes.

That felt like a million years ago. A trivial worry from a time long past. No one would be dropping any nukes anytime soon. No one would be doing anything anytime soon.

Charlie knew there was food down in the cellar. Jars of stuff that his mother had put up during canning season. Jugs of water from the well out back. He might be able to get by for a while before running out.

The things on the other side of the door seemed to redouble their efforts to get in, their moans angry yet pathetic, more of them now than before.

How long would they stay out there, he wondered. Would they lose interest in him? Forget he was there? Wander away in search of fresh meat?

Or were they as single-minded and determined as he suspected they might be? Maybe they'd just wait him out.

Charlie curled into a corner of the landing and wrapped his arms around his knees, sobbing into his t-shirt. He was supposed to be at Poppaw's Creek right now. Mom was supposed to be reading her Bible before her Bible Study class and Nora was supposed to be playing with her dolls in the yard and Pop was supposed to be drinking a beer and watching baseball and everybody was supposed to be alive and okay and not lying dead in the living room while strangers wandered through the house.

"I want to wake up now," Charlie whispered. He clenched his fists, drawing half-moons of blood in his palms. "This isn't happening. Please God...don't let this be happening..."

God didn't hear him, but the things on the other side of the door did. They scratched at the door, their voices bleeding together into one horrible, unending moan. Small fingers poked beneath the gap at the bottom of the door, desperately feeling for him. Charlie saw a Scooby-Doo bandage on one of the fingertips.

He remembered putting a bandage on Nora's hand when she picked up a splinter from the front porch. She'd cried until she saw the special bandage, and then they'd laughed and had ice cream before dinner and watched "Sponge Bob" and everything was okay again.

Nora.

Charlie covered his head with his arms and wept.

And wished there had been just one more shell.

Love Story in 7G

It started, as all great loves do, with a kiss. The fact that the recipient of the kiss had long since shuffled off this mortal coil was of little consequence. She was young, she was beautiful, and she was well loved by Murray Kindlebaum. Being dead was just a small flaw he could learn to live with. No one was perfect, after all.

But that was nothing for lovers to dwell upon. He gazed at her face, so perfectly serene, and felt his heart swell with his love for her. He had named her Jeannie, after his mother, and she was by far the most beautiful Jeannie yet. Her hair, flecked with leaves and bits of grass like that of a wood nymph's, flowed like molten gold over the crook of his arm as he held her. He'd carefully cleansed the mud and blood from her face and body, but left her hair as it was. It made her look wild, untamed. And he liked that. He really liked it.

Murray leaned forward, gazing at the sweep of her lashes over her high cheekbones, smiling at the faint scar curving from the corner of her mouth. She was lovely, but flawed. Just as they all were. But that didn't matter. Not now. Now when he had so much love to give.

He gently pursed her lips for her, imagining how pink and soft they must have been before turning such a stunning shade of blue, and then, with a touch like a butterfly's wings, he kissed her.

***

Across town, in a small apartment overlooking a brick wall, another love story was drawing to an end. It was a sad moment, but unavoidable, really. People just grew apart. They changed. And things went bad.

Really, *really* bad. Drawing flies kind of bad.

Nora Vanderkirk sat across from her love and wondered just how things could go so bad so fast. The heat was probably the main cause—that and the fact that he was too tall to stuff into the fridge. It was a shame, too, because Peter had been awfully handsome. She'd loved him best of all.

She sighed as she watched a piece of cartilage slowly slip away from what used to be his nose. It slid over his ruined cheek, hanging by a few threads of skin, and then plopped onto the plastic couch cover. Nora fought back a few tears; she'd really loved his nose.

This is just not healthy at all, she thought as she lifted her leg and stopped his slow, downward slide, bracing her foot against his squishy chest. He'd had nice pecs once. Shame. Hugging him now was like hugging a bag of Jell-O...and that just didn't do a thing for her.

Still, it had been nice while it lasted. Peter, once she'd shut him up, had been so sweet and kind. He'd never belittled her, never called her names, never said she was stupid...all he did was hold her when she wanted to be held, and listen to her when she needed to talk. So what if he'd had a little problem with...the other thing. Sex wasn't the only factor in their relationship.

But now he was leaving her, just like all the others had left her, and a part of Nora was relieved. She was a creature of change; she liked variety in her life and loathed routine with a passion. She didn't even buy a whole box of cereal at the store—she liked the packs of small boxes, one of each kind, just in case she felt like Fruit Loops instead of Rice Krispies. Change was good. Necessary, even. Peter was a wonderful part of her life, but now he was over and it was time to move on.

Nora smiled as she leaned back in her chair and thought about the new guy she'd seen at the office. Sure, he was just a janitor, and sure he leered at her every time she walked past, but she could see that he had some raw potential. He wasn't half-bad looking either—she liked his mouth and eyes, and he had the kind of squishy, teddy-bear body that was just made for cuddling. Usually, she went for the muscle-bound, thick-necked hunks like Peter...but there was just something different about this new guy. Something irresistible.

Sighing as Peter made the long, slow slide down the couch, Nora closed her eyes and imagined her teddy-bear janitor. He'd be an easy one. Because he wasn't the most gorgeous thing in the world, he'd be ripe for a pretty girl like her. A friendly smile, a few flirty words...he'd almost be *too* easy. She guessed that it would take a week, tops, to make him fall so totally and completely in love with her that he would do anything.

And then she'd do it. Nice and clean. Pillow to the face, maybe. Or a bottle of sleeping pills in his drink. Or rat poison...she'd always wanted to see how that would work. At any rate, she'd take care of him and then...then he'd be the perfect man.

Peter slid to the floor with a wet thwap of raw meat and Nora sighed. Great. Now she'd have to mop.

***

Murray stopped dead in his tracks when he saw her, his jaw dropping as he stared. Leaning against his broom, he unabashedly gazed at her as she talked with her co-workers, dazzled by the brightness of her smile, the glossy sheen of her golden hair. She was easily the most beautiful woman he had ever seen, and in the space of a heartbeat he knew that he had fallen totally and irrevocably in love with her. She was his reason for being, his destiny.

And the best thing was, he knew he could have her. All he needed to do was keep an eye on her, learn her routine, follow her home...and after a few weeks or so, he'd be ready to make his move. She was a frail little thing, anyway...virtually skin and bones. He could almost feel his hands fitting around that slender throat, almost hear the crackle and snap of her spine, the soft "Oh!" as she realized what was happening. And then she'd collapse gracefully into his embrace and be his forever and ever and ever...

Murray had to blink away sudden tears. He couldn't help it. Love made him all sentimental and mushy.

The woman—*goddess*, he thought—turned slightly toward him, presenting her flawless profile, and at that moment Murray would have sworn on a stack of Torahs that his heart actually, physically, literally skipped a beat. Did she have blue eyes or green? Not that it actually mattered—they got all cloudy and dull anyway—but he'd always been partial to blue-eyed blondes. She smiled again and he noticed a deep dimple in her right cheek. He had the fleeting mental image of himself flicking his tongue into that dimple and the force of the thought nearly staggered him. He'd never wanted anyone as badly as he wanted her. Never.

And he didn't want to wait for her, even though he knew he had to. Even though he knew that every moment he had to watch her without being able to touch or taste or hold her would kill him inside, he had to wait. But that was all right...he was a patient, patient man. His whole life had been spent waiting for one thing or another, always half-expecting the thing he wanted to never materialize or happen. He was good at waiting. Every woman he'd ever loved, he'd waited for, biding his time until the perfect moment arose and he could make his affections known.

Besides...the waiting, the anticipation, was almost as good as when it actually happened.

The boss, a hulking ape of a woman, looked his way and glared, so Murray gave the broom a nudge, pretending to be absorbed in his mindless task. He waited until he sensed that the ape had lost interest in him, then glanced back to the woman. His woman. His gaze took her in, lingering on the slim legs, the curve of her hip, the narrowness of her waist. Her skin was a lovely shade of peach that he knew wouldn't fade to that horrible fish-belly white that he hated. He could hardly wait to touch her hair, to wash and style it the way he wanted, the way he thought would look best. She shouldn't wear it pinned back so severely, he thought. It would look much better loose and flowing...

He hadn't realized he was staring so intently at her until she looked his way and their eyes locked. For an instant, Murray felt awestruck and paralyzed, almost trapped. Now he would have to make up excuses, avoid her, pretend that a slug like him couldn't possibly exist in the same universe that would allow such beauty. He cleared his throat and grimaced in humiliation, gripping the handle of his broom until his knuckles whitened and he felt the grain of the wood splinter into his palm. He knew he should look away but...he couldn't. And he didn't want to. He'd never seen a lovelier woman in his life.

He expected the look he always got from women, the *how dare you even glance my way, troll!* look that made him feel like the scum film in his mop-bucket. Any second now. Any second she'd be wrinkling her nose in disgust and flouncing away like she was queen of the damned universe.

And then she did the most amazing thing...

She smiled at him.

Murray didn't know what she was doing at first. His immediate thought was that she was so disgusted by the thought of him looking at her that she was baring her teeth at him. Then he saw the warmth in her eyes as her dimple deepened and felt a hot rush spread from his chest to his limbs, linger to do a few laps around his groin. She was smiling! At *him*! It seemed beyond his meager grasp of reality to think that a woman like her might actually acknowledge his existence, but...

She smiled at him. And kept smiling.

Murray suddenly found himself in uncharted territory. This wasn't the way things usually went. They never smiled at him. Never looked at him. What if she wanted to talk? What would he say? A woman like her was a zillion times smarter than he could ever dream of being...there's no way he could possibly hold a conversation with her without sounding like the stupid idiot he actually was. She'd never smile at him again.

He began to push the broom across the floor, quickly looking away from the blinding brilliance of her smile, concentrating on keeping his nice, tidy pile of dirt in an even row. His face, his entire body, felt greasy with flop sweat. His stomach gurgled at an embarrassingly loud decibel. He chanced a quick look her way and saw, with a start, that she had broken away from her group...

And that she was walking his way.

Fear spurred Murray to move at a speed he'd never thought himself capable of reaching. Without another glance, he scurried away, haphazardly shoving the pile of dirt out of his way. He caught a whiff of her perfume—something sweet and flowery that reminded him of springtime—and felt suddenly weak-kneed. He had to have more time to think about this. He wasn't in control of the situation anymore, and he didn't like that feeling one bit. He needed to plan, to follow her around and see that she was just as human as he was, that she was nothing special. Not a goddess or a queen. Just a woman.

And then...then he could do what he had to do to make her belong to him.

***

Nora wasn't sure why she felt insulted. She knew Janitor-Boy was interested in her—one look at those stupid cow-eyes of his told her that much. What she didn't know was why he skittered away and ran when she decided to give him a thrill and talk to him. Apparently he had no idea how many men would kill to be able to spend a moment or two in her presence. Apparently he was as dumb as he looked.

Which wasn't necessarily a problem. She happened to like them big and stupid. It made her life a hell of a lot easier.

Nora glanced at her watch and chewed on her lower lip for a moment. Ten to five. Ten minutes to make an impression on Mop-Boy that he'd never forget. She wouldn't be able to sleep that night if she didn't think she had his complete and total adoration.

Looking over her shoulder to make sure Ms. McGillicuddy wasn't snooping around, Nora hurried down the hallway and into the stairwell, following the trail of dirt and debris he'd left in his rush to get out of her path. As she trotted down the steps—he'd gone back to his hidey-hole in the basement, she'd assumed—she undid a few buttons on her blouse and let down her hair, giving it a quick toss and shake. Poor bastard wouldn't know what hit him.

The door to the janitor's lounge was half-open, and as Nora eased into the room—careful not to touch anything—she heard the sound of water running. He was probably rinsing out the mop. No matter. She'd surprise him. They were alone, after all...and she was feeling particularly lonely. She might even take him home with her, get the boring touchy-feely trust crap out of the way immediately so he would be completely comfortable with her. Of course, that meant she'd probably have to sleep with him...not her favorite part, but she'd endured it before and could endure it again. Luckily, most men couldn't hold out very long anyway. Five minutes of counting ceiling tiles and then the guy was sprawled out beside her, snoring and drooling and farting and doing all the other disgusting things men did.

Nora shivered despite herself. Men were *so* much easier to deal with after she'd taken care of them. They didn't tell her she wasn't slim enough. They didn't cheat on her with bimbos they'd picked up at work. They didn't tell her to cook for them or clean up after them or serve them. They just cuddled her. Held her. Listened to her talk about work without interrupting or ignoring her.

And even though they started to smell after a while, it was still far better than the alternative.

Nora draped herself over a ratty couch in the corner, suggestively crossing her legs and cocking her hip and digging her fingers through her hair. An instant later, Janitor-Boy walked in, a mop in hand. It took him a moment to notice her, but when he finally did, the effect was just as Nora had hoped: drop-jawed, wide-eyed, tented-trouser surprise.

"Hi," she said, turning the wattage of her smile up to full brilliance. "I noticed you today...were you looking at me?"

He pulled the mop in front of him. "Um..."

"It's okay." Nora slowly sat up and gestured for him. He didn't move. "Because I was looking at you, too."

"You were?"

"Of course I was. You're a handsome guy...I'll bet you have girls looking at you all the time." Nora managed somehow to keep the smile plastered over her lips. "My name is Nora."

"Muh-Murray..." He coughed, a strangled sound, and shook his head to clear it.

Nora fought her rising impatience. The shy guy act was cute the first two seconds; now it was just getting on her nerves. She maintained her smile, however. It was going to be a cold, lonely night and she didn't particularly feel like suffering through it alone.

"C'mere, Murray..." Nora patted the seat beside her and waited while he shuffled over to sit with her. He was heavier than she'd first thought, with a beer gut and a big butt that the overalls had camouflaged. She'd have some problems handling him once he was dead weight. Good thing she'd kept up with the Nautilus.

"You don't have to be shy with me, Murray honey." Nora trailed her fingers through his lank brown hair and surreptitiously wiped them on his shoulder. This one had definitely looked better from a distance. If she weren't so lonely, she'd bypass him for that gorgeous executive up in accounting, but someone might actually miss *him*.

Murray glanced toward her, then looked away, almost squirming with nervousness. He licked his lips and squeezed his hands together, fumbling his fingers over each other as he hunched his shoulders and tried to make himself small. His reaction was totally baffling to Nora. She'd assumed he was a normal man, with normal needs and wants, and that all she'd have to do was crook her finger and he'd come running. Instead, she'd found a man with all the emotional maturity of an eighth grader.

Murray's stomach rumbled loudly, and at that moment Nora decided that he would be a one-night stand. She wouldn't even bother to refrigerate him. She'd just take him home, let him have that one last two minute thrill, then take care of him while he was asleep. In a way, she felt as though she'd be doing the world a favor.

Before she could talk herself out of it, Nora grabbed Murray by the lapels and pulled him closer, kissing him roughly and trying not to taste the egg salad on his breath. As always, kissing opened up something inside Nora, and she lost the initial pang of disgust as the kiss progressed. Murray whimpered and remained absolutely still as Nora's lips moved over his, as if he'd never kissed anyone before and didn't quite know what to do. The thought gave Nora pause. Maybe he wasn't like the others. Maybe he'd be different.

Maybe she wouldn't have to *make* him love her.

Nora pulled away from him, unsure of the new feelings blossoming inside her. For a long time, she simply stared at Murray, at the thick lips, the droopy eyes, the chipmunk cheeks. He wasn't a gorgeous man by any means, but there was innocence about him that Nora liked. He could be molded into the man—the living, breathing man—she'd always wanted. No more plastic on the furniture. No more messy clean-ups when she'd lingered with them too long. She could make him be whatever she wanted him to be, and he'd be so grateful that someone like her loved him, he would never dream of betraying her.

The thought was almost too good to be true. She could start using her refrigerator for food again. She could go to the bridge just to sightsee and not to dump off a body. She could take him out in public without drawing flies.

"Come to my apartment," she finally said, voice shaky. He seemed to grow more handsome as she gazed at him. "Tonight."

Murray, dumbfounded, simply nodded.

"Hamilton Arms. 7G. Eight o'clock." Nora kissed him again, a smothering, breath-sucking, nerve-jangling kiss that left them both weak. Murray collapsed back on the couch as Nora stumbled to her feet.

"Make it seven," she said and smiled.

**

Murray really didn't want to have to kill her. She was so pretty, with her cheeks all pink with blush and her eyes bluer than his mother's favorite sapphire brooch. If she died, she'd lose that prettiness. Her hair would dry out and break if he tried to run his fingers through it. Her skin would roll up and fall away if he used too much pressure in his caress. Her eyes would grow cloudy and sink back into her skull.

And worst of all, she wouldn't smile anymore. No matter how much he tried to keep the smiles on their lips, it always looked like nothing but a grimace. And he never liked that.

The elevator ride up to Nora's apartment was the longest he'd ever had to endure. He gripped the roses in his hand so tightly that they'd begun to droop. Their smell—so sickly sweet and cloying—seemed to clog his nostrils. He'd never had a real date before. He'd never had to talk to a woman...and he'd never had a woman want to talk to him before, much less kiss him the way Nora had kissed him earlier.

He could still feel that kiss tingling against his lips. He'd kissed women before, but never one who had been able to kiss back. It'd been such a weird sensation to feel her mouth moving against him, her warm lips slip-sliding over his. And there had been nothing rotted or foul about her breath; she'd tasted like toothpaste, clean and fresh and minty.

Murray had liked it. A lot. It made him wonder how the other things would be. Warm instead of cold. Wet instead of dry. Alive, instead of—

The elevator shuddered and jerked to a stop and Murray opened the door to the seventh floor. There was a faint, familiar scent in the air, but he paid it no mind, too grateful to smell something besides the damn roses to care *what* it was. Her apartment was just at the end of the hall, and with each step Murray took, he knew that he was just one step closer to Paradise.

He'd just raised his hand to knock at the door when it opened and Nora stood there, angelic in a white dress—the dim part of Murray's mind still capable of rational thought realized with a heart-stopping thud that she was wearing a *negligee*—and a beaming smile. She took his hand and led him into her apartment, and Murray was too dumbstruck by lust to even notice that she had locked the door behind him.

Her apartment was as beautiful as he'd imagined it would be. Lots of pink frills and lacy curtains, a stuffed animal collection in the corner, fancy pictures on the walls. As a Frank Sinatra CD played softly in the background, she led him to the couch. He plopped down bonelessly, crackling the plastic over the cushions. For a moment he was reminded of his mother and his bright mood clouded. Nora wasn't like his mother. She wasn't like the others.

He clenched his fists and closed his eyes until the feeling went away.

"Can I get you a drink?" Nora asked, fluttering from place to place like a hummingbird. Murray grew dizzy just watching her. Her perfume smelled like the vanilla his mother used to cook with when he was a boy. The smell of it was so strong he could almost taste it.

"Um...I don't really drink..."

"Oh, come on...just a little drinky-poo." Nora flashed him another smile. "You can drink it if you want to. If not, I'll just water the plants with it."

"Okay then...sure..." Murray's back ached and he forced himself to relax a little. He watched Nora glide over to the bar and fiddle with bottles and glasses, pouring him a glass of something amber. He didn't know what he'd be drinking. Didn't care. She kept her back to him as she poured, and he was too enchanted by the fall of blond hair over her slender shoulders to care why.

"I hope you like scotch," she said and turned back to him, fixing him with a smile that made his entire body quiver. Murray dimly felt himself nod, even though the only scotch he was familiar with was butterscotch, which he hated. Nora joined him at the couch and handed him his drink, hesitating only a moment before relinquishing it to him. He set it on the coffee table, too nervous to drink.

"Do you believe in fate, Murray?" Nora leaned close to him, so close that he could see the huge pores dotting the bridge of her nose, the tiny lines around her eyes. She was older than he'd thought.

"I, uh…sure." Murray smiled faintly, but his attention had wandered from her breathtaking beauty, focused instead on a clump of mascara under her right eye. She smiled back to him and he caught a glimpse of scarlet-red lipstick on the corner of her front tooth…which wasn't quite as gleaming white as he'd thought.

Nothing was like he'd thought.

"I do," Nora said, oblivious to his stare. "I believe in fate…and I believe in raw, animal attraction between a man and a woman. Don't you?"

Murray's attention had snagged on a mole just beneath her ear. A single curling hair grew from its center. He hadn't noticed that before. "Uh-huh, sure…" he muttered.

"When I saw you, I knew that we should be together…" Nora leaned closer to him and took a sip of her drink. Murray heard a faint clicking sound in her throat as she swallowed. I knew that we could connect."

"Uh-huh…" Murray looked closely at her hair and noticed strands of dark brown around the roots. She dyed her hair. All that beautiful golden blonde came out of a bottle…

It was almost heartbreaking.

Nora cuddled beside him, her head on his shoulder, and suddenly every bit of attraction he'd felt ebbed away. She wasn't as beautiful as he'd thought she was. She'd lied to him—to everyone—and made them believe she was perfect.

Just like his mother had done.

"I can't believe I'm telling you this, Murray, but…" Nora sighed and fiddled with the buttons of his shirt. Her fingernail polish was chipped. "I think I've fallen in love with you."

"Um…great." Murray forced a smile and gently eased himself away from her. One hand found its way up to her neck, cradling the side of her throat. The night wouldn't be a complete loss…

"Great?" Nora's dazzling smile lost its luster. "What do mean, 'great'? I just said I love you!"

"I know. I heard you." Murray gently stroked the edge of his thumb over the pulse of her throat. He didn't need someone like *her* to love him…he needed someone pure, someone beautiful and perfect.

"What is it? Don't you…aren't you attracted to me?" Nora didn't notice his hand at her throat, too wound up in her own anger to care. That old familiar coldness opened up inside her, and for a moment her rage was directed at herself as much as it was to Murray. How could she have been so stupid?

Murray gazed at her for a few long moments, and Nora had never felt so vulnerable in her life. "Actually…" He shrugged and half-smiled. "Nope. Sorry."

Nora's cheeks ached as she kept on smiling. "Well, then…I don't suppose that's anyone's fault, is it? If you're not attracted to me, then…well…big deal. Right?"

"Right." Murray smiled—the first relaxed smile she'd seen from him—and Nora abruptly realized that he was stroking her neck. "But…"

"But what?" Nora stiffened beneath his touch. The pads of his fingers were rough, scaly.

"But I still want to…" He waggled his brows as his grin slanted. "You know…"

Bitter revulsion rose in Nora's throat. And if this wasn't just like a man. Not good enough to love, but he'd screw her if given the chance. How could she have ever thought he might be different?

"I know," she said and tightly smiled. He was too busy looking at her chest to notice the anger in her eyes. She didn't think she could bear to allow him to touch her, no matter how much easier it would make killing him. No one rejected her. No one.

"I want to, too…" she whispered, hoping she sounded at least faintly sincere. Not that he'd notice. "But could you do one itty-bitty favor for me first?"

His gaze never left her cleavage. Nora noticed that his breathing was getting faster, his hand on her throat pressing tighter.

"Sure…" he managed to say.

Nora leaned forward—further disabling him by flashing him a more generous view of cleavage—and took his glass from the coffee table, pressing it into his hand. "I like the taste of scotch on a man's breath…"

No sooner than the words were said, Murray upended the glass and gulped the scotch in one breath. The shy little boy personality was gone, replaced by an over-eager aggressor. He swiped his sleeve over his mouth, then dived atop Nora, pushing her back into the plastic cushions. Nora passively waited while he sloppily kissed her neck…

…and then…

Murray jerked away from her, one hand clawing at his throat as the rat poison worked its charms. Nora watched with detached fascination, mentally cataloging the pros and cones of Mouse-B-Gone. The frothing wasn't too pleasant, but his face was turning a lovely shade of blue…not too much swelling either, but it seemed to be taking forever for him to just die.

Murray kicked and spasmed, eyes bulging, rolling wildly as he felt his throat turn to fire. It hurt so bad…and it was her fault. She was making him hurt. She was killing him.

Killing him…

Murray had never actually hated a woman before—except for his mother, but he didn't like to think about her. But now he knew a hate so pure and blinding and all-consuming that he was, for just an instant, awed by its power. He wanted the bitch to die. He didn't love her. He didn't need her. He just wanted her to die.

Black blobs danced in his vision as he reached out to Nora with incredibly long arms, an eternity passing before he felt her slender throat in his hands, before he felt the throb of her pulse against his palms. She wriggled and tried to get away—normally his favorite part of the game—but Murray collapsed his weight atop her, squeezing and squeezing and squeezing…

Nora tried to scream, but nothing could get past the pressure of his hands. She bucked and fought, pushing at him, but he was too heavy, too strong. Even dying. She saw the familiar tightening of the features, the glassiness that glazed the eyes, the slackness that opened the jaw, and new that if she could just hold on a second longer…just an instant…she would be all right. If she could just wait…if the black sparkles would go away from her eyes…if he would just hurry up and *die*…she'd…be…

Both of them stiffened at the same moment, their mouths open in breathless screams, eyes rolling back as the world turned to black nothingness. Nora *whuffed* softly as Murray's weight fell atop her, forcing out what little air remained in her lungs. His slack mouth rested on her cheek, his hands cradling her face in an almost loving caress. Their bodies were carelessly intertwined, as close as lovers.

Their first night together blended into the next day…and the next day…and the next. "Strangers in the Night" played endlessly on the stereo as body fluids mixed and mingled and flies—drawn by the warm smell of Murray and Nora's love—met, mated, and flew away.

Fanboys

(originally published in Decadence of the Dead*)*

It was a long way down.

Terri dropped the hairbrush and leaned back in her chair, unable to look away from the wreck of her own reflection. Jesus. Forty-two years old and trying to pass for ten years younger. Hair bleached so blonde it felt crispy to the touch. Make-up caked on so heavy she could feel it weighing her skin down, just to hide the wrinkles deeping around her eyes and bracketing her mouth. Who the hell was she trying to fool, anyway?

She took a deep draw off her cigarette and watched tiny little lines form all around her lips. Once upon a time she had a mouth that would have given Angelina Jolie a run for her money. Once she had been given an award from some silly fanboy gore magazine for "Best Lips."

Once she'd had a career as Terri Stephens, Scream Queen Extraordinaire. Now…now she had the conventions.

This was her fifth one this year. So far, it was averaging out to one convention every other month. This one was in some podunk town in Pennsylvania, in a cheap hotel close to the airport. She'd flown in from L.A. and gone straight to her room, dreading each minute before she'd have to go downstairs to the so-called 'ballroom' and put on the Terri Stephens' show.

It never varied. She'd settle down at a table and pile VHS tapes of her movies in front of her, like a wall between her and her fans. She'd sign stacks of artsy black-and-white photos of herself that were taken when she was twenty-six years old—back when she could honestly say she was gorgeous—and sell them for ten bucks each. Sometimes she might take part in a panel discussion of women in horror or slasher movies from the '80s. And when it was over, she would have endured her fans' lusty jokes, their desperate, groping hugs during photo ops, their offensive jokes at her expense. Sometimes they even said they loved her.

Yeah. Right. They loved her back when her tits were perky and her ass was high. They loved the image they saw in the movies, the pretty girl who ended up naked and covered in buckets of corn syrup blood after having R-rated sex with some air-headed himbo. She wondered if that's the woman they saw when they finally made it up to her table, when they finally shook her hand and saw her face-to-face. Did they see a middle-aged woman struggling to pay her bills and remain relevant in an industry where younger, prettier girls blew into town every day? Or did they see the hot young thing she used to be?

Most of the time she tried to look through the guys when they ambled up to her table. The majority of them were her age, guys who had used her images to get them through puberty. They were the ones who seemed the most grateful for a smile, a handshake, a special comment on the signed photo. She could feel the loneliness pouring off them like heat. They still thought she was beautiful. They still thought she could hold her own against the young girls entering the business, the ones who took short-cuts to "stardom" by doing more extreme exploitation movies.

But sometimes she would look at the younger guys a little more closely. They could be cruel, gauging her age with a practiced, jaundiced eye. Occasionally they'd comment, compare her to the perkier girls in the room, complain that she wasn't as hot as she used to be.

And she'd have to keep smiling and signing and selling her movies. If she wanted to make her rent for the month, she had to put up with the shit and deal with it.

Terri reached for her drink and gulped it in one swallow. Yeah, that would help her look all fresh and dewy and young. Have another Jack and Coke and see how many auditions you get called for next week.

"Fuck you," she muttered. She just didn't know if she was saying it to the voice in her head or the fanboys waiting just outside the dressing room doors.

***

"…you were so fucking hot in 'Gravedigger 2'!"

"…I had your pictures taped right over my bed…"

"…would you sign it, 'To Gavin, thanks for the best sex of my life'?"

"…can I have a lock of your hair?"

"…dude, you looked really haggy in that last movie. What happened?"

"…you know, you're the same age as my mom!"

***

Terri glanced at her watch and sighed. Only nine-thirty? She felt like she'd been sitting there for days. A kid with glasses and a fake head bursting out of his gut ambled up to her table and grinned, pushing a VHS copy of "Blood War" towards her.

"Who should I make it out to?" Terri forced a smile and held her silver marker poised over the lurid photo of her twenty-year old self. God, she really did look good back then.

"Bobby." His voice cracked midway through the word, his blush turning his spotty face even pinker. "Bobby McCoy. I really liked your pictures in *Celebrity Nudes*. You used to be really hot."

Terri's cheeks cramped as she forced herself to keep smiling. She signed her standard signature—"To Bobby, All my love Terri"— and quickly pushed the video back across the table.

"My dad said he used to be a big fan of yours." Bobby scooped up the video, still grinning. "He said he didn't think you'd still be hot—"

"Okay," Terri snapped, smile wavering. "Thanks. Goodbye now."

Bobby frowned, confused, but moved on, stuffing the video into his backpack. Terri slumped back in her chair and rubbed at her forehead. She felt a migraine coming on.

"Oh! I didn't think you'd be here this year!"

Terri winced, keeping her eyes squeezed shut for as long as she could. She knew that squeally, little girl voice all too well. Steffy Nichols, the newest 'it' girl in the business. She seemed to be in every new release, showing off her perfect, surgically enhanced body in various forms of undress, and she had all the acting ability of a dead rat. Her self-esteem was unmatched, though. Since she was so sought-after by producers (mostly because she was willing to do everything short of hardcore porn—and even that was negotiable), she proclaimed herself to be the Queen of the whole 'scream queen' industry.

She'd taken almost a dozen roles that should have gone to Terri. Producers took one look at Steffy, compared her to Terri, and all bets were off.

"I decided to make an appearance," Terri managed to say, forcing a smile. "My fans—"

"That's so cute, that you think you have fans." Steffy smiled, hitching up her tube top to draw even more attention to her double Ds. "Do people really still remember you?"

Terri didn't answer. She couldn't. Her stomach had leapt into her throat and choked her with bile. How could someone be so effortlessly cruel?

"I hate these things," Steffy said as she perched on the edge of the table. She was wearing a skirt short enough to call for a Brazilian wax and every guy in the area watched her every move. Terri might as well have been invisible. "All these losers drooling over me...bunch of freaks."

"I'm feeling sick," Terri said and pushed away from the table. "Where's the bathroom?"

"In the back," Steffy said with a smile. "Maybe while you're in there you should re-do your makeup. Your wrinkles are really caking up."

Terri gritted her teeth and moved as quickly as she could, cutting a path through the grinning fanboys as they sniffed out Steffy's position and started surrounding her.

If they recognized Terri, they didn't bother to acknowledge it once they saw Steffy. And for a terrible, longing moment, Terri missed that kind of overwhelming attention. To be that wanted, that desired…

Bile rose in her throat, bitter and burning.

***

She actually felt safe in the bathroom stall. Even as she puked up her meager lunch and slumped over the toilet, she felt safer in there than she did out in the convention. There were no staring eyes, no judgement, no disapproval. Just her and the toilet and her puke. But now she had to go back. If she expected to pick up her appearance fee once this whole mess was over with, she had to go back.

She wished she prayed. Maybe that would make it easier.

Terri carefully washed her face, trying not to do too much damage to her make-up, and stared at her reflection for a moment. In any other world, she would be considered a knock-out. If she were a soccer mom in Ohio, she'd be the best looking woman in the minivan.

But she wasn't. She was a washed-up actress who was ashamed of every movie she'd ever done.

Terri closed her eyes and forced herself to turn away from the mirror. She forced herself to take deep breaths and open the bathroom door. She forced herself to step into the service hallway and face her adoring public once again.

The first thing she noticed was the silence.

Terri slipped into the rear of the ballroom, afraid of what she'd find because something deep inside her was screaming for her to run and get out now before it was too late.

The entire ball room was quiet. Dead quiet. None of the normal sounds of a crowd. No grunts or farts or coughs or sighs. It was as if the place had been deserted.

But it wasn't empty.

No, everyone was still there.

They were just…dead.

It looked like the old photos she had once seen of Jonestown. Bodies piled atop bodies, as if they had just dropped where they stood. Just a sea of corpses, unmoving and silent.

"Oh, my God…" Terri couldn't move for a moment. She couldn't look away from the bodies.

Until the explosions began.

She screamed and fell to the floor, cringing and covering her head until she realized that the ceiling wasn't going to fall in on her. The explosions were coming from outside.

Suddenly she had to see.

She scrambled for the fire door and opened it just as the belly of a 747 seemed to scrape the top of the hotel, hurdling helplessly toward the neighboring airport. She felt the impact in her bones. In the distance she saw other planes plummeting to the ground, slamming into the low mountains, into houses and buildings and highways. Just falling out of the skies.

Like there was no one flying the planes.

She stumbled back inside, shaking so violently that she could barely keep her balance. For a moment, she could only stand in the threshold of the main ballroom, staring at the sea of bodies. Such total stillness. Such silence.

And for a moment, she thought she might have lost her mind.

"Hello?" Her voice trembled, came out as a croak. She cough-gagged to clear her throat. She felt like she was going to vomit again. "Is anyone here? Hello?"

No response. She hadn't really expected one.

She waded into the bodies, gingerly stepping around them, unable to step over them for some reason. Men she had just talked to, smiled at, posed with…all of them now lying dead on the floor. Their eyes were open, looks of pure shock on their faces, as if they couldn't quite believe they were actually dead. Some of them still held her photos and videos.

The place smelled like piss and shit. She'd always heard that people did that when they died, but thought it was just a stupid story. Terri covered her nose and mouth, gagging. There were over four hundred people in the ballroom, and she was the only one left breathing. It was like the end of the world.

And the silence. Dear God, the silence. She'd never thought that silence could be so suffocating, so thick.

"Please…" she whispered, needing to hear something, even if it was just the sound of her own voice. "Please…somebody be alive…"

She accidently stepped on a man's outstretched hand and his fingers crunched beneath her shoe. She screamed and jumped back, losing her balance and sprawling over an overweight bearded man in a too-tight Star Trek t-shirt. He huffed out a dead breath as she fell onto him, his eyes wide and staring at nothing.

Terri scrambled to her feet. The touch of his skin…already cooling, already clammy and dead. She couldn't bear it.

She felt the tears on her cheeks before realizing she was crying. Part of her wished she had been taken by whatever had killed these people. All her life she had despised being alone, fearing nothing more than solitude. She had filled her life with friends and lovers and co-workers, needing them to see her, validate her, admire her. She had become an actress because she knew that would ensure a kind of immortality; as long as there were people to watch her films, she would be seen and loved and wanted. She needed, more than anything, to be seen.

But now...now would there be anyone left to remember her?

She heard a soft moan.

"Who's there? Hey! Who's there?" Terri forced herself to keep moving through the minefield of limbs. The moan came from the tables. She followed the sound, her lifeline, her only connection to an increasingly tenuous sanity.

She found Steffy Nichols crouching under the table, and a tiny, ugly part of her was disturbingly satisfied to see that she looked horrible. The smug mask of her beauty was gone now. Tears had caused her mascara to drip down her face, leaving her eyes naked and puffy. The smugness that she had always worn like a badge of honor was gone now.

Steffy took Terri's hand and shakily stood up. She moaned again when she saw the bodies, and Terri felt another awful wave of satisfaction; if nothing else, she was at least stronger than Steffy. "Why is everyone...what's wrong with them?"

"I think...I think they're dead." Terri swallowed hard, forcing herself to remain calm. "They're all dead."

Steffy faltered on her feet and began crying again. Terri felt an overwhelming urge to slap her. Now was not the time for her "look-at-me" melodramatics. Not that there was anyone left to look at her anymore.

"Listen to me..." Terri grabbed Steffy's thin shoulders and shook her. Hard. "Steffy! Calm down and listen to me..."

Steffy focused her eyes on Terri, shuddering but quiet.

"We have got to get out of here and find more people." Terri's voice sounded calm, much calmer than she actually felt. "Whatever's happening...it can't be everywhere. There has to be other people out there."

Steffy nodded, but Terri couldn't be sure how much she was actually comprehending. She wasn't the sharpest tool in the shed in the best of situations.

"Are you okay now?" Terri bent slightly so she could look Steffy directly in the eye. "Are you calm now?"

Steffy nodded, keeping her gaze only on Terri. That was good. If she looked around and really thought about where they were and what was surrounding them, she would lose her shit permanently.

"Good. Now come on…we're getting out of here."

She took Steffy's cold, bony hand—noticing the perfectly manicured nails and ostentatious rings—and wished that she had survived with a big, macho guy instead of this useless little girl.

She pulled Steffy along behind her, inexplicably annoyed by her meekness. She didn't need this. She didn't want to be responsible for a grown woman who should be able to take care of herself. Steffy had probably never had to do anything for herself her whole life. She'd been pampered and petted and praised since she was old enough to draw attention to herself. Terri hadn't been as lucky. She'd had to fight for everything she ever had. It wasn't fair that she had to be responsible for this little bitch now.

"What was that?" Steffy stopped, jerking Terri's hand. "I saw something move."

"Nothing. Now come on…"

"No! I saw something…there! Over there!" Steffy pointed toward the main stage where the panel discussions had been held.

Terri saw nothing, just bodies sprawled on the floor. No movement.

Except…

One of the men suddenly sat up, springing upright as if he had been shocked. Steffy screamed and hid behind Terri.

Terri couldn't move. For a few seconds, she couldn't even breathe.

One after another, more men began to sit up. They moved with a jerky hitch, like puppets on strings, animated by something outside of their bodies. Their eyes rolled wildly, unfocused, clouded and flat.

Terri realized that they weren't aware of her yet. She didn't want to think about what would happen when they saw her.

She glanced over at Steffy and saw that she was hyperventilating, a scream just waiting to erupt. Once she screamed and the men noticed them…

Terri had been in enough horror movies to know what happened then.

She slapped her hand over Steffy's mouth just as she began to howl. Steffy moaned against her palm, making enough noise to draw the attention of every man who had risen. Their heads swiveled towards them, moving in perfect synchronicity.

"Oh, God…" Terri took an involuntary step back, stumbling over a still dormant corpse. She felt a wall at her back. The door looked like it was a million miles away instead of a few feet.

Steffy gasped for air, impossibly loud in the silence.

The men rose, their arms twitching and flailing, their mouths slack-jawed and drooling. Some of them had trouble getting to their feet and stumbled over the corpses, falling and rising with disturbing speed.

Every one of them stared at Terri and Steffy, their eyes fixed and unblinking, yet somehow aware. Some of them still clutched the photos Terri had signed earlier. Some of them still carried Steffy's DVDs in their hands.

Their fans.

One of the men raised his arm and reached for Terri, his fingers opening and closing at air, as if he were trying desperately to touch her. He moaned and took a shuffling step closer.

A few of the others answered his call, blindly moving forward.

"What's happening?" Steffy's voice, shrill with fear, slashed at Terri's nerves. "Terri? What do we do?"

"Fanboys," Terri said softly. She couldn't look away from them. Only minutes ago they were alive, laughing, walking around the room and having fun. Now they were monsters.

"What do we do?" Steffy's grip on Terri's arm tightened, bony fingers squeezing hard enough to startle Terri out of her daze. "Terri?"

"I don't know…" Terri murmured, more to herself than to Steffy. She had no idea how to process what she was seeing, much less what to do about it. If they ran, they would be chased. If they hid, they would be found. If they were caught…

Terri couldn't let her mind go to that place. What *would* the men do to them? Kill them? Eat them? Rape them?

They were all on their feet now, unsteady but standing. All of them turning to face Terri and Steffy. They made no sound, and the silence was smothering.

Terri reached down and took Steffy's hand, drawing cold comfort from the contact.

The men shuffled closer, every face slack and empty, every pair of eyes staring but unseeing.

Steffy huddled closer to Terri, slobbering with tears. Terri felt the wall pressing against her back. From the corner of her eye she could see the open door that led to the hallway…and away from the ballroom.

She could smell them now, an overwhelming stench of body odor and bad hygiene, cheap cologne and expired deodorant. Their hands twitched at their sides, as if they were already touching her.

Terri put her arm around Steffy's shoulders, holding the sobbing girl close…

…and pushed her out into the mob, so fast that Steffy didn't realize what was happening until the men fell on her in a hungry pack, swallowing her whole as she screamed.

Terri didn't wait around to see what they were doing. She ran. She ran for the door and didn't look back. She leapt over bodies on the floor and dodged the outstretched hands of the men who hadn't been distracted by Steffy and ran until she felt her heart would explode and her lungs were on fire.

And then she was in the hallway, and there were more bodies lying everywhere. Women. Men. Children. Collapsed and still in the golden light of the setting sun that shone through the window at the end of the hall.

Steffy's screams grew rougher.

Then they abruptly stopped.

Terri couldn't remember how to get out of the building. She knew it was shock fogging her mind, made worse by the sounds of the men following her from the ballroom, but she didn't know where to go.

So she fell into the stairwell, fighting her way up the steps to her fifth floor room. Maybe they couldn't climb steps. Maybe they wouldn't bother to follow her. Maybe Steffy—

oh, God...what did I do?

--would be enough to distract them. Maybe she could get to her room and call 911 and everything would be okay, everything would be all right, and she could use this to write a book and get famous again and she'd never have to go to another goddam convention ever again...

The stairwell door slammed open.

Terri could hear them moving below her, clattering against the metal steps, their moans and grunts echoing in the stairwell. She didn't want to see, but she had to look. She edged closer to the handrail and peeked over the side.

Dozens of them. Dazed but determined to climb the stairs.

One of them, a spotty-faced boy with glasses, raised his head just before Terri could duck back into the shadows. She recognized him. Bobby. Bobby with the dad who thought she used to be hot.

And Bobby saw her.

He opened his mouth wide and moaned, drawing the attention of the others.

Terri felt tears burning her eyes as she stumbled up another flight of stairs. One more and she'd be on her floor. Just ten more steps. Now five more…

They were only a few flights beneath her. How were they moving so fast?

She threw herself against the door to the fifth floor, fumbling for the handle, almost unable to find the strength to yank the door open. They were right behind her now, so close she could smell them again, that thick warm stench of unwashed bodies. She glanced over her shoulder and saw that they were on the landing just below her.

And then she was through the door and running down the hallway to her room, dodging the bodies that littered the floor, trying not to see their faces, their open eyes. She fumbled through the pockets of her jeans, hands trembling, feeling for the keycard.

The stairwell door opened. The men flooded through. So fast. How are they moving so fast?

Terri choked on a sob. The keycard wasn't working. She turned it around, rightside up, watching the men stumble closer.

Their clothes were covered with blood.

Steffy.

The keycard slid into the lock and the little red light blinked green.

She thought she felt someone's hand in her hair but then she was inside the room and slamming the door behind her and throwing all the locks and oh, God…how many were out there now? She peeked through the spyhole and saw at least half a dozen men within her field of vision.

They beat at the door with the palms of their hands. Some of them used fists. One of them rattled the doorknob.

How long would it be before they figured out they could break the door down?

Terri backed away from the door, vision blurred with tears. She looked around the cheap room. A bed. A dresser. A balcony looking out over the inferno of the airport. A mini-fridge. No weapons. No way out.

The door shook in its frame. Their moans had turned angry now, without the pathetic confusion of before. They wanted in so badly. They wanted her.

She had nowhere to go.

Terri screamed in pure frustration and the sound made the men on the other side of the door frenzy. She could see the wood splintering in the frame. The locks wouldn't hold. They couldn't.

If this was one of her movies, she would have a machine gun stashed under the bed. Or the hero would come through the door and save her.

If this was a movie, she would have never thrown a woman into the middle of those men.

She half-stumbled across the room, pulling open the sliding balcony door. The air stunk of burning flesh and black smoke from the airport. The sun was setting behind the mountains, washing the nightmare of the world in the most beautiful golden light that Terri had ever seen.

The last sunset she would ever see.

She looked below the balcony. She was five stories up. Nothing but asphalt beneath.

She could jump. Maybe she'd land okay.

Maybe she'd shatter her legs.

Maybe she'd break her neck.

But maybe she'd be okay.

The doorframe shuddered again. She could hear the wood cracking beneath their fists. It sounded like they were throwing themselves against the door now. They'd be inside in a few minutes.

She almost wished she'd stuck around to see what they did to Steffy. Then she'd know what to expect.

What she deserved.

Another crack. The door was coming down. A bloody hand tore through the shattered wood, reaching blindly for her.

All she'd ever needed was to be seen. To be wanted.

She kept her eyes on the door as she swung a leg over the edge of the railing, straddling the narrow brick wall, waiting. She glanced down again. It didn't seem that far down. Not really.

The door seemed to explode inward, slamming back on its hinges so abruptly that the men on the other side seemed momentarily stunned.

Terri eased her other leg over the railing, perching on its edge.

They saw her. Their flat eyes seemed to glow in the growing shadows of the room. Terri could see their silhouettes, hulking shapes gathering, pouring through the door of her room. They reached for her, fingers grasping. They moaned, agonized but triumphant. She was theirs now. They had her.

As they staggered into the light of the fading sunset, Terri could see that some of them had blood on their faces…and she suddenly knew what they'd done to Steffy. Touching her hadn't been enough. Their hunger for her had gone far beyond that. They had wanted Steffy for so many years that she had become a part of them.

Just the way they wanted her now.

They surged forward, flooding through the open balcony door. So close.

Terri twisted to face the men, smiling at them for one frozen moment as she pushed off the edge of the railing. She smiled at them for all their years of devotion to her. For all their love. She owed them that much at least.

One last smile for her fans.

It was a long way down.

Nympho

(originally published in **Love, Damned Love***)*

At first he thought he'd had one too many beers.

Frank stood at the water's edge for a few minutes, unable to do anything but stare at the woman as she lazily backstroked over the gentle waves. She was nude, and the unexpected sight of her breasts skimming along the surface made him tremble so fiercely that he nearly spilled his beer. The moon was bright enough for him to see that she was spectacularly beautiful.

She wasn't anyone he knew. Women like her didn't run with his crowd, and he knew he hadn't seen her around the bonfire earlier. The only girls at the party were the sorority sisters who thought that Daisy Dukes and baby tees were the height of naughty sexiness, and all of them had already attached themselves to his frat brothers. He was on his own, as usual. If the girls needed somebody to write a term paper or do a few pages of calculus, then he was the big stud on campus. Any other time, well...it just sucked to be the token smart guy.

The party was winding down behind him, their beer-soaked whoops and yells fading into wetter sounds of sex in all its varieties, and Frank still stood in the softly ebbing waves, transfixed by the woman as she swam so beautifully.

"Hello."

Her whispery voice carried over the water, startling him into sharp embarrassment. Busted. Now she'd chew him out and send him packing. He knew the drill.

"I'm sorry...I didn't mean to stare...I mean, I saw you swimming and..." Frank's voice died in his throat as he watched her swim towards him. She stood in the waist-deep water and suddenly Frank forgot how to form words. Spectacularly beautiful wasn't adequate enough to describe her. He knew he was staring at her breasts—knew that he should at least look up and into her eyes—but he couldn't even make himself blink.

"Why don't you come out and talk to me?" She smiled as she spoke, and Frank finally managed to raise his gaze to her face. Dear God...she was every beautiful woman, every hot actress, every wet dream he had ever known. Her eyes were huge, and even in the moonlight he could see that they were blue. And her mouth...just thinking about her mouth would give him fuel for a thousand jerk-off sessions to come.

He wanted to walk out into the water, but couldn't make his legs move. He was so hard it almost hurt.

She cocked her head to the side and her smile slanted in a way that seemed to share a secret joke between them. Holding out a hand to him, she whispered, "Please...?"

Suddenly Frank was moving, tossing away the beer can, sloshing clumsily through the waves until he stood directly in front of her. His hands twitched with the desire to cup her breasts, to thumb the nipples that peeked out from ropy strands of her wet hair.

"You can touch me, if you want." She gazed into his eyes as she reached out to him, hooking her fingers in the elastic waistband of his trunks. "I want you to."

Frank's mouth went dry. He felt outside of his body as his hands rose and actually, really, oh God yes it's happening cupped her breasts. He'd never done as much before, and he felt awkward as he pressed his palms against her hardening nipples. But dear God...he never wanted the moment to end.

Her hands slipped beneath the waistband, and as she kept his gaze locked on hers, she began stroking him, her touch so soft and slow that he closed his eyes for a moment, afraid that he'd lose it right then and there. This wasn't happening to him. Couldn't be happening.

But her hands were on him, and his hands were on her breasts, and when he opened his eyes again, her face was so close to his that he could feel her breath against his lips.

No one could be that beautiful. It wasn't possible.

She kissed him, teasing his lips with the tip of her tongue, and he felt her sighing into his mouth, melting against him as her grip tightened pleasurably around him. That first kiss went on forever, their lips parting only long enough to change the angle as she somehow worked his trunks down to his knees.

He knew the others were on the beach, knew that they could be watching him, even laughing at him, but he didn't care. This could all be a big joke, but this woman would be worth every smirk and laugh. Nothing mattered but the slick warmth of her as she guided him into her body, the tightness surrounding him as she shifted and rode him beneath the waves.

Gasping, he opened his eyes and saw that she was watching him. Her expression remained placid, but a faint smile drew up the corner of her lips. Her hands on his shoulders gripped him tightly—

...oh shit...no rubbers...I don't have anything on...

—but he could not stop, could not do anything but grip her narrow waist tighter.

And still she watched him. And he was helpless.

He cried out without any concern for the others hearing him, finally closing his eyes as the world exploded. It felt unreal. Nothing he'd ever imagined, nothing he'd ever experienced, had ever prepared him for that.

She slid away from him as he struggled for breath, and that felt lonelier than anything he had ever known. He opened his eyes, startled by the sudden coldness, and felt her pull away from his embrace.

"Wait...!"

She smiled, teeth shining white in the moonlight, and languidly backstroked away from him. Watching the water sluice over her breasts and belly made him immediately want her again.

"Don't go!" He clumsily swam towards her, into deeper waters, but his legs were bound up by his trunks and he flailed helplessly in the waves. "I don't know your name!"

Her smile widened and she effortlessly turned away from him, swimming with a speed that left him awed.

And more alone than he'd ever felt in his life.

***

He went back the next night. And the next. And the next. A week passed by without a sign of her, and every day of that week was more miserable than the last. He dreamed of her, could still feel the weight of her breasts in his hands and the heat of her body as he plunged inside her. He looked for her on campus, but no woman compared to her.

And he didn't even know her name.

I'm crazy, he thought as he stared at the waves, hoping to see her emerging from the ocean like his own personal Venus. This is why they're called one-night stands. They last one night. No matter how good it might have been. One night.

But maybe it wasn't any good for her.

He hadn't considered that.

She hadn't made any sound, hadn't given him any encouragement. He'd been quick, selfish, coming too fast for her to climax with him. No wonder she'd swam away so fast. She couldn't wait to get away from him.

It made sense. And it made Frank feel as if his stomach had turned hollow. The thought of never seeing her again, never feeling her body again...

"Hello..."

The night was much darker than the first night he'd seen her, but he knew that voice, had heard it in his dreams every night. She'd come up behind him, and when he turned he saw that she was lying in the tide, supported on her elbows with her legs parted to allow the waves access to the dark vee between them. She smiled and licked at her lips, as if she were suddenly, ravenously hungry.

Frank stumbled towards her, transfixed as she idly strummed her fingertips over her nipples, as she flexed and arched her back to enjoy the force of each wave washing over her. She kept her eyes on his, and when he was close enough, she rose onto her knees, keeping her gaze fixed on his as she undid his jeans and yanked them to his ankles.

He felt her breath against him, and this time, when he came he felt as if he were having a heart attack. Every muscle tensed, every nerve ending felt as if it were exploding with pleasure/pain. He heard himself screaming with the intensity of it.

He hit the sand on his knees, gasping as if someone had punched him in the belly, unable to even speak. She smiled that same funny little smile and crawled into the waves again, presenting him with a momentary view of her perfect ass as she dove into the water.

Even drained so thoroughly, Frank felt another twinge of painful desire shooting through him. He fell onto his side, then rolled onto his back as the waves lapped against him, lulling him into a dark, deep sleep filled with dreams of her.

***

Torture.

Every day was a new torment. Every moment away from her was an eternity of pain and loneliness. Now that he knew what he had been missing for so many years, now that he had felt such unbelievable release, he could think of nothing else. When he closed his eyes he saw her on her knees before him, so submissive and pliant and desperate for him. He felt her mouth on him, felt her tongue and her breath and her hands on his body.

That was when he was alive. When he was with her. Inside her. The rest of his life was nothing compared to those moments.

He went back to the beach every night, haunting the shores until dawn, sometimes sleeping on the sand in the hopes that he might wake up with her beside him.

Nothing. No sign of her. And every day that passed made him ache even more to feel her again.

Frank realized that he was acting like an addict, like a junkie in search of his next fix, but he felt an almost physical need for her. Whoever she was.

And sometimes that need enraged him. Did she even care what she was doing to him? Was he just a quick fuck to her? Was he nothing but a game? She didn't even want to know his name.

He knew that if he could just talk to her, if he could just spend some time with her, he could make her want to be with him. Didn't women want guys who were serious about a relationship? He wanted that with her. He wanted to be with her every night and day, to know everything about her, to be able to do whatever she wanted him to do. He wanted to make love to her properly, to make her come beneath his hands and mouth and know that he wanted her, body and soul.

If he could just *talk* to her. That's all he needed. Just to talk to her.

He could make her listen. Make her understand.

So every night he went back to the beach—their special beach—and sat on the rocks until dawn. He watched the waves so intently that he found himself holding his breath in anticipation of seeing her again. He masturbated into the tide pools swirling around the rocks, unable to help himself once he started remembering the way he felt inside her. And as he waited, as he remembered, he wept.

It was when he was weeping that she returned to him.

She slid her hands over his shoulders, along the sides of his arms, and leaned down to kiss the top of his head.

Frank choked on his tears, so relieved to have her back that for a moment he thought he might be dreaming. He turned around and she was standing behind him, completely naked, more perfect than he'd even remembered. Her hair hung in wet curls over her breasts, down to the curve of her hips, and as she held her arms out to him, Frank felt as if he couldn't move fast enough, couldn't look at her long enough.

And he couldn't get inside her again soon enough.

He lost control. Conscious thought dappled in and out of his mind. He pulled her down to him, beneath him, pinning her against the rocks as she spread her legs for him and stretched her arms over her head. He couldn't wait, didn't want to wait, and suddenly he was slamming against her, unable to stop, needing to do it harder and harder, to make her see how much he wanted her, how desperate she had made him.

And she let him. She let him do everything. Smiling, watching his every move, she spread her legs and moved against him and did everything he wanted before he even knew he wanted it.

Frank lasted longer than he expected, and when he came, he felt as if every ounce of strength exploded out of him. He felt her moving, ready to run away again, and he lowered his weight atop her body.

"Please don't go..." He raised his head and gazed down at her. She was so beautiful. So perfect. "I need to talk to you."

She shook her head. "No...I need to go. Now."

"Do you have a boyfriend? Is that why you can't stay?" Frank felt that familiar panic rising at the thought of losing her again. "What's your name?"

"Let me go!" She weakly pushed at him, but Frank didn't move. "I don't want this..."

"You started it!" Frank reached up and pinned her arms down at the wrist. He knew he was a heartbeat away from going too far, but God help him...he couldn't stop. Not now. "Please...just talk to me. That's all I want."

"I have to go!" She squirmed, bucking against him, and the feel of it made him hard again. The easy seduction in her eyes was gone now, replaced by...fear? Panic?

Shame burned through him, but it wasn't enough to make his erection go away.

"Don't make me do this," she whispered.

"I'm not going to hurt you," Frank said, near tears. "I just want to know who—"

Something stung him.

The pain encircled his left thigh, like a jellyfish tendril had wrapped around his leg, and Frank cried out, rolling off her. She didn't move, lying perfectly still.

"What did you do?" Numbness moved quickly, deadening Frank's left leg. In the darkness, the faint silver glow of moonlight, he couldn't see the wound to his leg, but he could feel the warmth of his own blood ebbing away.

"I told you to let me go..." She moved over him and now he could see what had stung him. Her legs—those beautiful, perfectly shaped legs—were not legs anymore. As he watched, he saw the skin—gelatinous, grey-mottled flesh—splitting, dividing into dozens of smooth, rounded tentacles. They moved independently of each other, frenzied as they stroked over his legs with a wet slickness.

"I liked you," she said quietly. "But now I'm hungry. You should have let me go."

Frank screamed.

And abruptly shut up when he saw her face again.

Her true face.

Her eyes had elongated, all black pupil now, and stared lidlessly at him. Her mouth was no longer a mouth; it was a huge hole, lined with rows of needle-sharp teeth, lipless and drooling as she moved closer to his face. He could see something like gills opening up along either side of her swanlike throat, globules of thick discharge dripping from their fluttering edges.

"No..." He pushed at her shoulders, felt his fingers sink into her cold, jellied flesh. She moved closer to him, skimming his chest with her open mouth, slithering her tongue over his skin. Frank couldn't move. His lower half felt dead, too heavy to move. He watched her lower her head over his penis, felt it engulfed in the pricking circle of her mouth and screamed at the thought of all those teeth...

But she moved lower, dragging her mouth down his left leg.

"Please...I'm sorry..."

She slid down to his feet and raised herself over them. Her torso held the barest remnants of breasts. Her flat belly melted into that mass of tendrils and tentacles, all of them moving independently of each other, blindly roaming over his legs, wrapping loosely around his dick, probing between his thighs.

Frank felt the tears on his cheeks and realized he was crying. "I'm sorry! I said I was sorry!"

But they were beyond words now. He raised his head and watched her engulf the toes of his left foot in her needle-lined mouth. Her tongue teased and danced around each toe, and then she was swallowing his foot to the arch. He could feel the teeth grinding into his flesh and screamed.

She took him even deeper, swallowing his foot up to his ankle. Her black eyes held his.

Unreal. This isn't happening. This can't be happening.

She opened her mouth wider, slid upwards, and suddenly she had swallowed his leg up to his knee. Frank screamed again, feeling her needle teeth slashing and grinding against flesh and muscle and bone. He felt the crunch, and when she raised her head, the muscles of her throat working mightily to swallow every last bit, he saw that she had taken his leg with him.

Frank's screams died.

She crawled atop him and he felt razor-tips slashing and digging into his belly and sides as the tentacles swarmed over his chest and arms. The salt of his blood smelled like the sea, and he gagged as he felt tendrils worming inside his gut, searching blindly, hungrily.

"I..." He choked, shook with pain, gasped for breath that wouldn't come. "I...loved...you..."

She cocked her head curiously as she hovered close to his face. Now he could see nothing of the woman he thought she had been. Her eyes were so black, so unreadable, that he felt dizzy gazing into them.

He had loved her. Whatever she was. He really had loved her.

She stroked his cheek with the pads of what had once been her fingers, her touch gentle. Frank could almost believe, in that moment, that she might have felt the same for him.

And then she opened her mouth wide to kiss him one last time.

The Beautiful People

(originally published in **Decadence of the Dead***)*

They were still out there.

She'd lost count of how many waited restlessly just outside the doors, pressing their faces against the glass, hungry. They wanted to get inside. And they were getting impatient.

Just the way London Wyatt liked it.

London sensed that the paparazzi had waited long enough, so she gestured to the bodyguards to escort her through the rear entrance of the boutique. She stumbled through the door, unsteady on her stiletto heels, and giggled at herself.

The explosion of flashes was her reward, and London gloried in it, striking her signature pose—one shoulder cocked high, eyes half-closed, tongue peeking from the corner of her lips—and knowing that her picture would appear in every tabloid and gossip website in the world. She hadn't seen herself in *L.A. Star* magazine in two weeks, and that was totally unacceptable. London liked being known as the "bad girl," and she went out of her way to raise hell.

She saw her personal assistant, Viki, grimacing and couldn't help but laugh at her. Bitch needed to buy a sense of humor.

"What's your problem, Vik?"

"You've got a photo shoot for *Maximum* magazine at three and—"

"And they'll wait for me. Jesus, Viki. Chill."

London bent over to check a price tag, giving them a flash of ass as her micro-mini skirt rode up, and knew that the photo would be all over the Internet in minutes. It was all part of the job. Give them what they want and they would give her what she needed.

"She's out there again."

London gave the paps a coy smile over her shoulder before turning to Viki. The smile immediately disappeared. "Who?"

"Your biggest fan." Viki jerked her head towards the glass at the front of the boutique and London turned around, sparking a new barrage of flashbulbs. She had to fight to plaster a fresh smile on her face.

"Shit…" she hissed. "I thought you arranged for a restraining order or something."

"I did. That doesn't mean she'll obey it."

London laughed falsely and cocked her head to the side, keeping an eye on the creepy woman standing amid the photographers. The little troll was just standing there, mouth gaping open as she watched London's every move. She had thick features—wide nose, rubbery lips, bulgy eyes, all framed by lank, greasy hair—and was as round as she was tall. She was every loathsome thing a woman could possibly be, and she didn't just want to be London's best friend, she wanted to *be* London.

The thought of it made her want to puke.

"I want her gone. Now." London's smile fell away when she turned back to Viki. "Get the bodyguards on her or call the police or whatever. Just get her away from me."

"But she's harmless—"

"She's gross. And I don't want anyone taking a picture of me even close to that troll. Now do what I say and quit arguing, bitch."

Viki took a deep breath and closed her eyes for a moment,

"Now smile like a good little bitch and let's give them what they want." London slipped into her second favorite pose—head tossed back, open mouth smile, eyes sultry and knowing—and felt the hot waves of lust and envy as her fans worshiped her. Right now, she was the hottest thing on Rodeo Drive.

And all was right with the world.

***

Maggie leaned her forehead against the cool glass, wishing more than anything that she could pass through it and magically be a part of that wonderful, beautiful world on the other side. She would be tall and slim and beautiful, and she and London would be best friends. She knew London would like her if they ever met. She knew all of London's favorite things, and she knew her *real* history—not the vicious lies that were published in those trashy tabloids—so they would have tons of stuff to talk about.

She just wanted to be friends. That's all. If she was friends with London, then everything would be perfect. People would smile when they saw her and want to take her picture and men would want to talk to her and everything would be so much better.

But she couldn't talk to London anymore. The police had warned her that she couldn't email her or call her or try to talk to her in person ever again. They didn't understand that their friendship was just in its early stages, that London was just getting to know her.

Maggie watched London disappear through the back of the store, followed by that slut Viki. She had a feeling she knew exactly what just happened in there and she cheered London on as she watched her take Viki down a notch or two. London was so cool.

As the photographers drifted away, in search of their next target, Maggie felt that familiar sense of loss as the moment between her and London ended. She stood on tiptoes and watched London's Humvee merge into traffic, heading back to Beverly Hills. She waved, just in case London was looking for her. She knew she had seen her— the electric shock of making eye contact with London was one of the biggest thrills she'd ever had—and she knew London had gotten her psychic message. She told London that she was always going to be there for her, no matter how many paparazzi were bugging her or how many bad stories floated around in the tabloids. She was always going to be her best friend.

Maggie smiled as she made her way to the bus stop.

***

"I think you should take the python to the party. Or the kinkajou. *Nobody* carries Chihuahuas anymore."

London ignored her stylist and studied her reflection, making sure her nipples were visible. She hated staying at the Chateau Marmont—the rooms were too small and there was never enough closet space—but it was all part of the game. She was expected to stay there, just like she was expected to stop into the Bar Marmont to have a drink and throw some free publicity their way. Then everything is comped and everybody gets their picture in the tabs.

"I don't like this." London pulled her blouse over her head, standing topless amid a crowd of strangers who walked in and out of the room. They were on her payroll, so they might as well have been invisible. And besides, it wasn't like they hadn't seen her boobs before. "Give me the silk one."

That was better. Not only was the top totally see-through, but it was low-cut enough to give her plenty of opportunities for flashing the paparazzi. The boys loved their tit shots.

"How much am I getting for tonight?" London sat in a throne-like chair and was instantly attended to by her hair guy. He was new, and she hadn't bothered to learn his name. Why waste her time. She didn't like his look, so she'd probably fire him after tonight.

"Fifty thousand," Jackie, her manager poured a glass of champagne and hurried over to London with it. London sighed and rolled her eyes. Why was she always surrounded by such boring twats? If it wasn't Viki bitching at her about what she couldn't do, it was Jackie telling her that she had to actually go to work somewhere. "Sixty if you stay for an hour."

"An hour?" London sighed. "Jesus…what do they want from me?"

"I've also got you booked for the party for the "Blood Gun 3" premiere at the Arcadium Theater after you hit the opening of the Vodka Tap on Sunset."

London pushed the hair guy out of her way. "Fuck that, Jackie. I'm not doing two in one night."

"Not what I heard," the hair guy muttered.

"Okay, asshole. You're fired. Leave now." London stood and stomped over to Jackie. "And you…either I get a hundred thou for the second party, or they can get somebody else."

"Well…" Jackie cleared her throat. "Kinsey Malone is going to make an appearance, so maybe they won't notice if you don't make it."

London went icy. "Kinsey? That bitch is going to be there?"

"Yes, but—"

"Get me a hundred thou for the party, or you're fired. Can you understand that, or do I need to speak slower?"

Jackie scurried from the room, already dialing someone on her cell, and London could hear the desperation in her voice. Good. Bitch needed to remember who she worked for. She was paid to do what London wanted, whenever London wanted, and if she couldn't do the job, then her ass was out.

London re-checked her hair. The extensions were looking ratty, but they'd do for tonight. She wanted to look a little rough, a little slutty. She'd gained half a pound, so she felt like a porker, but the mini-skirt was just short enough to flash a little cooch and a lot of ass when she danced. If this outfit didn't get her into the gossip blogs, then nothing would. Maybe she'd find some girl to make out with, too. That would definitely take the attention off Kinsey. She'd have to fuck a donkey to get more press than London.

London smiled at her reflection. Perfect.

"Hey, London…your video's on!"

The synthesized opening notes of her latest single blared from the TV and London spun around in her chair. She never got tired of watching her videos, and this one was especially hot. The whole video was just her writhing around on a beach in a wet t-shirt, and it was already number five on the daily countdown.

She began singing along—an extra little treat for her entourage, who loved hearing these impromptu personal concerts—and was right in the middle of the high note when the video cut out.

"The fuck?" London opened her eyes, ready to murder whoever turned the channel. Instead of her video, now there was nothing but a blank screen and a scroll across the bottom advising viewers to turn immediately to the cable news channels.

"Oh, my God..." one of the hair girls, a fatty with hot pink streaks in dyed black hair, quickly turned the channel to CNN. "Guys! Get in here!"

London was ignored as her staff of stylists and assistants flooded into the suite and circled around the plasma screen, where the shot of the anchors cut to jumpy video footage of bloody people running around like idiots.

Everyone was talking at once.

"Oh, shit...is that New York?"

"They don't know if it's some kind of biological weapon or not."

"Terrorists, probably."

"Did you see the footage from Washington?"

"I heard that they've stopped all the flights coming into Chicago."

London looked around, saw that no one was even aware that she was among them, and felt like screaming. Did they not realize whose suite they were in? What was wrong with these people?

"Jackie!" London yelled. "Get in here, now!"

Jackie slowly entered the bedroom again, her face ashen. "I've got to go…"

"Like fuck you will." London swept her arm out towards the group of people around the television. "What is going on?"

"I'm leaving," Jackie murmured, moving past London to collect her laptop and Blackberry, shoving it all into the huge Prada bag that London had handed down to her. "I've got to check on my kids…the news is saying it'll probably start happening here…"

London felt as if she had entered some kind of parallel universe. Nobody was acting the way they were supposed to act. "I don't pay you to check on your kids, Jackie—"

Jackie brushed past her. "Then I quit."

And just like that, she was gone.

London turned to the crowd around the television. "Somebody tell me what is happening!"

A mousy woman with ridiculous pigtails in her hair and hipster glasses turned away long enough to glance at London. "They're saying it's the end of the world."

"Bullshit." London pushed her way to the television and turned up the sound. All she saw was a bunch of ugly people running around like extras in a cheap horror movie.

"I've got to get home," the hair guy said, backing away from the television, as if he were afraid to turn his back on it. Others followed him, nearly stampeding out of the room. Nobody had even asked her if they could leave.

Pouting, London turned back to the television, trying to understand what was freaking everybody out so badly. So what if something was happening in New York? Did they not understand that New York is a long way from L.A.?

"…early reports are coming in from Washington stating that the President has safely boarded Air Force One after the attack within the White House." The news anchor's voice trembled as he gazed into the camera. London recognized him after a moment; she had met him once, and they had done some lines in the bathroom of some club in SoHo. "Some witnesses to the attacks in New York are stating that the mobs are…this can't be right…*eating* their victims…"

London looked away from the television screen and realized that she was alone in the room.

"Religious groups are calling it Judgment Day, while the CDC is investigating the possibility of biological attack—"

London turned off the television and grabbed her purse. Whatever.

***

Maggie clutched her London scrapbook close to her chest as she stared at the television. It wasn't a plasma screen like London's, but the images were just as clear and just as disturbing. When she was a little girl, Momma had told her that the world would end when Jesus came back. He would raise the dead and judge the sinners and only the worthy would be able to go to Heaven.

The things they were saying on TV sounded an awful lot like the things Momma used to tell her. Maybe it *was* the end of the world. But it was happening so far away from her, all the way over on the other side of the country. It seemed like if Jesus was going to come back, He would come back everywhere at once.

It was probably nothing to worry about. So Maggie wasn't going to worry. London probably wasn't worried about it. London was fierce. She could do anything.

Maggie felt better thinking of London. She flipped through her scrapbook and smiled at all the photos of London she had carefully trimmed out of tabloids and magazines. She always looked so pretty, so perfect.

It was almost time to leave. London had a party to attend tonight, and Maggie wanted to be there to give her all the emotional support she could. She had read that Kinsey was planning on being there too, and she hated the thought of London getting upset.

She hoped that London would see her there, but even if she didn't, she'd know that Maggie was there. They were soul mates, after all.

***

"So where is everybody?" London frowned as her Hummer approached the main entrance of the Vodka Tap. The red carpet was in place, but only a handful of photographers stood waiting for their photo ops. "I'm not the first one here, am I?"

"Oh, my God…London, look at this." Viki held her palm TV out to London, offering her one of the earbuds. "They're saying that they're closing all the airports."

"So? It's not like *I'm* flying anywhere," London said as she glanced at the TV. Jesus…wasn't there some kind of rule against showing so much blood on the news? "What do you think Kinsey will wear tonight? I'll look hotter than her, right?"

Viki didn't answer, staring at the TV screen instead. "They're saying that New York is on fire…"

"Oh, God…there's Stalker Girl.…" London laughed. "I can't believe that bitch! Why can't she just get a life, anyway? God."

Viki turned off the TV, trembling as she dropped it into her purse. "Maybe we should go home tonight."

"Are you kidding? Home? On a Saturday night?" London rolled her eyes and had the door open the moment the car stopped. The flash of cameras was immediately blinding. Plastering the smile on her face, she unfolded herself from the backseat and presented herself to the adoring public.

***

Maggie's eyes filled with tears when she saw London smiling. With everything going on in the world right now, it was amazing to know that London could still smile and make everyone around her so happy. But that was just how London was. Always thinking of other people.

An obnoxious photographer pushed her out of the way to get a better angle, and Maggie pushed back, knocking him to the ground. The paparazzi suddenly circled them, snapping photos as the red carpet was momentarily forgotten. Some of them were laughing. Maggie couldn't tell if they were laughing at her or the jerk on the ground. It didn't matter. She could feel the rage building inside her anyway.

"What's your problem, bitch!" The asshole rolled onto his side, trying to get to his feet. Two hundred extra pounds on his frame didn't help his cause. "I'll sue your ass!"

They were all laughing at her now.

Maggie turned around and saw that London was craning her head to see what the commotion was. She pointed at Maggie and made a face, shaking her head as she laughed and turned away.

London was laughing at her. Laughing.

At that moment, Maggie wanted—more than anything else in the world—to just lie down and die.

Instead, she hung her head and shuffled down the street to the bus stop. She knew where London would be headed next. Maybe she could talk to her, explain what happened. Maybe London wasn't laughing at her after all, but at the stupid photographer. That had to be it. London wouldn't make fun of her.

Maggie felt the heaviness in her chest lighten. London was her friend. She'd never laugh at her. Never.

***

The party was dead.

So unbelievable. London didn't have anyone to hang with, and there were no cameras from "Entertainment Tonight" or even "Extra." Even the wannabe celeb bloggers weren't there, and they usually went everywhere. The club was mostly empty, and everyone who *did* attend were hanging around the bar, drinking as they watched the news on the wall mounted TV.

So boring.

London twirled in the middle of the dance floor, whooping and yelling and singing along with the music, but no one looked at her.

Even Viki wasn't watching, and Viki *always* watched.

Pissed, London threw her glass to the floor and stomped over to yank on Viki's sleeve. "Come on. I'm ready to go."

"Hold on, Lond…" Viki didn't even turn around. "In a sec."

London pouted prettily, but no one was paying attention to her, so she threw her purse onto the bar and grabbed the nearest drink. She looked around at everyone as they watched TV, smirking at their dumb expressions. Bunch of losers. They looked like they were going to shit their pants.

"New York's totally closed off," Viki murmured, voice trembling. "Everything east of the Mississippi is crazy. Everybody's killing each other…"

"And that's because they're all a bunch of stupid rednecks." London drained her drink and motioned for another. "Who cares?"

"This is serious, London."

"And I'm seriously bored. Now come on…let's go to the premiere. I want to get there before Kinsey."

London grabbed Viki's bony arm and dragged her away from the bar. Maybe things would be livelier at the next party.

***

"… you think is happening, Miss Wyatt?"

It took London a moment to realize that the Humvee driver was actually daring to speak to her. Marty knew the rules. No eye contact, no direct conversation. She looked over to Viki to share her disbelief and saw that she was watching that stupid little TV again. Bitch.

"I tried calling my mom out in Queens, and she said that the streets were getting pretty bad out there. She saw one guy walking around with a knife sticking out of his neck." Marty's eyes kept cutting to the rearview mirror, searching out London. "I told her to lock her doors and not to let anybody in, but Momma's too friendly. I know she'll let one of 'em inside."

London sighed. "One of *who*?"

"Jesus, Miss Wyatt! Don't you know what's going on?"

She definitely didn't like the tone of his voice. His ass would be fired by tomorrow morning, that was for sure.

"It's all over the news. They're saying that dead people are walking around and shit!" Marty half-turned his head to look at her in the back seat. "It's all over the East coast, and they think it's starting out here now, too."

London laughed. "That's so stupid. You're stupid. Everybody's acting all stupid over noth--"

A woman dressed in a glittery red dress came out of nowhere, lurching into the middle of the road from between two parked cars. Marty stomped on his brakes just a fraction of a second before hitting her, and she slowly turned around to look at him. Even London could see that there was something very wrong. The woman still wore her jewels—gaudy diamond earrings, a huge ruby necklace—and was in full evening makeup. But her eyes were milky white, and her jaw looked as if it had been unhinged by a hard blow.

And her throat looked…chewed.

Viki screamed a little, covering her mouth with her hands like a bad actress in an even worse movie.

"Oh, fuck…" Marty breathed, hitting the power locks on the doors.

The woman began to crawl onto the hood of the Humvee, her filmy eyes rolling madly as she moaned and drooled blood and bile onto the windshield. She scratched at the glass, gnawed at it with broken teeth, trying to get inside.

Marty threw the Hummer into reverse and the woman slid sideways off the hood, hitting the road hard enough to bounce. He slammed to a stop and London leaned forward to get a better look.

The woman was standing up. Her arm hung dead from a dislocated shoulder, and her forehead was split in a bloodless gash, but she stood up.

"Oh, God…" London whispered. "What's wrong with her?"

They were beginning to draw a crowd. Tourists, mostly, gawking and pointing and whispering. As the woman turned around to face them, they began to applaud, looking around for the cameras. The woman seemed unaware of them, staggering slowly away from the Humvee. Heading toward a fat man in a Hawaiian shirt.

Then things happened very quickly.

The woman had her face buried in the fat man's throat before he could even scream. And then he couldn't scream, because his windpipe was being chewed. Blood sprayed the crowd as the man fell backwards, the woman riding him all the way down to the ground.

"Go!" London shouted, pounding at the backseat. "Just get out of here!"

It seemed like it took forever for the Humvee to back up and pull out. London watched the woman pull stringy, stretchy gobs of bloody meat out of the fat man's throat with her teeth as the tourists surrounding them took photos and pointed video cameras.

Nobody tried to stop her.

***

Viki wouldn't stop crying, and it was pissing London off. The driver babbled and swore as he drove, air raid sirens were beginning to blare all over L.A., and traffic was a bitch. Fat, ugly people were running all over the place, abandoning their cars in the middle of the road.

London watched it all from behind tinted windows, drinking deeply from a bottle of Jack she had carried out of the last bar. In a way, it was like watching a really bitchin' movie. A few more of the weirdos had popped up, attacking anybody who got close, and after the first few spurts of blood, London felt like what she was seeing wasn't real.

She couldn't wait for everything to be over with so she could get back to normal. She was supposed to fly out to the Bahamas with Tyra and Niki next weekend, and she wasn't about to cancel.

Viki rocked back and forth on the seat beside London, weeping as she watched the little TV. Now *that* was just boring. She was ruining her makeup and making her eyes puffy, and it wasn't like it would do her any good.

"I'm hungry," London whined. "Aren't we there yet?"

"I can't believe you're still going to the premiere." Viki finally looked up from the TV, her mascara running over her cheeks. She looked like shit. "We need to get home—"

"It's not that serious, Vik."

"Are you kidding me? Have you looked outside?"

"I'm not letting Kinsey get all the attention tonight."

"Jesus, London…what is wrong with you?"

London tuned her out and looked out the window again. People were on foot, running along the freeway with bags and suitcases in their hands. A few of them had guns. They were followed by the weird-looking ones, the people who walked funny and attacked anyone who got too close.

"This is really happening, and it's really serious, and you'd better pull your head out of your ass and deal!"

London leaned forward. "Stop the car."

The driver glanced over his shoulder. "It's not safe to stop...they'll swarm us—"

"I said, stop the fucking car, idiot!"

The Humvee slammed to a stop. People started towards them, desperate and afraid. The others were close behind them, gaining ground with each second.

Viki saw them coming, knew what was going to happen. "London...what are you doing?"

"Get out."

"What? No..."

"If you don't like riding with me, then walk! Get out of my car, bitch!" London swung at Viki, landing a hard slap against her cheek. "Get out, get out, get out!"

Viki fumbled with the door handle while trying to fend off London's blows, screaming as the driver shouted at London to stop. She fell out of the car on her hands and knees.

London slammed the door and locked it again. "Drive."

"You can't just leave her—"

"I can do whatever I want to do!" London screamed. "Now just fucking drive!"

Viki managed to get to her feet just as the Humvee pulled away. London turned around in the seat to watch her grow smaller in the distance, surrounded by those weird-looking, ugly strangers.

London waved goodbye. She didn't need Viki's shit anymore.

"Miss Wyatt...we've got to get to one of the shelters." The driver glanced into the rearview mirror. "Please...I've got a family. I have to go home."

"Just keep driving."

"But—"

"I said, keep fucking driving." London chewed on one of her manicured fingernails as she stared out the window. Every once in a while one of the things would notice the Humvee and slam against the hood or the roof, but the car kept moving fast enough to keep them from overtaking it.

"Where do you want to go?" The driver's voice cracked and London realized that he was crying.

"The Arcadium Theater." London drained the bottle of Jack, closing her eyes as the world around her grew a little more muffled. Better. That was better.

She was going to go to the premiere and fight with Kinsey Malone and flirt with cute boys and maybe do some blow in the bathroom and everything was going to be okay and normal again and all this ugliness was going to go away.

It was going to be okay. She was London Wyatt, and she always got her way. It had to be okay.

They kept driving. London couldn't look away from the chaos in the streets. It was like L.A. had turned into a war zone in just a few hours. As they got closer to the theater, London noticed that the caliber of people wandering the streets had changed. They weren't the ugly, poor people who lived in the Valley and shopped at Wal-Mart. These were people she knew. She'd fought with some of them. Partied with a few of them. Fucked most of them. They were dressed better than the others, but they had the same dead look in their eyes. They stumbled over the bodies lying in the road as if they were blind, stopping only to drop to their knees to bite and tear at the corpses.

These were the people who had been adored, the stars who made the movies that the whole world worshiped. They had lived in mansions, spent money on useless, flamboyant junk, indulged their every desire and made millions envious of their every move.

And now they wobbled up and down the streets of L.A., covered with blood and dirt, aware of nothing. Now they were no different than the people who had paid to see their movies or bought the tabloids to gawk at their photos. Now they weren't special anymore.

London felt the numbing buzz of Jack Daniels rapidly burning off. And she didn't want to be sober now. She didn't want to have to think about what was happening. She wanted things to be the way they were supposed to have been. She wanted normal back.

***

Maggie held her scrapbook close to her chest as she slowly rocked back and forth, watching the world on the other side of the bus window go insane. There were only a few people on the bus with her, all of them looking out the windows, no one speaking.

All of them were scared. She could feel it like a blast of cold air. Bad things were happening and no one knew exactly what they were. All they knew was what they saw happening on the streets. And what was happening on the streets was very bad.

Maggie felt far away from everything. People were screaming, running wild in the streets, attacking each other. She saw a woman tear the throat out of a little girl. She saw a guy take down a man twice his size and gut him in the middle of the street. She saw things she never imagined she would see on the streets of Los Angeles.

And all she could think of was London. Was she safe? Was everything okay with her? Where was she now?

The scrapbook felt good and solid in her arms, and she rested her cheek on it as she gazed out the window.

She saw a billboard with London's face, for the perfume she had just relased, and the sight made her smile. It was a sign. London was with her.

The thought calmed her, and she closed her eyes for a moment, thinking of her favorite daydream where she's as thin and beautiful as London, and together they shop and party and dance and are best friends. London accepted her, and didn't mind that she wasn't that smart or worked at a Taco Hut or had to buy her clothes from Goodwill. In Maggie's daydreams, the world was perfect and so was she.

The bus driver suddenly shouted and Maggie snapped awake, looking ahead to see a crowd of people standing in the middle of the street. They didn't even try to move. Even with a huge bus hurdling towards them, they just stood there, like they were waiting.

The bus screeched to a stop, but not before it plowed into the crowd. They went down without a sound, but even as they were crushed below the wheels, the others were swarming the bus, slamming their fists against the windows. One of them pressed its face against the glass just outside of Maggie's window, and she could see that whatever it was, it wasn't alive anymore. She couldn't look away from its gaping mouth, the teeth broken and dripping blood. It had eyes like a shark, flat and black and utterly focused on getting to her.

They were pounding at the bus door, pulling at it, opening it inch by inch. The driver fought to keep the door shut, but there were too many of them. They surrounded the bus now, rocking it as they struggled to get inside. And they kept moaning, like their souls were in Hell but their bodies remained here.

Maggie shrunk back in her seat and tightened her hold on the scrapbook. The hydraulic door slammed open and suddenly they were on the bus, swarming down the aisle, using their teeth and clawed hands on everyone in their path. The driver was yanked out from behind the wheel, his screams ending in a wet crunching sound. Everyone was screaming now, pleading, begging for mercy from a God that was not listening.

Maggie saw it all as if she were watching a movie. It wasn't real. She was not watching men and women murder and eat other men and women. She was on her way to the theater so she could watch

London enter the premiere. She was going to take more pictures to glue in her scrapbook, and then she was going to go home and dream that she was best friends with London.

That's what she was supposed to be doing. Not this.

A man she had never seen before, who had probably been a tourist only hours before, stumbled down the aisle, fixated on her with an intensity that made Maggie tremble. His mouth fell open as he reached for her with blood-covered hands.

Sliding out of her seat, she backed up, dizzy with nausea as the stench of blood slammed into her. More of the things had noticed her now, and they gathered behind the tourist, moving slowly but steadily down the aisle.

Maggie hit the back of the bus. Trapped. Nowhere to go.

Something dug into the small of her back, and she realized she was pressed against the emergency exit.

She didn't want to turn around to open it, afraid that the moment she stopped watching their slow advance, they'd leap forward with hellish speed. And crazily, she didn't want to leave the bus, knowing that there were so many of those things out there, waiting.

But if she stayed…if she stayed, they'd tear her apart.

Clutching the scrapbook to her chest, Maggie pushed open the emergency exit and jumped to the ground, skinning her hands and knees on the asphalt. She stood quickly and looked around. Most of those things were at the front of the bus.

But they wouldn't stay there.

Maggie limped away, keeping her distance from the slow moving things around her. She couldn't think of them as people. They were *things* now. Whatever had happened to them, they weren't people anymore.

In the gathering dusk, Maggie realized that she was only a few blocks away from the Arcadium. That was where London would be. She'd be safe there.

They'd *both* be safe. And that was all that mattered now.

***

The Hummer jumped the sidewalk, and London screamed as bodies crunched beneath the wheels. She couldn't tell if they had been normal people or the other ones, and at that moment she didn't care. She could see the Arcadium Theater just ahead, and that meant things were almost normal again. She'd get a drink and watch whatever stupid movie was premiering, and then she'd party. She'd even get her photo taken with Kinsey Malone, if the paparazzi wanted. She just wanted to forget everything she had seen and party.

The street ahead was surprisingly empty, with only a few of the slow weirdos bumbling around. So maybe it was almost over.

"Get out of the car!" Marty stomped on the brakes hard enough to send London onto the floor of the backseat. "I did what you wanted and got you here. Now go on, get out!"

"You can't talk to me like that, you asshole!" London slapped at his shoulders, screaming inarticulately as she pummeled him with her fists. "You fucker! You're fired! You're *fired*!"

Marty half-turned to face her and grabbed her wrist hard enough to make her shut up. "Fuck you, London. Now get the fuck out of the Hummer."

London wrenched herself out of his grasp and fumbled her way out of the back of the Hummer, stumbling out to the pavement. Marty shot her the finger and stepped on the gas, screeching away from the theater.

"I hope your family is dead!" London screamed. "Do you hear me! Dead!"

A tortured moan was her reply, and the sound of it echoing through the unnatural quiet made London realize that she was not alone. The weirdos were coming out of the clubs and boutiques lining the street, and as the wind shifted, London could smell the thick warm stink of blood. They seemed to zero in on her in an instant, and they seemed to move a little faster now that they had a target.

London couldn't breathe. She couldn't breathe and she couldn't scream and she couldn't run. From the safety of the Hummer, she had seen what the weirdos had done to anyone they caught. She had seen throats bitten out and eyes gouged and stomachs ripped open. No amount of Jack Daniels could blot those memories from her mind.

And at that moment, standing exposed in the middle of the street, London realized that there was no going back to normal. These things didn't care who she was or how much money she had. No one cared anymore.

If she died, no one would even know. There'd be no special announcements on E! or "Entertainment Tonight." Because nobody would give a shit.

"Goddamn it!" she screamed, balling her hands into fists as she stomped the pavement. "Leave me alone!"

They kept moaning, stumbling closer from all directions, reaching out for her. London backed away from them, wobbling on her spiked heels. She glanced behind her and saw that the doors to the Arcadium were closer than she thought. She could get inside and hide, then she'd be okay.

The weirdos were getting closer, all of them reaching out for her, like they wanted a piece of her. Like her fans.

"London!"

London spun around, frantic. She saw a flash of fiery-red hair that she recognized instantly. Kinsey Malone was at the doors of the Arcadium, leaning out. Her mini-dress was soaked with blood, and she looked like she'd spent a night snorting bad coke, but she was alive, at least.

A few of the weirdos stood between her and the theater, but London was able to sprint past them, shuddering as their fingertips grazed her arms. Kinsey opened the door and London collapsed inside, squinting against the sudden dimness. She saw a lot of people she recognized, but they were all crying and moaning and huddled together.

"I thought you were dead for a minute," Kinsey said as she hugged London. "I couldn't tell—"

London grimaced as Kinsey backed away. Something had taken a chunk out of her upper arm, and the wound was still bleeding heavily. "Jesus Christ! What happened to you?"

"Some fat woman bit me when I got out of my limo." Kinsey smiled wanly. "I self-medicated."

London noticed the white residue around Kinsey's nostrils and nodded. "Got any more?"

"Yeah…come on."

They made their way to the back of the theater lobby. If anybody else knew that Kinsey was holding, they'd be mobbed. Everybody would want to get out of their heads. They quietly entered the ladies room and sat in a corner. London closed her eyes and leaned against the wall.

"This is so fucked," she said as Kinsey dug a small glassine envelope out of her purse and handed it to her. "I was going to fly out to the Bahamas this weekend, too."

"Guess that's cancelled."

"Guess everything's cancelled." London dipped a pinky nail into the coke. "Thank fuck you had this," London said, snorting up one nostril, then the other. "I just want to go to sleep and wake up when it's over."

Kinsey shifted uncomfortably against the wall. For the first time since entering the theater, London noticed how pale she was, how grayish-blue her lips had become. The bite on her arm looked even nastier than it had before, like it was instantly infected.

"I'm gonna have to get plastic surgery," Kinsey said and closed her eyes. "Don't think make up will cover that."

"I'll give you the name of my guy," London murmured, feeling suddenly very tired, even after the coke. "He did my nose and my boobs. He's great…"

London's voice trailed away as she drifted to sleep. She dimly felt Kinsey falling against her but didn't push her away. Bygones were bygones, and if the bitch wanted to sleep on her lap…

In an instant, she was asleep.

***

Maggie staggered forward slowly, feeling as if her entire body were going numb. Her legs felt weak, but she forced them to move, even as she stumbled. She tasted her own blood in her mouth and had to stop to spit it out. She couldn't look at herself. There were too many bites, too many holes, too much blood. She only had four fingers left on her hands, but she still clutched the scrapbook to her chest. It was wet with blood, but she held onto it. She was so close now. So close.

There had been too many of them, and even though they were slow and spaced out, they were still too much for her. They'd bitten off her fingers as she tried to push them away, and sank their teeth into her arms before she could shake them off. Once they had a piece of her in their mouths, they seemed to forget the rest of her was still there. That was the only way she was able to get away from them.

Maggie sobbed, but she kept walking. The Arcadium was in sight, and she was so happy, so relieved, because now she could be with London. London was there. She knew it. Felt it.

There were more of those things in front of the doors, but Maggie pushed her way through them, silent even as they bit at her, grabbed at her, tried to pull her down. She fought them back, even though she was so tired now, even though she had no strength in her arms and her entire body felt like a raw nerve ending. A little boy sank his teeth into her forearm and Maggie screamed, an eternity passing as she felt his sharp little teeth sawing into the flesh of her arm. She hadn't known she could even feel any more pain.

More of them clawed at her, grabbing handfuls of her hair and tearing it from her scalp, trying to eat even that. They took ribbons of skin from her cheeks and throat, chewing it from beneath their fingernails, licking her blood from their hands.

But she forced her way through them, feeling the pain but pushing past it. This would all be worthwhile once she saved London. She'd take care of herself later. Right now, that was all that mattered.

She fell against the door and closed her eyes for a moment, gathering the strength to pull it open. She felt them bunching up behind her, pressing her against the door, and she moved as quickly as she could, opening the door by inches until she could slip through.

There weren't enough of them out there to break down the doors, and they weren't smart enough to figure out how to open them yet. Maggie tripped over her own feet and fell onto the carpeted floor, rolling onto her back, wanting to cry with the sheer pleasure of being able to rest for a moment.

But she wasn't finished yet. She still had to find London.

Maggie crawled to her hands and knees, wincing as she put weight on her chewed palms and shakily stood up. Her head felt light, the room spinning around her as she struggled to see in the murky light. The last bit of sunlight was fading, and the lobby was pooled with shadows. She could see people huddled against the walls, some of them dressed in expensive gowns and tuxes. Others in lightweight touristy clothing. Some of them were faces she recognized from TV.

Everybody was covered with blood. Everybody looked shell shocked and terrified.

None of them was London.

Maggie bit back her tears. No, London had to be here. She had to be.

She spat blood again and forced herself to move forward.

***

London didn't want to open her eyes, but her back ached and her butt was numb and the last thing she needed was for the tabloids to get a picture of her passed out in a bathroom. She felt a weight in her lap and dimly remembered Kinsey passing out against her. Bitch needed to get her ass up now.

"Hey…wake up." London looked down at the mass of red hair. Kinsey moved her head slightly, but didn't sit up. "Come on, Kins…I want more coke."

A sharp pain suddenly shot through London's inner thigh and she cried out as she slapped at Kinsey's head. "Bitch! Did you just bite me? I told you I'm not into that shit!"

Kinsey didn't move her head. Instead, she burrowed deeper, and another, even more agonizing pain paralyzed London for a moment. She actually felt the flesh being bitten away, and the very idea of it was so incredibly ludicrous that she almost wanted to laugh.

Then Kinsey raised her head, matted strands of red hair hanging over eyes that had gone black and dead and flat, and opened her mouth. London could see bits of her own skin stuck in Kinsey's perfect white teeth.

London screamed and pushed away from Kinsey, scrambling back against the cold tiles of the bathroom floor. Kinsey crawled after her, dripping blood from her open mouth. Her long, salon-manicured nails clicked and clacked against the tiles.

London couldn't stop screaming. She felt her throat tearing on the inside, but still she kept screaming, even as she pushed herself back into the corner of the bathroom, trapped as Kinsey kept crawling forward. She could feel blood pumping out of her thigh with each heartbeat, so much of it that she was sitting in a puddle of her own blood within seconds. She watched it spreading beneath her, funneling into the grout between the tiles.

Kinsey reached out and grabbed London's foot, pulling herself forward as she tugged London closer, dragging her through the blood.

London feebly kicked at her face as Kinsey sank her teeth into her ankle, gnawing at the bone.

The bathroom door opened, and another one of the things staggered in, heading straight for London. Kinsey kept chewing, even when the other one grabbed her by the hair and yanked her away. London curled up in the corner as the two of them fought over her, still trying to scream even though she could make no sound. A book fell from the other one's arms, splattering in the blood on the tile.

The thing slammed Kinsey's head into the mirrored wall over the sink, over and over again.

Then it let her go, and Kinsey hit the floor hard. She didn't move.

London whimpered as the thing turned to look at her.

And then she recognized it.

The creepy woman who stalked her. The troll.

"London..."

For a moment, London didn't know how to react. The woman wasn't one of those things. She was still normal.

She extended a hand, and London saw the bloody stumps of her fingers. She didn't want to touch her, but she took her hand anyway.

"My name...is Maggie..." Her words came in sharp exhalations, and she staggered, leaning against the wall as she struggled for breath. "I came...to save you..."

She helped London stand, taking on her weight as London limped along on her wounded leg. London closed her eyes, suddenly woozy as blood gushed down her leg.

But it was okay now. Now she had somebody to take care of her. It was okay now.

***

The stairs were a struggle, but Maggie barely felt the pain. She couldn't stop looking at London, so beautiful even as she cried out in agony. She coaxed her up each step, pausing to rest only at the landing, until they were finally at the door to the roof.

Please be unlocked, she prayed. Please, please…

The door opened.

Maggie limped out onto the roof, pulling London along with her. London's head lolled as she faded in and out of consciousness. She murmured nonsense, and Maggie couldn't help but smile. Silly girl, dreaming out loud.

They collapsed against one of the walls, and Maggie marveled at the perfect crimson sunset. She could see the Hollywood sign, and she lifted London's chin so she could see it too.

"Isn't it pretty?" Maggie cooed. She snuggled London closer, best friends forever. "I thought you'd like it better up here."

London said nothing. Her eyes fluttered, but stayed shut. Her skin had faded a sickly grey color, but she was still beautiful.

"You're so tired…you need to get your sleep," Maggie said, resting her cheek against London's matted hair. "I knew we'd be friends. I always knew. We're soul mates."

Maggie stroked London's shoulders as she watched the sun sink behind the faraway horizon. Everything seemed very far away from her now.

And when London opened her eyes again, Maggie was so, so very happy.

Ground Floor

(originally published in **Cold Flesh***)*

"Close the doors! *Now!*"

The last guy dove headfirst into the elevator, slamming against the back wall as one of the things reached for him, so close that it got halfway into the elevator before the doors finally started to shut. I swung my pocketbook at it, afraid of getting too close, but afraid that if the doors touched it, they'd automatically spring open…and then it'd be another eternity before we could close them again. My bag caught its face, knocking off its lower jaw, sending the thing reeling back just as the doors closed.

And then we began the descent.

No one spoke for a few moments. We all stared at the digital readout as the floors flashed past. Ninety-eight was the nightmare we'd just escaped. We had a long ride ahead of us.

I looked around at everyone. All strangers. I wouldn't even have been in the building if not for a meeting with my divorce attorney. But because my ex-husband decided that I should pay for his new Porsche in the settlement, I ended up in the middle of New York fucking City during the end of the world.

The people around me looked like typical white-collar wageslaves. Five in all, counting me. All of us in our own little worlds of shock. One other woman. Three men, including the guy who'd made the last-second dive. He huddled in the corner, one leg sticking straight out. He wore bike shorts, the silly-looking spandex kind, and I could see a huge hole in his thigh. Blood pumped out of the wound in steady rhythm. It took me a second to realize that it was spurting out with each heartbeat.

I closed my eyes for a moment, fighting the first creeping whispers of claustrophobia. I thought of wide open fields. Endless prairies. Ocean horizons.

It wasn't working. I could smell the blood. I could feel the warmth of these people pressing against me. I could hear the whines and groans of the elevator cables. My little tricks weren't going to work this time. I couldn't escape it.

And I could feel the panic coming on, like a slowly-building drumbeat in the back of my mind. Even the piped-in Muzak—a horrible string-arrangment of a Beatles song—couldn't distract me.

"Does anyone know what's happening out there?"

This from one of the men, the short guy in a three-piece suit whose comb-over now stuck out at all angles from his bald head. He looked pissed-off, impatient by the interruption in his Type-A lifestyle.

I couldn't answer him. All I knew was that I'd spent the entire day cloistered in her lawyer's office. No TV. No radio. I didn't even know something was wrong until people started spilling out of stairwells and elevators, babbling about the end of the world. They had come up from the bottom floors of the building, desperate to get away from the things that were flooding into the place. I just wondered where they thought they could run.

Just like I wondered why we so desperate to go down. It felt like descending into a snake pit. At least being on the elevator was better than the hell they'd left behind.

"The TV went out while I was watching CNN." The other woman spoke softly. She kept looking at the numbers flashing on the display. Floor eighty-one and counting. "It started this morning. Now it's everywhere."

"*What's* everywhere?" Comb-over's face was getting redder and redder. "I want to know what the hell those things are and why they're going crazy—"

The elevator suddenly lurched, the lights dimming for just a moment. Everyone froze, waiting. For something.

The floor display clicked to seventy-nine. Still on the descent.

"I saw one of them tear my secretary's throat out." The taller man—who, in another lifetime, probably looked very natty in his red suspenders and power-tie—spoke so softly that I barely heard him over the Muzak. "It ate her. And then it tried to eat me."

No one had much to say after that. We'd all seen those things attacking people.

Seventy-four. Almost there.

"My name is Mindy Underwood." The woman beside me held out her hand. For a moment I couldn't understand why. Amazing how quickly your manners disappear when the world ends. "I'm with Johnson, Quigley and Bradshaw on ninety-three. Junior partner. They say I could be full partner by the end of the year."

The conversation was beyond me. I limply shook her hand, not sure if I should respond. Mindy, in her perfectly tailored suit and sensible heels, looked like she was operating in some other reality where people still made polite chit-chat and didn't try to rip your throat out.

"Anne Crenshaw," I said quietly, looking from Mindy to the others in the elevator.

"Mitch Vernon," the little man with the comb-over muttered.

"Tom Donaldson." This was the tall guy with the suspenders. He looked down at the other man, who was curled up in a fetal ball. "I don't know his name…"

"It's Petey," Mindy said as she knelt beside him. "He's a messenger…he comes up to the offices all the time.." Her voice trailed away as she got a close up look at the ragged tear in his thigh. "Oh, God…"

"Jesus…I think one of those things bit him."Mitch seemed suddenly panicky. He looked like a heart attack waiting to happen, his skin waxy, slick with sweat.

"What are they?" Mindy's stood up again. Apparently she realized that a law degree couldn't help poor old Petey one bit as he bled to death. "What do they want? Are they terrorists?"

"Don't be stupid," I muttered. I didn't look away from those glowing green numbers. Sixty-two. Sixty-one. Sixty.

And then the numbers stopped.

The elevator settled into place.

The doors were going to open.

"Oh shit…" I moved back from the doors as the elevator dinged. Everybody seemed to realize what was happening at the exact same moment. We all pressed against the rear of the elevator, waiting.

The doors slid open just as smoothly as ever.

And on the other side…oh, God…

Whoever had pressed the button was gone now, but his blood remained. Great pools of it all over the tasteful Italian tile floor. The elevator opened into the reception area for a plastic surgeon's office, once one of the most sought-after doctors in the city. Now the receptionist lay sprawled over her marble-topped desk, torn open from the chin down. Blood dripped from the ceiling. A hand, chewed to pulp at the wrist, lay palm up just in front of the elevator doors. In another time, the office would have been chic with its dimly lit with recessed lights intended to flatter even the most haggard of faces. Now the lights just cast a lot of shadows.

And a few of them were moving.

They must have smelled Petey's blood, because we could hear them coming, shuffles and moans, nothing human. I edged closer to the door as it began to close. I had to see them. It wouldn't be real unless I saw them.

I peeked out, glancing to the right. And then to the left.

They were right there. Right fucking there.

I fell back into the elevator just as they rushed forward. Dozens of them. All of them reaching. All of them looking hungry.

The doors closed. The elevator hummed to life again. Descending.

No one spoke for at least ten floors. I couldn't stop shaking. Mindy wept silently, curled up beside Petey as he bled out beside her. His blood puddled around him, soaking into her expensive linen suit, but she didn't even notice. Now she really was in her own little world. I envied her. I didn't want to be here, either.

"So what do we do?" Tom's voice trembled. He held a hand to his mouth and chewed furiously on his thumbnail. He brought blood but didn't notice. "We can't…what if…what if that happens again? What if the doors open?"

"I say we push him out to distract 'em," Mitch glanced back at Petey and grimaced. "Bastard's dying anyway."

"We can't—" I caught myself before I could finish saying the words, because I knew we *could*. If it meant a chance at getting the hell out of this elevator, we'd be capable of doing damn near anything. The rules had changed between heartbeats. And if I insisted on making some kind of stupid moral stance about murder, I could find myself being thrown headfirst out the doors.

Amazing how quickly a person's mind can adapt to a brand new reality, how quickly we can accept it when we have no other choice.

I looked at Mitch and Tom, sizing them up. Either one of them could overpower me. Mindy and Petey were useless. I was on my own. I either had to go with the majority or…

Or suffer the consequences. And I most definitely didn't want that.

The numbers continued to flicker past. Forty-two. Forty-one. Forty.

I tried to estimate how much longer we'd be descending. It felt like we'd been on the elevator for an eternity already. If there weren't any more stops, we might reach the ground floor in five, six minutes. Ten at the most.

The stench of Petey's blood was suddenly deepened by another odor—he'd released his bowels. I knew that wasn't a good sign. His body was shutting down.

"Maybe we should stop the elevator and put him out," I said quietly, hating myself as I spoke. "He's dying—"

"I'm not opening these doors until we hit the ground floor," Mitch said, moving to block the row of buttons. "We don't know what's on the other side."

"That's right," Tom said, still chewing on his thumbnail. His lower lip was smeared with blood. "We can't stop the elevator. I'm not opening those doors. I'm *not*."

I moved to the farthest corner of the elevator, trying to put as much space as possible between us. My pulse pounded in my skull, my chest so tight it felt like someone had reached into my chest to squeeze my heart. The elevator, muggy now, stinking of blood and shit and sweat, felt like a coffin.

I couldn't stop it. I couldn't help it. I had to get out. Do something. Move.

Mitch never saw it coming. I swung my bag with all my strength, catching him across the back and knocking him to the floor. I wasn't thinking of anything but getting out, getting some air, getting away from these people and this smell and this nightmare. I lunged at the panel of buttons, aiming for the emergency stop. If we could just open the doors for a minute, just let some air in here and breathe for a second, everything would be okay. Everything would be better.

The elevator jerked to a stop. The lights went out.

I hadn't hit the button. Something else was wrong.

"What did you do?" Mitch's voice sounded shrill in the darkness. I felt his hand grip my upper arm, squeezing hard. I yanked away from him, moving back to my little corner.

"I didn't do anything!" I couldn't breathe. Too dark. Too close.

"The power's out," Tom said quietly. "Listen…"

No one spoke. Now that we didn't have the distraction of the hum of the elevator or the sickly-sweetness of the Muzak, we could hear what we'd tried so desperately not to hear.

Moans. Scratching. Just on the other side of those doors. So close. They could probably smell Petey's blood. They wanted in here so badly…

It felt like forever before anyone spoke again. All we could do was stand there and listen to the sound of those things on the other side of the door. In the darkness it was all too easy to imagine what they'd do if they managed to get to us.

"Maybe…" my throat caught, so dry I could barely swallow. "Maybe we should climb out."

"And how do we do that?" Mitch was to my left, standing uncomfortably close to me. I could feel his soft stomach pressing against my arm. "We got no light. We don't even know if there's a hatch—"

"There's a hatch," I said. "I always look for one when I get in an elevator."

"So then what do we do?" This from Tom, who I imagined was still gnawing at his bloodied thumb. "We climb out the hatch and then what? We can't get past the elevator to get down—"

"Maybe we can climb up to the roof—"

"Are you fucking kidding me, lady?" Mitch grabbed my arm again. I jerked away from him. I didn't like the idea of him being able to touch me in the darkness. "This is a hundred and two story building."

"Then maybe we can pry the doors open on another floor. Those things can't be everywhere, can they?"

I heard Mitch huff, felt him move away from me. The darkness inside the elevator was so total, so deep, that I had to lean against the wall to keep my balance. The blackness felt thick around me, drowning me. I knew that I only had a few minutes before I lost whatever control I'd managed to hang onto. The darkness was too much. It felt like being dead.

I dropped to my knees, trying not to be so aware of the warmth of blood pooling on the floor of the elevator, and felt for my pocketbook. I had a lighter in there, leftover from my latest smoking jag. I'd quit because I was afraid of cancer, but I always kept a pack of Winstons and a butane lighter with me just in case I backslid.

I closed my eyes as I dug through the purse, identifying everything by feel. Keys. Checkbook. Tampon. Lipstick. Winstons. Lighter.

Please work. Please, please work.

I held my breath and thumbed the button. A flicker. And then a small, steady flame.

The light wasn't much, but it helped me breathe again. Everyone looked different, the shadows distorting their features. I glanced over to the corner, where Petey now lay motionless. Mindy sat beside him, staring at nothing, not even blinking. Completely gone. Again, I envied her. Whatever happened to us, she wouldn't be aware of anything but what she saw in her own private world.

"Gimme that!" Mitch made a move to grab the lighter and I let the flame go out, snatching the lighter close to my chest as the darkness surrounded us again. Thicker this time.

"Don't do that again." I could hear the fear in my voice and knew that Mitch heard it too. I knew his type. Hot-headed. Impulsive. Mean. "We don't know how long this will last. We have to save the lighter—"

"For what?" Mitch somehow found my arm in the pitch black and pushed me against the back wall of the elevator. "We're not going nowhere. We're stuck. The power's out—"

"It might be temporary," Tom said quickly. "We don't know what's happening."

"Exactly. We *don't* know." Mitch gave my arm one last hard pinch and let go of me. "And this bitch is gonna give us enough light to open the hatch or else—"

"Or else *what*?" I was almost screaming now, and the sound of it made the things on the other side of the door go crazy. They knew we were in here. I didn't care. I struck out in the darkness and felt my fists hit pudgy shoulders. Mitch. "What are you gonna do? Huh? What are you gonna *do*?"

"Get off me! Stop it!" Mitch moved away from my flailing hands and I forced myself to calm down. Deep breaths. The air felt warm. Thick. The stink of Petey's blood made my eyes water.

I went back to my corner and curled myself away from the others, pressing my cheek against the cool wooden panels. My head throbbed with each heartbeat.

"Okay, listen…" Tom's voice sounded weak but steady. "Maybe we can do this. Let's open the hatch and get some air in here at least. Can we do that?"

Mitch mumbled something.

"Fine, then…" Tom reached out blindly, gingerly touching my shoulder. "Lady, we're going to need to use your lighter."

"No—"

"*Please.*"

The need to get out of that coffin was stronger than my fear of losing the only thing that could connect me to sanity. Even if I was only trading one tomb for another.

"Only if I go up first," I said.

"Fine."

I touched Tom's hand, still grasping my shoulder, and gave him the lighter. I didn't trust him. I just wanted out.

Tom thumbed the lighter and the elevator was suddenly intensely bright, the orange glow of the flame throwing flickering shadows onto our faces. Somehow we managed to coordinate ourselves without speaking. Mitch laced his fingers for me to step into and boosted me a few feet into the air, just enough for me to reach the hatch. I gave it a hard push. Nothing.

"It's stuck…" I pounded the hatch with my fists. "I can't—"

"Ow! Shit!" The light abruptly died. "I burned my hand. Wait a second…"

Vertigo hit me hard. I laced my fingers into the grill of the light fixtures to hold on, to anchor me until the dizziness passed.

"Hurry it up!" Mitch staggered slightly and pitched me forward. I would have gone into the wall if I hadn't been holding on to the grill.

"I'm trying…" I kept pushing at the hatch, my hands slick with sweat. The sound of their moans seemed louder now, echoing all around us.

But now it was different. Now it sounded like it was in the elevator with us.

And there was another, softer sound. A wet sound.

Chewing.

I realized what was happening just as Tom flicked on the lighter again.

Mindy slumped over Petey's body, her eyes open and glassy. Petey's face was buried in her throat, tearing out strips of flesh and muscle as blood coursed over their bodies. And he was eating her.

Panic slammed into us. I clawed at the hatch, desperate now, fighting to keep my balance as Mitch side-stepped away from Petey.

"Oh, God…" Tom moaned. "Oh, God…oh, God…"

The hatch abruptly gave way and opened just as the elevator jerked and the lights flickered back to life again, blinding me for just an instant. The light made it worse. Now we could see everything.

Petey raised his head from Mindy's neck, his face masked in her blood but perfectly blank. Perfectly expressionless. There was nothing human to him anymore.

But he was aware of us now.

Suddenly I felt two pairs of hands pushing me up into the hatch. I glanced down and saw Petey shoving Mindy's body away from his and struggling to stand.

My head cleared the hatch and I suddenly felt like I might vomit. The elevator was moving too quickly, the walls of the shaft flying past . I looked up and could only see a tunnel of darkness lengthening behind me.

But then I was climbing on top of the elevator, rolling onto my stomach as I looked back through the hatch and reached for Mitch.

The elevator slowed and settled into place.

We were stopping.

I grabbed Mitch's hands just as Petey lunged at Tom, going for his throat, snapping at him. I saw a gout of blood splatter across the button panel, so dark it was almost black.

My hands slipped on Mitch's forearms as he tried to jump and grab the hatch. I tried not to look at Tom, tried not to see Petey burrowing into his stomach with his bare hands.

The doors opened.

They flooded in, at least a dozen of them at once, all of them grasping, snapping, desperate. Mitch jumped again and managed to hook his arms over the edge of the hatch. I grabbed him under his armpits and pulled…but they pulled back.

He slid away from me, the look on his face so lost, so sad.

Below the hatch, the things were already chewing on his legs, ripping at his soft belly.

Mitch didn't scream. He just let go.

I peeped over the edge of the hatch, terrified that they would see me there and somehow climb up to get me. There were so many in that small space, all of them dead and decaying, monsters from my worst nightmares. The stench of blood gagged me but I held my breath until the urge to vomit passed.

I watched them feast until I couldn't bear any more. I don't know how many hours it took them to finish. I lost track of everything but the glow of light from the open hatch as I curled up against the elevator cable and wrapped my arms around it. I couldn't move. I couldn't climb the ladder and pry open the doors by myself. I couldn't even force myself to close the hatch and shut myself into the blackness again.

So I waited. Listening to them. The moans, so tortured and hungry. The slurping, wet sounds of eating. The shuffle-drag of their feet as they moved in and out of the elevator.

And then, finally, I heard nothing at all except a dull thumping sound.

I slowly moved to the lip of the hatch and looked inside. Empty. Blood dripped from the ceiling, covered the walls. An arm lay in the elevator door, blocking it from closing.

But they were all gone. Mindy. Mitch. Tom. Petey.

I didn't think they had been dragged away. I think they turned into those things.

I wondered if they would remember that I was hiding on top of the elevator. If they'd be back for me.

I took a chance and crawled out further, looking through the open elevator doors to the hallway on the other side. The things had moved on for the moment.

But they'd be back. The blood would attract them. Like sharks.

I moved before I could talk myself out of it, sliding feetfirst through the hatch while I lowered myself back into the elevator. There was a bad moment when I couldn't see beneath me. I could imagine one of the things coming through the doors, sinking its teeth into my thigh—

But then I was hanging from the lip of the hatch, completely inside the elevator again. Still empty. Still none of the things in sight.

I dropped the last few feet and landed hard, sliding on the blood.

And then I could hear them again. Coming back.

I kicked the arm out of the way and the elevator doors finally closed just as a greenish-gray skinned woman stumbled closer, her fingertips only inches away from the elevator.

And then I was descending again. Alone now.

I hit the button for the ground floor and closed my eyes.

Dominion

"I don't think this is going to work…"

"Shut up and close your eyes, Carl." Patty placed her black-polished fingertips on the edge of the plastic white planchette. "Turn up the music."

Even with her eyes closed, Patty knew he was staring at her, so she ran the tip of her tongue over her lower lip, adding a soft little moan for good measure. Guys like Carl were so easy. Rich frat boys looking to add a little danger to their white bread lives. She knew exactly what the rumors said about her—she was a witch, she worshiped Satan, she ate babies, blah blah blah—and she enjoyed living up to the expectations when she brought guys home. It made her forget that she was once just as white bread and bland and boring as Carl and all the others.

Plus, it was fun to freak them out.

"Mmm…can you feel the spirits, Carl? They're all around us…" Patty smiled, eyes still closed, and moved along with the planchette as she guided it around the board. Carl laughed, the sound catching nervously in his throat, and Patty opened her eyes to study him. Poor little boy was in over his head now. He looked almost ready to bolt.

"You okay, Carl?" She smiled and cocked her head to the side, knowing exactly what kind of reaction she'd get from him. "You're not getting scared, are you?"

"No." He pulled his hands away from the planchette, suddenly defensive. Patty's smile faded and she leaned back on her elbows, knowing that his gaze would be drawn to the way her considerable breasts jiggled beneath the spaghetti strap tank top she wore. And she was right. Of course.

"Um…" He shook his head to recover his thoughts and forced his gaze back to hers. "I was just wondering…"

"Yeah?"

"What's with all this…demon stuff?"

Patty glanced around her small apartment. It was suitably—if not obnoxiously—Goth. Black fabric covering the couch. Sketches of demons taped to the walls. Plaster gargoyles and plastic pentagrams everywhere. She liked the way it all looked, and the way it made her look to others.

Patty grinned. "Don't you like my decorating style?"

"Some guys in my Spanish class say you're a witch."

"Yeah...heard that one before. Your friends should really try to be more original." She studied him for a moment. "Ever think it would be cool to be possessed?"

"Possessed?"

"Yeah…*possessed*." Patty sat up, eyes wide and shining as brightly as the hoops dangling from her brows. "Having a demon get inside you, taking over, making you powerful and shit."

"Like 'The Exorcist'?"

"Exactly!" Still smiling, Patty reached beneath her bed and pulled out a shoebox, lifting the lid to produce a baggie of mossy pot. Another reach beneath the bed and rolling papers appeared. "Want to know what my fantasy is?"

Of course he did. She could tell by the way his pants tented and his breathing suddenly quickened.

"My fantasy," Patty said as she prepared a fat joint, "is to open myself up to…whatever…and be possessed. You know, spewing puke, levitating, the whole thing. I've been working on my demon invocations for, like, a couple of months now. The last one I did called for blood."

"Whose?"

"Mine," she said, silently adding *you idiot*. She would have said it out loud, but she needed Carl to help her with the sex magick she needed for the newest invocation. Plus she really wanted to get laid.

"Why?"

Patty slowly smiled. "Who knows. Who cares. The world's fucked up anyway. Wouldn't it be better to be, you know, powerful?"

"But how would that make *you* powerful?"

"You become, like, bigger than yourself because you've submitted your will to something stronger. So you get powerful because you're weak. Know what I mean?"

Carl nodded. He didn't get it.

"I've got a feeling it's going to happen real soon. The world's going to shit anyway, and there've been all kinds of signs. Prophecies coming to pass. Stuff like that makes it easier to open yourself up."

"So what are you going to do if you get possessed?" he asked as he took the joint. "Float around in a nightgown and puke on priests?"

Patty smiled. "Maybe. I just think it'd be really wicked to be possessed and go through the city, scaring the shit out of people."

"Uh-huh," Carl said and took a deep hit. "And then what? What about your soul?"

"The fuck do you mean, what about my soul?"

"Aren't you afraid of going to Hell?"

Patty thought about that for a moment. How could Hell be any worse than her life now?

"Better to reign in hell than serve in heaven, right?" Patty grinned crookedly and took another drag off the joint. "So come on...we gonna screw or what?"

Carl grinned.

***

Well *that* was a waste of latex...

Patty stared at the cracked plaster of the ceiling and listened to the yahoo snoring beside her. Of course he could sleep…hell, *she'd* just about fallen asleep while he was floundering around on top of her.

Patty rolled onto her side and stared into the dimness of her apartment, listening to the familiar sounds surrounding her. The constant murmur of her neighbors' arguments. The thump of a bed frame against the wall. The sharp slap of belt leather and the begging sobs of a woman. The constant scratch of rats scurrying within the walls and the whisper of roaches skittering in the darkness. The price she paid for living on her own, for the privilege of living a life that her parents would have never chosen for her.

Everything was as it always was, as it always should be…except for the jerk sleeping beside her, and he'd be out of there soon enough.

Patty closed her eyes, drifting into a light sleep.

And that's when she realized that everything had gone silent.

Patty sat up, holding her breath, listening. The familiar sounds were gone now.

Totally gone.

Even the sounds of the city were gone. No traffic in the street, or blaring of car alarms or fire trucks.

She sat up and reached for the bedside lamp.

"Hey…wake up…" Patty grabbed Carl's shoulder and shook him. "Come on! Wake up!"

Nothing.

Then he twitched and rolled onto his back.

But it wasn't him anymore.

His skin wept thick pus from raw wounds. His cracked lips pulled back to reveal yellowed teeth that looked more animal than human. And his open eyes, glittering silver, shone with horrible glee.

Patty scrambled out of the bed, stumbling backwards as Carl began to rise, hovering inches above the mattress. The sheets were drawn up with him, dangling over his body. His arms fell out to the sides, hanging loosely in mid-air as he rolled his head forward, his entire body straightening out vertically, until he looked as if he had been crucified on an invisible cross. He scanned the room until he saw Patty. Then he smiled, and it was the most horrible thing she had ever seen.

"We hunger…" His voice boomed through the silence, echoing with thousands of other voices, underscored with screams of agony. It didn't sound human.

Patty scrabbled backward on the floor, cracking. She backed onto her Ouija board, cracking the planchette. That's when she realized what she had done.

She'd invoked a demon. It had worked just like she'd hoped. Only it hadn't gone the way she'd wanted. It had gotten Carl instead.

And Carl didn't look like he was having such a good time being possessed.

His naked body twitched, suspended high in the air. His arms remained out to the sides, his legs dangling loosely below him. His chin dropped to his chest. For a few long moments, Patty could only hear the animal-like growls of his breathing. He didn't move.

Carl's left leg trembled. A crack of splintering bone suddenly exploded into the silence and Carl's leg snapped backward, the knee joint bending the wrong way. And somehow he laughed and screamed at the same time.

"Oh God…" she whimpered, tugging on a t-shirt, fighting her way into jeans, shoes. Another crack, and then horrible splintering sounds as his right leg shattered.

Carl screamed again, forcing Patty's attention back to him, and she saw claw marks appearing in the middle of his chest, down his stomach. She heard the sound of him coming apart, a wet unzipping of his flesh.

His eyes, cloudy with death, looked through her. And even as he screamed, the thing inside him forced his mouth to move into a smile.

Patty didn't stick around to see anything else.

***

Twelve blocks later, she stopped running.

She staggered, breathless, and finally fell against a lamp-post, gasping as she slid to the dirty pavement and covered her face with her hands. This wasn't what she wanted. It wasn't the way it was supposed to be. She was supposed to call the demon into herself and then she'd be cool and powerful and…

And it was all a lie. It wasn't like the movies. Not like the movies at all.

Patty's breathing slowed to normal, even though her heart bumped and raced erratically. She chewed on her thumbnail as she looked around her. No one on the street. No cars. No cabs. The lights were on, but nobody was home. In the entire city.

It's like the end of the world.

Patty forced herself to stand up, her entire body trembling. She looked up, craning her neck as far as she could. There was no moon. No stars. Lights burned in the windows of the canyon of buildings surrounding her, but there was no movement or sound. It felt like everyone in the entire world had suddenly disappeared.

Just like the Rapture.

Oh God…the Rapture.

In the space between heartbeats, all the old memories came flooding back. All the nights of being dragged to revival meetings, of hearing wheezing preachers rage against sin and human frailty, warning of the day when God himself would send His mighty armies down upon the earth to strike down the sinners. She remembered all of the sermons about the Rapture, how God would take the true believers up to Heaven in an instant and leave the world to the damned.

She remembered why she left home at fifteen. Why she had never gone back. She had always thought all the preachers had been full of shit. Telling stories about the Rapture was just a way of keeping ignorant hillbillies in line, making sure they followed all the rules and lived like good little Christians so no one would be bothered or make trouble.

But now...

"Hello?" she shouted into the silence. She looked around frantically, hoping for some glimpse of movement, some sign that she wasn't as alone as she felt. Never in her life had she ever sensed such a complete absence of presence. "Anybody?"

A piece of paper scraped over the sidewalk, pushed along by the wind. It was the only sound Patty could hear.

But with the wind came the sense that she wasn't alone anymore.

She noticed the smell first, the sweetly-tinged, meaty stink of rot. It reminded her of summer days spent driving along old country roads, when the world could be all freshly cut grass and honeysuckle one moment, and sun-baked, rotting road kill the next. Patty covered her mouth and nose with her hand, gagging at the sudden, overpowering intensity of it.

And then she heard the whispers.

Hundreds of voices, male and female, buzzing in and around her head like flies. Some moaned. Some screamed. Some cursed and ranted. All of them sounded tormented, terrified.

And suddenly, with the whispers, they came out of hiding. Women with their breasts slashed away, screaming as they held the lifeless lumps of flesh and fat in their hands. Men with their bellies slit open, trailing yards of their own intestines behind them as they staggered endlessly. Bodies that were no longer male or female, so mutilated and torn that they looked barely human. And the blood. All of the blood, washing over everything...

She clapped her hands to her ears, anything to drown out the awful whispers, but was too afraid to close her eyes.

She began to move, half-walking, half-staggering, with no idea of where she was going. Nothing looked familiar anymore. The buildings looked even more decrepit than before, as though they had aged and rotted in the few moments she had been there. The air felt thicker, heavier.

How could I have done this? I couldn't have done all this...not me.

She caught a glimpse of movement ahead—a whore in black spandex and torn hose staggering out of the mouth of an alley.

"Hey!" Patty lunged forward. "I need help! Please..."

The woman raised her head and smiled at Patty, rotted, broken teeth gleaming beneath blood-red lips. Her rheumy eyes wept thick yellow tears.

And as Patty watched, the woman's skin began to move, as if thousands of maggots wriggled just beneath the surface.

"Thank you..." the woman said, her voice echoing with thousands of other voices. "Thank you all for calling us back..."

She took a shuffling step forward and dropped to her knees before Patty, reaching out. The whore's spidery fingers brushed against the back of Patty's hand, the touch more loathsome than anything she'd ever felt before.

And before she could look away, the whore raised her head and smiled up at Patty, her mouth stretching wide in a monstrous smile, exposing sharklike rows of sharp grey teeth.

Patty screamed. And she ran. She ran until the whore was long behind her, until she was alone again.

The air felt thicker now, hotter and drier than it should be, and Patty had to stop to catch her breath, almost collapsing onto the sidewalk as she leaned forward and put her head between her knees to settle her dizziness. Once the worst of it faded, she looked up and around, trying to reorient herself. She had no idea where she was now. The city had changed along with the people. The buildings had decayed in seconds, like rotting corpses beneath the summer sun. Everything seemed poisoned, tainted.

Patty stumbled over her own feet, falling heavily to her knees. Shoulders bowed, she wept, curling into herself as she covered her head with her arms and shuddered.

And when she caught her breath, when her own keening wails finally eased, she heard it. Close, but faint.

A baby.

Patty stood, turning, listening, straining to hear it again. A baby meant life. Normal people. Help. Something this awful couldn't happen to a baby…

There it was again. A throaty, healthy scream.

Patty ran towards the sound, following it into a small grocery store. She paused at the threshold, unable to force herself to take a step inside. The lights were still on, which made everything that much worse.

Because with the lights on, she could see what had happened inside the store.

Half a dozen bodies. Torn. Ripped. Brutalized. Bloody shells that barely looked human anymore. Lying in a heap like so much dirty laundry.

And their faces…whatever had killed them, whatever had ripped them apart, had possessed them first. Their faces had changed just like Carl's, just like the whore's, just like all the things wandering in the streets.

"Oh God…" Patty whispered, holding her hand over her nose and mouth, gagging as she tried to look away from the pile of corpses but found that she couldn't. If she looked away, even for a moment, they might move...

The baby wailed again, snapping Patty back to awareness. She forced herself to enter the store, stepping carefully through the puddles of blood. She glanced over her shoulder to the pile of bodies—

...did the woman on the bottom move her arm?...

—but kept going, forcing herself to look away, knowing that if she stopped, if she looked at the pile hard enough, she *would* see them moving. She would see them untangling themselves, silently creeping up behind her, crawling through their own blood as they reached out for her...

Suddenly unnerved, Patty turned around again.

The bodies were gone.

"Oh, shit..." she murmured, her heart suddenly triphammering. Where was the goddamned baby?

It cried again, but this time there was nothing remotely human about the sound. She spun around.

It was hovering right in front of her face, waiting for her.

She'd never considered that a baby could be possessed.

Its eyes bulged out of their sockets, bloodshot and bleeding, as its toothless mouth widened in a gummy grin. The baby's skin had cracked like sunbaked mud, its entire body oozing blood and pus. It reached for Patty with its tiny hands, and for a moment—just a moment—she almost let it touch her.

Because in that moment, she almost lost her mind.

A black, fuzzy tongue snaked out of the baby's mouth, and that was all Patty needed to break the spell. Crying out, she spun around, stumbling over her own feet, sliding in the puddles of blood, and lurched toward the door. Laughter rumbled through the silence, coming from above. She glanced up and saw a young girl with the face of a monster crouched atop the doorframe, giggling softly as she hovered close to the ceiling, her arms dangling between her legs, her fingers wiggling independently of each other like slender snakes.

Close enough to grab Patty as she passed through.

And Patty definitely did not want to pass through.

Something moved behind her and she turned to see all the others, standing shoulder to shoulder in a wall of unmovable flesh. Their bodies had been broken, twisted, reformed into grotesque parodies of humanity by whatever had reanimated them. And they watched her. Without making a sound. Without making a move. They just watched her.

She could almost feel their muscles tensing, preparing to strike. All she had to do was move and they would be on her.

And the thought of those things touching her was more than she could bear.

Patty screamed and launched herself toward the door, towards the squirming fingers of the girl perched atop the doorframe, sensing the movement of the things behind her as they lurched forward. She kept screaming as she passed beneath the girl, felt those cold, slick fingers tangling in her hair, in the hoops pierced through her eyebrows, ripping out whatever they touched. Patty's scream caught in her throat, the pain so great that for a moment she could not make a sound, but she barreled through the doorway even as blood trickled into her eyes and over her scalp and did not stop until she was out in the street again, in air that smelled of green rot and acid bile.

She chanced a quick look over her shoulder. The girl hung upside down in the doorway, chewing on a scrap of Patty's hair and scalp. The others pushed past her, moving single-file into the street.

But they weren't the only ones.

They streamed out of alleys, out of apartment buildings, out of storefronts. Men and women. Children. Old people. All of them twisted, their limbs resculpted, their movements jerky and unsteady. All of them with those runny yellow eyes, with lips skinned back from teeth that looked more animal than human. All of them looking at her with such hate…

It wasn't the Rapture after all. It was something much worse. And it was all her fault.

Patty sobbed, stumbling as she took a step, afraid to turn her back on the things but terrified of facing them. So many of them…

And she had nowhere to go.

Patty ran anyway, wiping the blood from her eyes, catching glimpses of movement all around her. Everyone had been possessed. It hadn't mattered what kind of life they'd lived, hadn't mattered how often they'd gone to church, hadn't mattered how good they might have been…

In the end, nothing had mattered. And that terrified her more than anything.

Nothing fucking mattered.

She stumbled over something and went down hard on her hands and knees. And suddenly she couldn't run anymore. She couldn't make herself get up. Couldn't make herself move. She could hear those things getting closer, but…

But there was no use. It didn't matter. Nothing mattered.

Patty stared up at the sky as the first milky streaks of dawn appeared against the starless dark. She wished she could just die. That an aneurysm would explode in her brain or her heart would stop pumping…something quick and painless and merciful. If she could have willed it upon herself at that moment…

But she couldn't. She continued to live and breathe and wait for those things to reach her.

Even though she knew that they would touch her, that she would feel their wormy hands on her body and their hot breath against her skin and…

And she couldn't bear the thought of that.

Patty struggled to her feet. They were so close, closer than she had thought. And so many of them.

She began to run again. Somewhere just ahead, church bells began to peal, the clear, sweet notes a sudden shock after the growls and screams and endless tormented cries of the possessed. Patty instinctively followed the sound. Church bells meant hope.

She staggered up the stone steps to the church. Catholic, she thought. St. somebody or other. She didn't care. Maybe those things couldn't go into a church. Maybe she wouldn't have to run for a while. Maybe she could find someone else who hadn't been possessed.

At least, that's what she prayed for when she pushed open the heavy wooden doors and fell into the cool, candle-lit dimness. It was the first time she had prayed in years. And the first time she had ever so fervently meant it.

But just in case, she pushed a heavy wooden pew in front of the doors. God helps those who help themselves.

She backed away, tearing her gaze from the shuddering doors and turning towards the altar. Hundreds of candles flickered, the sound of flames popping and wax dripping almost too loud in the silence. Hanging directly behind the altar was a large crucifix, the sculpture of a crucified Christ so lifelike that Patty could almost see the beads of sweat and blood on His brow, could almost smell the blood that dripped steadily from his nailed wrists…

She was almost at the altar when she realized that the blood was still dripping.

And that it wasn't Jesus hanging on the cross.

The man was in his sixties, soft and paunchy and gray all over. Seeming to sense Patty's presence, he rolled his head forward to look at her. His eyes were agonized. Clear, not that rheumy yellow of the possessed. And fully aware. Even though something had stripped him naked before crucifying him, he still wore his clerical collar. It looked oddly obscene now.

Patty dropped to her knees, suddenly unable to take one more step, to resist one more moment. If there was no shelter in a church...

Then there would be no shelter anywhere.

"We've lost all..." The priest's voice barely carried over the cacophony of screams and moans from outside the church doors. Patty raised her head, wiping tears away with the backs of her hands.

For a moment he looked like her own father.

"No..." she whispered, shaking her head. Behind her, the doors trembled in their frame as more of the possessed gathered. "I didn't want this...I never wanted this..."

"It's...over..." The priest wheezed, each breath coming harder and harder for him now. "We...lost...the...contest..."

Patty could see the imprints of monstrous, invisible hands on his body, pushing, prodding, manipulating his flesh. The crack and splinter of bones sounded obscene, but not as horrible as the man's screams.

Patty fell back, watching as chunks of bloody meat were dug out of the priest's stomach, as deep, gaping wounds split across his chest. The priest howled in agony, the sound abruptly cut off as his throat suddenly disappeared in a spray of red mist.

And then there was silence. For one still, eerie moment...silence from within and without.

Patty turned toward the doors again.

Just as they exploded inward.

The things rushed in like a swarm of hornets, each of them reaching for her, each of them honing in on her like there was absolutely nothing else on this earth. The sheer number of them overwhelmed her for a moment. She felt completely paralyzed, unable to even breathe.

Until she heard the sound of wet ripping.

Followed by the priest's shrieks.

And then a warm rain of blood.

Patty's head snapped back as the priest was tossed through the air by those invisible demons, blood spraying everywhere, falling into the open mouths of the possessed like drops of consecrated wine. For just an instant, their attention was diverted from Patty as they wallowed in the priest's blood.

It was enough for Patty.

She broke for the closest door she could find, barreling into the priest's office and then out the rear of the church, heaving for breath as she stumbled down the steps and glanced up to the sky. Dawn was breaking, and for a moment she could believe that everything would be better, that once the sun rose, the world would go back to normal.

But she couldn't really believe that. Not now. Not after what she had seen.

Choking, heaving for breath, she staggered to the closest car she could find, a beat-up BMW that had seen better days. Judging from the crucifix hanging from the rearview mirror and the plastic Jesus on the dash, Patty guessed it had belonged to the priest. She tried the door. It swung open easily, without a sound.

And God must have been her co-pilot, because the keys were in the ignition.

Patty dove into the car and closed the door as silently as she could, wincing at the sound of the engine as it roared to life. As she expected, it brought the possessed out of the rear of the church, falling over themselves in their rush to get to the car.

She slammed the BMW into reverse, tearing her eyes away from the crowd of monsters just long enough to make sure she didn't back into a telephone pole, and then turned the car around. She knew where she had to go.

She glanced in the rearview and watched the demons fall into the distance.

***

It took less than an hour to get home.

The old neighborhood was just as normal-looking as ever. The good part of town, where all the doctors and lawyers and respected church elders lived. Every lawn was manicured, every house was freshly painted and guaranteed to inspire just the right amount of envy to outsiders.

It was the world Patty had known for the first fifteen years of her life. And until now, she hadn't realized how much she had missed such…normalcy.

She stopped the BMW in front of the house, cutting the engine but leaving the keys in the ignition. She eased out of the car warily, looking all around, expecting to see the demons flooding out of every house, from every alley.

Nothing. Just a normal dawn in a normal neighborhood.

Patty felt like crying. Maybe it hadn't spread here. Maybe it was just in the city. Maybe it was a terrorist attack...some kind of nerve gas…maybe...

She removed the rings and hoops and piercings from her face, tossing them into the gutter as she glanced at her reflection in the car's window. Without all the metal in her face, she looked like she had on the day she left home.

She wiped at the tears in her eyes and walked up the front steps, wondering if Momma was up yet, if she was sitting in her nightgown and robe watching the Today show while drinking her first cup of coffee of the day. And Daddy…by now he'd probably be singing hymns in the shower and rattling the house with his horrible, off-key baritone.

The memories made Patty smile even though her tears.

She knocked, her heart hammering in the space of seconds it took for Momma to open the door. For a few moments, they just stared at each other. Momma looked older than Patty remembered, with more gray in her hair, more lines around her eyes and mouth. She looked old and tired and sad beyond anything Patty had ever seen.

But she was Momma. She wasn't one of those things.

Without a word, Momma opened her arms. And in that instant, Patty knew she had been forgiven. She fell into her mother's arms and hugged her tightly, feeling how frail she had become, how old.

"Momma…I'm so sorry…" she whispered, burying her face in her mother's hair, smelling the good, familiar scent of Aqua-Net hairspray and baby powder.

"I know, baby." Momma's hands rubbed Patty's back, comforting her the way she used to years before. "You're back, and that's all that matters."

Patty sniffed, half-laughing through her tears, and raised her head. "Where's Daddy?"

Momma's smile widened as her embrace gradually tightened around Patty's shoulders. Her gaze flicked up to the ceiling.

Patty didn't want to look.

Her father skittered spider-like across the ceiling, his joints bent at impossible angles, his face destroyed, malformed by those demonic hands. A long, curling tongue flickered from between his cracked lips.

Patty screamed as her mother began to laugh.

Dumping Ground

(originally published in **Decadence of the Dead***)*

"Mom*mee*...I'm hot!"

Jackie Yavarro nodded wearily as she squinted into the distance. "I know, baby. Just sit still and be quiet for Mommy, okay?"

Katie must have heard the quaver in her voice, falling silent as she stared at Jackie with huge eyes. Jackie fiddled with the radio again, praying for a signal, for someone to explain what the hell was happening. But they were out in the middle of nowhere, just a few miles outside of the Everglades, and radio reception faded in and out with every curve of the road.

Not that it mattered. Jackie knew she'd gotten Katie out just before things got really bad. They'd been on the road for two days, just driving from one town to another, looking for a place that felt safe. Jackie didn't think 'safe' existed anymore. Not after the things she had seen at the club.

She'd gotten out of there just before the place was overrun. Just barely. It had been a regular night—she'd danced her five sets, did a few lap dances, pocketed enough money to buy a big-girl bike for Katie for Christmas. The news had been weird all day, with reports of people going crazy and attacking each other in the cities, but that was a whole world away from the Pink Pony Club and Messer, Florida. Jackie just did her act, stared at the big light over the DJ booth, thought about what she needed to pick up at the grocery store, and waited for her shift to be over.

But then Bubba Greeley stumbled into the club just before midnight, with his gut ripped open and his eyes milky white and all wrong. He tore through Vinnie, the bouncer, and Pat at the bar before anyone realized what was happening. Jackie was backstage getting dressed when it happened, but she heard the screams and knew instinctively that she needed to get away. All the other girls rushed out to the stage to see what the fuss was about, but Jackie headed straight for the back door. She didn't look back, just got in her car and drove home. She didn't want to see what she was leaving behind.

The radio was crazy, with people calling in with 'eye-witness' reports and lists of emergency stations that people were supposed to report to, if they were able. Jackie drove as fast as she dared, passing bodies on the road that just lay there like so much road kill, and cars that looked like they'd been through a demolition derby. She'd gone stone cold during that drive, seeing that people were killing other people, seeing that they were ripping chunks of flesh away with their teeth...but allowing herself to feel nothing at all. She turned herself off, just as she did when she had to do the lap dances. Her main goal was to get home and get Katie. That was it.

The door to her house was wide open when she'd pulled into the driveway. She had virtually flung herself out of her car, taking the steps two at a time, afraid to shout Katie's name in case anyone was in the house but afraid that if she didn't scream she'd go insane. The fucking babysitter had deserted Katie, left her home alone, with only a note of apology taped to the phone. Jackie flew through the house to Katie's bedroom and opened the door with a horror too real to contemplate dancing through her mind.

But Katie was in bed asleep, her stuffed cat tucked under her arm, her covers pulled up to her nose.

Sobbing silently, Jackie stuffed a few of Katie's clothes in a duffle bag and scooped her up, covers and all, to carry her to her own bedroom. Katie didn't even stir as Jackie threw whatever clothes she could find into a couple of Wal-Mart bags. Jackie felt time closing in on her, like she'd been damned lucky up to that point but that her luck was going to crap out at any second. She kept Katie with her as she tore through the small house, grabbing boxes and cans of food, cases of Coke and a couple of gallon jugs of water. It took forever to load up the car, carrying Katie with her on every trip, but she wasn't about to leave her baby alone again. Never again.

She drove non-stop until sunrise, listening to the stories on the radio, feeling more and more like she were in a waking nightmare. She drove until she stopped passing dead bodies lying on the sides of the road. She drove until she stopped seeing anyone at all. She and Katie camped in the car at night, and Jackie learned quickly how to pilfer gas out of abandoned cars. The constant terror became almost commonplace, the fear keeping her from sleeping too soundly, from ever believing they were safe.

Eventually, the radio offered more static than information, but she believed the news reports that had called those things the walking dead. Anyone who said that they were just infected with something hadn't ever seen one of them up close. Once you saw those milked-over eyes, smelled that stench of week-old road kill, heard those noises coming out of their mouths, that moan of hunger and anger and something even darker...once you saw all that, you wouldn't doubt for an instant what they were. Jackie had seen them up close, had watched them tear people apart with their bare hands. She knew what they were.

They were the dead. Somehow, God had closed His eyes and allowed the dead to rise and create Hell on earth for the living.

But Jackie had a little girl to protect, to spare the reality of this new, horrible world. And if that meant driving halfway across the goddam country alone, until she could find some halfway decent people to make camp with, then that's what she would do. She just hoped there were still good people left alive out there. From what she'd already seen, the worst of humanity were coming into their heyday, wallowing in the confusion and chaos and creating new kingdoms where civilization held no place.

Katie reached over and put her hand on Jackie's arm, startling her out of her thoughts. After all the years of struggling alone, drifting from one bastard to another, dealing with the memories of a father who had forced her to run away before she'd even turned fourteen, having Katie with her now felt like a miracle.

"It's okay, Mommy." Katie petted Jackie's arm and leaned over as much as her seatbelt would allow. "It's okay. Don't be scared."

A sob escaped Jackie and she suddenly couldn't see for her tears. Jesus Christ...what was she doing? She had no idea where they were going, no clue about what was happening to the world, no hope of ever finding a safe place for Katie. And right now they were in the middle of swamp country, miles away from civilization, such as it was.

Something exploded beneath the car and both of them shrieked. Jackie stomped on the brake as she flung an arm out to hold Katie in her seat, knowing almost immediately what the sound meant. Blow out.

The car settled to a stop, and for a moment the silence that engulfed them felt as thick as the humid air. The road was little more than a dirt path carved through the more solid parts of the swamp. She'd chosen to take this shortcut because she knew they'd be less likely to run across anyone, living or dead.

God help me, she thought, closing her eyes just as tears threatened to overwhelm her.

"What happened?" Katie's voice trembled, on the verge of hysterical tears, and Jackie snapped to, undoing their seatbelts so that she could pull Katie onto her lap. Ever since Katie was born, Jackie had marveled at how tiny and delicate her little girl felt in her arms. Now she just felt fragile. Breakable.

"I think our tires wore out," she said, forcing a lightness to her voice. "We drove an awful long way."

"Where are we now? Can we go home?" Katie raised her head, her honey-blonde hair plastered to her forehead, a thin runner of snot dangling from her nose. "I want to go home, Mommy."

"I know, baby, I know." Jackie wiped Katie's nose with the sleeve of her t-shirt, smoothing her hair from her face. "But remember what I told you about the bad people?"

Katie nodded, and the shudder that shook her shoulders broke Jackie's heart.

"Now I'm going to look at the tires, but I'll be right back, okay?"

"Okay..." Katie reluctantly moved away from Jackie, shrinking back in her seat.

Jackie looked around carefully before unlatching her door, grabbing the tire iron as she climbed out of the car. The air felt slightly cooler out of the car, and she took a deep breath, realizing that for the first time in days, she didn't smell decay on the wind. Her muscles ached, her joints creaking as she stretched her legs. She could barely walk.

"Can I come out too?" Katie had crawled into the driver's seat. Jackie nodded and held out her hand, scanning the road and bushes and beyond for any sign of movement. Nothing yet. It wouldn't hurt for Katie to stretch, too.

It was a beautiful day, the sky so blue and pretty it was almost too perfect to look at. The sun dappled the dirt road through the overhanging canopy of leaves, and the wind held the first hint of the approaching autumn. It was the kind of day that should have been spent in a park eating a picnic lunch of peanut butter sandwiches and fried chicken, playing on the slides and swing sets with Katie and her friends.

Jackie looked down at Katie, saw the exhaustion in her little girl's eyes and the streaks of dirt on her cheeks, and knew that those days would never come again.

"Stay right here," Jackie said as she walked to the front of the car. For a moment, she couldn't believe what she was actually seeing. Both front tires had exploded.

But that couldn't happen. Unless...

Jackie turned around and looked at the road behind them. A spike strip lay across the single lane, covered with dirt and stones.

Oh, Jesus...

A trap? Why would someone deliberately do this?

Despite the thick heat of the morning, Jackie suddenly went cold. She stood still for a few moments, listening to the crickets and birds, to the whisper of wind through the mossy trees. Someone was watching her. She knew the feeling all too well from the nights dancing at the club, the sick uneasiness of having strange men looking at her, being studied, evaluated. Wanted.

"Mommy, I have to go pee." Katie tugged at her blouse, insistent and almost whiny.

Jackie peered into the shadows of the swamp. He was out there. Somewhere. Whoever had put down the spike strip was out there watching and waiting.

"Not now, baby." Jackie took Katie's hand tightly, backing away from the spike strip, scanning the empty road, the thick undergrowth of swamp edging both sides of the path. "Get in the car."

"But I gotta pee!"

"Now, Katie. No arguments."

Jackie opened the driver's side door and held it as Katie scrambled inside. She knew that her tone of voice had probably scared her, but Jackie could not shake the horrible sense of urgency, the need to run, that she had felt back at her house. Time and luck were running out.

Jackie scanned the swamp and road one more time before ducking behind the wheel again. The windows were only half-rolled down—despite the heat, she wasn't comfortable with them completely open—and she reached over Katie to close her window and lock the door. She did the same to her door, her hands shaking so badly that it took her several attempts to just find the lock and push it down.

Once they were locked into the smothering heat of the car, Jackie closed her eyes and leaned her head against the wheel.

And then she realized that she had no idea what to do next.

"Mommy, can we go now?" Katie stroked Jackie's forearm, urgent. "I want to go."

Jackie opened her eyes and took a deep, shuddering breath. She could drive on the rims. What difference did it make now? She'd drive on the rims until she found another car somewhere and then they'd be okay. That's all she had to do. Just drive.

"Yeah, baby...we're going." Jackie managed a faint smile for Katie as she started the car again. "Seatbelt."

Katie busied herself buckling her seatbelt as Jackie pulled onto the road again. The ride was bumpy, but as she slowly accelerated, she could feel her chest loosening up, the tightness in her throat easing away. It was going to be okay. She just had to find another car that ran and then they'd be fine.

"Mommy, I can't get it locked."

As they reached a crossroads, Jackie looked away for a moment to reach over and click Katie's seatbelt into place.

And then the van rammed them.

***

The world exploded in a burst of pain and glass, an eternity trapped in the moment of impact. Jackie saw the grill of the van just outside Katie's window, and then it was on top of them, plowing into the side of the car, crushing it, brutal in its abrupt attack. Jackie's head smacked into the frame of her door, and everything went black for a few terrible moments.

And then there was nothing but silence. Silence and the rumble of the van's engine, like a monster chuckling in the dark.

"Katie...?" Jackie shook off the disorientation and reached for Katie's seatbelt. She slumped against the chest strap, horribly still. "Katie! Wake up, baby! Come on...please!"

Jackie undid the belt and pulled Katie into her arms, realizing with a fresh burst of panic that Katie wasn't moving on her own. Her small face was dotted with dozens of sparkling shards of glass, so very pale against the trickles of blood.

Jackie's breath caught, her chest suddenly so hollow that every heartbeat was agony. God, no...not like this. Not like this.

Katie suddenly, sharply inhaled and opened her eyes, jerking in Jackie's arms. And then she began to cry.

Jackie sobbed right along with her, holding her tightly, rocking her as best she could in the small space behind the wheel. She caught a glimpse of movement outside the car and twisted in her seat to follow it. Jesus...if it was one of those things she wouldn't be able to fight it off...

"Looks like you had a little accident." The voice preceded the man, and as he climbed out of the van, Jackie felt a fear that was suddenly unmatched by any that she had felt up to that point. There was something terribly wrong with this man. His eyes were unblinking, black, as he walked toward the driver's side door. He was tall, skinny in a way that made him seem deceptively weak. His face reminded her of a vulture's, with a prominent beak of a nose and a heavy brow over those horrible black eyes.

Jackie slowly slid Katie off her lap, blindly reaching for the tire iron.

The man ambled closer to the car, obviously in no hurry. He wore a filthy t-shirt and crud-caked jeans, and his arms were covered with crude black tattoos—skulls and thorns and snarling, grinning demons.

"Ain't that just like a woman driver, though." He grinned, exposing greenish-black teeth and rotted stubs. "My daddy always said that when you put a woman behind a wheel, you might as well go ahead and put your car in the junkyard."

Jackie tried to open the car door, but the impact had done something to the frame. She couldn't get out. But then again, that meant he couldn't get in.

"Boy, ain't you pretty. You sure are. Damn, girl...I don't get to see anything like you anymore." The man leaned against the car, peering through the window. His skin was a patchwork of ingrown hairs and yellow-headed pustules. Up close, his eyes reminded her of a shark's. Totally soulless. Dead.

"My little girl is hurt," Jackie said quietly. Her voice trembled, but she managed to keep it together. "I need to find a doctor—"

"Nope, nope, nope..." The man shook his head and chuckled. "You ain't goin' nowhere, sweetie."

Slowly, with awful deliberation, he rubbed at his crotch as he stared at Jackie through the window. He sucked on his upper lip as he shook his head, a slow smile pulling at his mouth.

"That's a pretty little girl you got there," he said, his gaze flicking over to Katie for a moment. Jackie wanted to claw his eyes out. She didn't want him looking at her little girl, didn't want him even acknowledging her existence.

"Just let us go." Jackie heard the rage in her voice but tried to temper it with fear. She knew men like this all too well. They wanted to be feared. They wanted to be obeyed. If a woman challenged them, she'd be beaten down until any spark of fight was destroyed. She'd grown up with men like that. Married men like that. Danced for men like that. "Come on...please. I won't tell anybody about the accident."

"What makes you think I care if anybody knows about this?" He laughed and shook his head at her. "Lady, you might not have noticed, but things ain't the way they used to be out there. Nobody cares about nothin' but saving their own asses."

He bent down further, until those cold eyes were only inches away from hers, separated only by that thin layer of window glass. "I can do whatever the fuck I want to do now."

And suddenly he was swinging something at the window. Jackie closed her eyes just as a shower of glass flew into her face, each tiny piece slitting and cutting and tearing her skin. She heard Katie screaming, heard herself screaming, and then his hand was around her throat and she couldn't scream, couldn't breathe.

"Come on out of there, baby."

Before she knew what he was going to do, he reached into the car, his movement as precise and sudden as a striking cobra, and grabbed Katie's hair, pulling her across Jackie and out of the open window. Katie shrieked, struggling to break free of him. Jackie was paralyzed by disbelief and shock, but only for a moment. Once he had stepped away from the door, she was out of the car and on top of him, yanking at his greasy hair, desperately trying to jam her fingers into his eyes, rake her nails down his cheeks. He yelped and released Katie's hair, dropping her as he bent backward and tried to shake Jackie off. She clung to him like a tick, still screaming as she forced him away from the car, battering him about the head and shoulders. She wanted to kill him. He touched Katie. Made her scream. She wanted him to die.

"Katie, hide!" Her voice sounded like a madwoman's in her own ears. She couldn't see her little girl, didn't know where she had gone. "*Hide!*"

"Get offa me, bitch!" The man threw himself backward, slamming Jackie into the side of the van. She held on, so he did it again and again, each time more viciously than before. The back of her head connected with the side mirror and fireworks exploded in front of her eyes. She was vaguely aware of Katie's screams, the shrill keening blending into the buzz that was filling her head as she took blow after blow against the reinforced side of the van. She didn't want to let go, but she couldn't hold on anymore. Before she could catch herself, her arms were suddenly sliding away from him and she felt herself falling. It was a nightmare. A fever dream. It couldn't be real.

The man spat at Jackie as he jumped away from her, as if afraid she'd attack him again. Jackie struggled to sit up, but her body wouldn't cooperate with her brain. "Ain't nobody does that to Earl Ray. Nobody!" He punctuated his words with a flurry of sharp kicks, catching Jackie in the stomach and thighs. "You gonna answer for that, bitch. You gonna pay."

Jackie managed to raise her head just as the man who called himself Earl Ray opened the van's sliding side door. The stench hit her first--metallic and rotten, green with decay--and she retched, rolling onto her side. Oh God, she thought, an agonized prayer as she saw what awaited her within. Knives. Guns. Blood-crusted baseball bats. A nail gun. It was a modern traveling torture chamber, splashed with rusty dried blood and littered with human debris.

God help us, Jackie thought. God help my little girl.

Earl Ray reappeared in the doorway with something that looked like a medieval ball and chain in his hand. He grinned, showing his stubs, and Jackie understood at that moment that she was looking into the face of evil. And somehow it was worse than any of the dead things she had seen. They couldn't control their nature. He could.

"I *told* you you was gonna pay," he said and swung the mace.

***

The pain woke her up.

Jackie moaned low in her throat as she opened her left eye, blinking away crusty specks of dried blood, and saw the full moon peeking over the trees. She'd thought she was dead. After the fifth swing of the mace, she hadn't been able to stay conscious any longer. She'd passed out with the sound of Katie's screams muffled by the thud and crack of her own bones breaking.

Katie...

Jackie rolled to her right side, using her arm for leverage as she struggled to sit up. Her left arm was broken, hanging against her side like a bag of glass shards. She coughed and tasted blood in her mouth. He busted me up, she thought and spat out the blood before she vomited. She felt as if something had reached into her stomach and squeezed her internal organs until they were nothing but paste. He must have kept swinging that mace long after she'd passed out. And judging from the torn condition of her blouse and jeans, he'd done other things to her while she was unconscious. But she didn't want to think about that. She was afraid she might remember something better left unknown.

Jackie finally managed to sit up in the scummy swamp water, but she barely felt the chill. She'd never seen a night so mercilessly dark. Even the light of the full moon didn't reach into the depths of the swamp. She'd never find her way out.

But what about Katie?

The thought of her baby alone with that monster opened up a fresh well of agony. Jackie doubled over, suddenly unable to stem the flood of tears as she cradled her shattered arm to her chest and wept. Katie couldn't be alive. The bastard wouldn't care that she was only five years old, that she could sing the ABC song and read along with "Sesame Street". He wouldn't care that he was snuffing out the life of a baby who hadn't even had the chance to live. Katie was Jackie's world, but she would mean less than nothing to that monster. They were just victims. Toys for him to play with and discard.

Jackie dimly heard her wails answered by the swamp frogs, her cries echoing in the darkness surrounding her. She wanted to die. If Katie was gone, then she wanted to go with her. She couldn't bear the thought of her baby all alone and scared.

She wept, rocking to and fro as the brackish pond water seeped into her mangled jeans. What had he done to her before finally ending it? What kind of terror did Katie have to endure before he finally killed her? God help me, she thought. Please.

But there was no heavenly blaze of light, no gentle hand reaching out to guide her from the darkness. Jackie opened her eyes and saw nothing but the jagged stumps of trees protruding from the swamp, the water catching only the faintest bit of moonlight and reflecting it back to the sky. She was alone.

She closed her eyes and a cold calmness settled over her, stopping her sobs in mid-hitch. The pain in her arm and chest faded into an almost comforting numbness, her nerves either dead or dying as the calm spread through her body, into her mind. All she could feel now was razor-sharp grief for her little girl...and a bone-deep rage.

She slowly got to her feet, each movement a struggle for her bruised and broken body, but she didn't feel the pain. He'd shattered her knee with a swing of the mace, but she walked on it anyway, ignoring the scrape and crunch of bone. It didn't matter. She didn't care. All she wanted was to find the bastard and hurt him.

Jackie staggered through the shallow pond water. Her eyes had adjusted to the darkness, and now she could make out other shapes lying on the banks of the pond. At first she thought they might be sacks of garbage, abandoned by some swamp-dweller. Then she got close enough to catch a whiff of their stench, like road kill on an August day. Like the inside of that bastard's van.

Bodies. He'd brought her to his dumping ground.

They seemed to be everywhere, sprawled helplessly among the undergrowth and trees, all of them in various stages of decay. Some had been skeletonized by the elements. Others were so badly bloated and burned by endless hours in the Florida heat that they didn't even look like human beings any more. Men, women, or children...she couldn't tell. There were just so many of them.

And they were writhing in the swamp mud, some of them crawling. Some of them staggering to their feet. Some of them so rotted that they could do nothing but moan.

The comforting numbness that had settled in wasn't enough to block out the horror surrounding her now. How could one man do all this?

Jackie knew she should be afraid, surrounded by so many of the dead, but she felt no fear as she walked among them. They watched her with flat eyes, and the ones that could walk began to follow her.

She took another unsteady, shuffling step forward and nearly stumbled over another body, this one lying in the shallow edge of the pond. The pressure of her foot released a gout of body gasses, and Jackie gagged as she struggled away. It had been a woman once, and what remained of her long blonde hair shone against the whiteness of her skull. It rolled its head from side to side and cried out, a guttural croak full of misery.

Jackie stumbled back to the shore just as the stagnant water parted and a rough-hewn log floated to the surface. The log opened its eyes and mouth, snagging the water-bloated corpse at the waist and dragging it beneath the surface again, disappearing without a trace, its cries swallowed up by the water.

Jackie laughed, a shrill, gobbling sound that was only barely sane. Dear God...she was in Hell. This couldn't be real. It could only be Hell.

And before she knew it, the swamp suddenly became a living, breathing thing. The croaking of frogs seemed to double in volume, joined by the click and chirp of cicadas and crickets. Snakes slithered beneath her feet, sliding silently into the underbrush, gliding gracefully on the water's surface. The canopy of cypress trees overhead blocked the moon almost purposely, keeping her in darkness as she stumbled through the human wreckage.

And the moans. The moans surrounded her. So much pain.

Katie, she thought, gagging at the overwhelming stench of the dead. Was Katie out here with the others? Had that bastard left her out to die?

Then it occurred to her: the bastard thought she was already dead, or else he wouldn't have left her alone. He'd left her in the swamp for the gators. As far as he knew, she was already in the bottom of the pond, wedged between the branches of a fallen tree by a hungry alligator. As far as he knew, she couldn't come after him.

Music drifted into the night, faint beneath the endless cacophony of the frogs, but Jackie somehow recognized the tune: Lynyrd Skynyrd. "Freebird." She'd always hated the song, always felt unreasonably depressed whenever she heard it, but now it was like a lifeline in the darkness. She followed the sound, moving clumsily through the swamp, climbing awkwardly over fallen trees. She felt like a blind woman trying to navigate her way through a razor-lined maze; each step was a leap of faith. She half-expected to feel the sharp strike of a cottonmouth as she sloshed through ankle-deep muck, but she passed through unscathed. She just kept following the music. Music meant people. People meant help for Katie.

A veil of hanging moss brushed against her face as she stepped into another clearing. About two hundred yards away was a ramshackle hut, pasted together with tarpaper and sheets of rusted siding. It stood on stilts in the middle of a pond, leaning precariously towards the water, and looked uninhabitable...but the music was definitely coming from there. A shadow passed in front of the sickly yellow light shining from one of the windows: someone was home.

Please have a phone, Jackie thought as she crossed the clearing as quickly as she could, half-dragging her busted leg as she struggled to run. Oh, God...please don't let it be too late for Katie. Please, God...

A woman screamed.

Jackie stopped so abruptly that she nearly fell, realizing with a burst of fresh horror that the scream had come from inside the shack...and that now she was too close to it to get away without being seen. Another scream was followed by a man's derisive laughter.

Jackie's rage rekindled. She recognized the laughter. She'd found the bastard. She should have known he'd stay close to his dumping ground.

All thought to her own life disappeared, swallowed by a bitter rise of hate. Dragging herself up the cinderblock steps, she had no idea of what she would do or even if she would have the strength to do it, but she didn't care anymore. She'd tear the bastard's throat out with her teeth if she got the chance.

Breathing hard, she threw herself against the shack's door, pounding on it, clawing at it. She felt her fingernails snap and peel away, but the pain only made her more aware. She screamed, unable to form words, raging as she slammed herself against the wood.

Skynyrd abruptly stopped in mid-guitar solo, and a thick silence rushed to fill the vacuum. Even the swamp frogs and cicadas had stopped singing. Jackie kept pounding on the flimsy door, screaming with rage and frustration. She finally managed to knock it off a hinge and it swung open before her, crashing to the floor.

For what felt like an eternity, she simply stood there in the doorway, glaring through a haze of blood at the bastard as he straddled a girl who looked no older than fifteen. The girl's face was a mass of bruises, her short brown hair matted to her skull. Her eyes were open but sightless. She was gone.

"What the fuck...?" His piggy eyes widened as he stared back at Jackie, his mouth dropping open in an oafish gape of surprise. He held a blackjack in one hand, his arm still cocked back to deliver a blow. "You're dead, bitch! I killed you!"

Jackie shuffled into the shack, feeling more dead than alive as she breathed in the ever-present stink of human decay. Just as the van had been, the one room hovel was filled with bloody weapons and rotting body parts. Trophies. Jackie saw a woman's head resting on a tabletop and told herself that it wasn't really real. None of this was real. She was in hell.

 Jackie tried to speak, to tell him to get off the girl, but her lips felt swollen, her tongue three sizes too big for her mouth. She couldn't see him very well--her left eye felt as if it had been glued shut with dried blood--but she moved forward, her broken arm hanging dead at her side, dragging her shattered leg. The sudden fear she saw in his eyes was intensely gratifying; she smiled, feeling her lips crack and bleed with the movement.

The bastard made a sound that was almost a scream and scrambled away from the girl's body. Jackie reached out with her good arm and picked up the first thing she saw: a baseball bat that he had driven nails through, creating a crude but effective torture device. It felt good and heavy in her hand. It would hurt. It would hurt him intensely.

Jackie laughed, the sound bubbling out of her bloody mouth on a pinkish froth, and swung the bat. Even with one hand, she knew she could land a good, solid blow.

She swung the bat and knocked over a stack of pornographic magazines, scattering them across the filthy floor. The bastard held his hands out as he stumbled toward the back of the shack. The floor tilted away from him slightly, and he lost his balance as he tried to put a chair between him and Jackie. The chair was a flimsy dinette seat, and Jackie knocked it easily out of the way with a swing of the bat.

Jackie tried to speak, forcing the words out. "How many?" she asked, approaching him slowly--more slowly than she would have liked. It was beginning to be a struggle to keep her broken leg moving; it felt like so much dead meat now, completely numb from the hip to the ankle. "How many people did you kill?"

He shook his head savagely, moaning low in his throat as his back finally came up against the back wall. Surrounded by the souvenirs of his cruelty, he had reverted back to the pathetic little boy he'd always been. Tears spilled from his eyes as his lower lip wobbled and his chin quivered.

"Please...don't hurt me...please..." He slid to the floor in an almost fetal crouch. "I didn't want to kill you...the voices made me do it..."

Jackie spat at him, swinging the bat. It caught his left knee, and she could almost feel the shatter of bones reverberating up the handle of the bat. It felt good.

He howled in agony and clutched at his leg. Jackie swung the bat again, catching the back of his left hand with the jagged spikes. She thought of what he had done with those hands, how many people he had violated and mutilated, and swung the bat again, shredding his fingers and palm as he raised his arm in defense.

But it wasn't enough. She thought of all the bodies she'd left out in the darkness, all the families grieving for them, all the pain and terror and fear this one man had caused. If he lived, he might never be caught. He'd go on killing until he died. And how many more children might he kill? How many more lives would he destroy?

"You're dead!" he screamed, a little boy's voice in a man's body. "I killed you! You can't come back!"

"Yes," Jackie whispered, smiling through bloody lips. "I can..."

She swung the bat, planning to bury its spikes deeply in the bastard's head, but he rolled out of the way at the last moment and the nails slammed into the wall instead. The impact wrenched the bat out of Jackie's hand, and before she could grab something else, the bastard had pulled up a trapdoor and slithered through. Jackie heard a splash beneath the shack and dropped to her knees at the edge of the trapdoor. No...He couldn't get away...not now...

He let out a half-assed rebel yell, laughing as he gazed up to the shack floor. He'd fallen only ten or so feet, landing in waist deep water.

Jackie whimpered, clutching at the edge of the opening. The light from inside the shack shone onto the water's surface, giving it an oily, brackish quality. The bastard pushed his wet hair away from his face and grinned, flashing that mouthful of repulsive stubs.

"I know you didn't think I was actually scared of you!" he yelled, grinning. "Don't you think I know what to do when I'm finished with y'all?"

As he spoke, Jackie saw the water behind him stir, saw shapes silently rise to the surface behind him. Their faces shone ghostly pale in the light from the shack.

"Aw, but that's okay. It's alright. I'm gonna finish the job this time," the bastard said and giggled. "I'm gonna chop you up into little bitty pieces and feed you to the fuckin' gators, bitch."

Black eyes watched him. Mouths opened, flashing yellow teeth.

"Dead or not, I'm gonna make you screa--"

They were on him all at once, so many that Jackie couldn't see where they ended and he began. They tore at him with teeth and nail, their agonized moans now filled with fury. His eyes, wild with fear yet filled with realization, met Jackie's for just a heartbeat before the dead dragged him into the water and his screams became gargled gasps.

Jackie watched until they had torn him to pieces, until they had gorged themselves on his flesh and blood and left what remained to float to the bottom of the swamp.

She watched until she realized the reason why the dead hadn't tried to touch her. And for a moment, just a moment, she wept.

***

She walked, like all the others, moving towards some great unknowable end, feeling nothing. By dawn, the swamp was behind her. Ahead was the remains of her car.

Everything that had happened in that car happened a million years ago. It meant nothing to her now. She felt nothing now. Her thoughts were gone, her mind empty of everything but a sense of gnawing hunger.

Jackie kept moving, dragging herself along, staring ahead at nothing.

She didn't even see the small figure wriggling in the dirt beneath the car, crawling out.

"Mommy! I hid like you told me to...I got scared, but I did what you told me to do."

Jackie stopped for a moment. She stared at Katie.

Katie ran to her, wrapping her arms around Jackie's waist, hugging her tightly. Jackie lolled her head to the side, looking down at Katie, and then she dropped down to her knees beside the girl, wrapping her arms around her, holding her tightly. Katie, so trusting, hugged her back.

Whatever remained of Jackie's mind realized that she could not leave her child alone in the world. Dimly, like an almost forgotten memory, she knew that she vowed she would never leave Katie alone again.

Mommy?" Katie raised her head to look up at Jackie. "Mommy, what's wrong?"

Jackie opened her mouth but no words would come.

Then she gave her baby one last kiss.

When We Are As We Once Were

"Mrs. Mallory just died."

Megan Edwards closed her eyes and slumped back in her chair, suddenly too exhausted to deal with another one so soon. "Jesus..." she whispered, a prayer that she couldn't even finish.

"What do we do with her?" Bobby, the nurse's aide who had joined the small core of nurses in the break room, looked ready to panic. Megan knew they would have to watch him closely. With everything going on outside the walls of the nursing home, they definitely didn't need more chaos. Not that they'd be going anywhere soon. The National Guard had already begun blocking the highways with tanks. No one had actually said the words 'martial law' yet, but the news reports kept showing soldiers with guns. The news called it a "shelter-in-place"—nobody allowed on the roads for any reason but the worst emergency.

But who was defining 'worst emergency,' Megan wondered. Right now it *all* seemed pretty damn bad.

She shook away the other thoughts for the moment. She was the only doctor on call that night, so for some reason everyone had automatically decided to defer to her. She wished they wouldn't. It made her feel responsible for them, and she didn't want that kind of load on her shoulders.

But somebody had to be. And it was either her or that jackass janitor Earl, who thought they should just desert the patients and strike out to save their own asses. He would be trouble when things started getting worse...and Megan had a feeling they would start getting worse very, very soon.

"Wrap her in sheets," Megan said as she stood, wobbling slightly. "Do it tight, so she can't get out, in case she..." She stopped and took a deep breath, shaking her head as a pulse of fire shot through her temples. Migraine was coming, she realized. "Just take her down to the basement and put her in the cold room."

The cold room. The polite way they referred to the nursing home's makeshift morgue. Sometimes, in bad weather, the funeral home couldn't pick up the bodies right away, so they had to store them down in the basement. Three air conditioners ran at all times, keeping the room chilly, but it wasn't intended for long term storage.

But it had a heavy door on it that locked. And Megan was afraid they might have to use it.

Bobby and Lucy, one of the sturdier nurse attendants, nodded and hurried out of the room. Megan swallowed back a wave of nausea and closed her eyes again, trying to will the pain away. She had suffered from migraines ever since high school. Stress usually triggered them, and the bigger the worry, the worse the migraine. This one felt like her head was cracking open, like something was reaching inside her skull and squeezing her brain to mush.

The thought reminded her of what had started this whole panic, and the nausea rose again. She didn't want to think about how they found Mr. Stoller and Mr. Henks. She didn't want to think about the way Mr. Henks shoved handfuls of Mr. Stoller's intestines into his toothless mouth, gumming them as he swallowed.

And she didn't want to think about the way Mr. Stoller's eyes had opened while Mr. Henks was chewing on him.

"Has anyone tried the television yet?" she asked weakly, forcing the images away.

"I will, Meg." Janey, one of the younger nurses, crouched in front of the breakroom television and flipped channels. It was such an old TV that it didn't even have a remote control. That was all the nursing home could afford.

The black screen blipped to life and a buzz of static exploded into the room, momentarily masking the unbearable moans and cries for help echoing through the halls. The residents had no idea what was going on. They were like children, frightened and helpless and badly needing comforting.

Once again, the burden of responsibility settled on Megan's shoulders, momentarily paralyzing her. Six residents between the ages of 70 and 95 remained after the initial panic. Five staff members, including herself and Earl the janitor, remained to care for them. The nursing home had been at its lowest capacity in years, thank God. Megan couldn't imagine what she would have done if all the beds had been full.

She just wished she knew what was going on. Mr. Stoller had been dead when she opened that door. The wound to his stomach was too severe, and at 78 he would have never been able to survive the blood loss. And why had Mr. Henks done such a thing? He and Mr. Stoller had been roommates for years, best friends since before the nursing home. They used to play chess outside on sunny days and work on jigsaw puzzles together in the winter.

So why would Mr. Henks tear the guts out of his best friend?

"CNN's on!" Janey suddenly shouted, startling everyone into silence. Megan, Earl, and Janey huddled around the television, stunned by the images on the screen.

It couldn't be real. Not this.

The talking head newscaster, usually an attractive blonde, was disheveled and wan, the circles beneath her eyes stark against her paleness. Megan's first thought was that the world really *was* ending if nobody cared about putting on make-up before going on camera.

"…early reports state that there is an epidemic spreading throughout the East Coast," the newscaster said, her voice shaky and not modulated at all. "At this time we have no details about the nature of this epidemic, but we are expecting a statement from the Director of the Center for Disease Control within the hour. We *do* have this footage shot by amateur photographer Ed Dillon from Monroe, Pennsylvania. This footage has not been edited, so viewer discretion is advised."

Suddenly the screen was grainy, the picture shaky and out of focus. A family picnic. Mom's laying out the food while brother and sister chase each other in a game of tag. A perfect summer day.

Megan's stomach soured as she watched the family on the screen. She remembered waking up that morning and looking at the sky and wondering if she should take the day off and take Andy and Hannah to the playground. They had been begging her to play hooky and spend more time with them before they had to go back to their father. The custody agreement gave Frank the kids during the school year, but they were Megan's all summer long. She'd thought they would have plenty of time together over the next few months. She'd even saved her vacation and sick days so she could take the entire month of July off. They'd go to the beach and hit the amusement parks and go on picnics and do all the fun stuff that they wanted to do.

So she'd decided against taking the day off, and she'd taken Andy and Hannah to her parents' house and headed in to work as usual. She'd planned to bring a pizza and a couple of videos home to them to make up for it.

But that was before.

Megan covered her mouth as the video began to turn bad. The happy family on the screen was being stealthily surrounded by dark figures coming up on them from behind. Why didn't he see them? Megan wondered. First there were two of them stumbling over the rise behind the kids. Then another three stepping out of the trees. By the time Ed Dillon focused his camera on one of them and zoomed in on its face, it was too late.

The thing had maggots in its eyes. And it was tearing out the woman's throat.

Mercifully, Ed dropped the camera before the things got to his children, but the background noises—the screams, the begging, the shrieking—were still agonizingly sharp on the soundtrack. The camera, on its side now, kept recording. A child in sneakers ran past the lens, followed by a man's dirty bare feet. Then nothing but blades of grass. And the screams.

The CNN anchor reappeared on the screen. "We will return in a few moments," she said somberly. Rousing drums and violins underscored the flashy graphic on the screen, "EPIDEMIC OF TERROR."

"Jesus Christ..." Megan whispered, shaking her head.

Janey turned the sound down on the television as the commercials began. Seeing them gave Megan a strange comfort. Things couldn't be that bad if they were still playing commercials on TV.

"I think it's bio-warfare," Earl said as he stood up. "It's some kind of terrorist attack that's making people go cannibal."

"I drove past a funeral this afternoon on my way into work," Janey said quietly. "It was at Overland Park, you know...the big cemetery next to the highway?"

Megan nodded, only half-listening as she fumbled her cell phone out of her lab coat.

"The casket was just sitting there," Janey continued, her voice soft and far away. "And it was open. But there was nobody around."

Megan called her parents' number, closing her eyes as she waited for the beeps that meant that she had a signal. It was the tenth time she'd attempted to call. The line was busy on the other side.

Her parents lived about a mile from Overland Park.

She didn't want to think about it.

Bobby and Lucy came back into the lounge, both of them breathless and sheened with sweat.

"She started moving right when we were tying her up," Lucy said as she hit the freezer and took out a hidden bottle of vodka. "Goddam if she didn't."

"Save me some of that," Bobby said as he reached for the bottle.

Megan noticed that his forearm was bloody. She turned off the phone and dropped it into her pocket, never taking her gaze away from Bobby's wound.

"What happened?" she asked.

"Old bitch bit me." Bobby laughed, but it was a nervous, desperate sound. "She had one tooth left in her head and she bit me."

"Let me clean that out." Megan started working on Bobby's arm, grateful for the distraction. She glanced up at Lucy, who was chugging from the vodka bottle. "I wouldn't do that."

"Why not?" Lucy's eyes narrowed, making her look even fiercer than usual. She was a big woman, with close-cropped black hair and masculine features, and had a personality that swiveled between bitchy and slightly less bitchy. Megan had heard a few stories about the way she treated the residents and was planning on dismissing her. Now it was too late.

"We don't know what's going to happen," Megan said evenly, meeting Lucy's stare head-on. "If you get drunk, you're on your own."

Lucy didn't look away for a few moments. Then she capped the bottle and slammed it down hard on the countertop of the kitchenette.

For a few minutes, no one spoke. The sounds of the residents echoed through the hallways.

"I don't like having everyone so separated," Megan finally said, running a hand through her hair. It felt greasy and clotted, even though she had just washed it that morning—a lifetime ago. "I think we should bring all the residents into the sunroom."

"Beds and all?" Janey asked.

"Yes. Bring their wheelchairs or walkers, too. But bring the beds. I don't know how long this is going to last."

As everyone filed out of the breakroom, Megan went to one of the windows and looked outside. The nursing home was several miles outside of town, stuck in the boonies so guilt-ridden children could stash their parents and grandparents away in the peace and quiet of the country. It was a beautiful setting for a nursing home, but the isolation had always spooked Megan a little.

She shook the thoughts away and hurried out to help gather up the residents. It looked like they were going to be in for a very long, dark night.

***

Megan hated to do it, but she sedated the remaining residents and had Lucy and Bobby restrain them once they'd fallen asleep. She hated those restraints, but if someone had a heart attack and died in their sleep...

They'd what? she asked herself. Come back like Mr. Henks did? Try to eat us the way he was eating Mr. Stoller?

It was impossible, so far beyond the norms of reality that it felt more dreamlike than real. Dead people did not move. They did not attack. They were dead. The dead stayed dead. That was the way it was, the way it had always been.

There was just no earthly way the dead could come back to life. No matter what she had witnessed at the nursing home, no matter what she had seen on the news, Megan could not believe it was true.

And yet...

Her head throbbing in time with her heartbeat, Megan had finally sat down once the last resident had been sedated. She was forcing herself to use her cell phone only once every half-hour, futilely calling her parents' house even though she knew she would only hear the prickly burr of a busy signal. She couldn't convince herself that the phone had been left accidentally off the hook or that her mother had gotten into a gossipy chat with one of her church friends.

Civilization was going under, a little piece at a time. First the blockades on the highways. Then the news blackouts. Then the phone lines. Whatever was happening out there was huge, and it was everywhere.

Earl and Lucy sat off to the side, listlessly playing Hearts with a greasy deck of cards. Bobby and Janey were curled up together on the couch they had brought in from the breakroom. Megan hadn't even known they were dating. Maybe they weren't. Maybe they just needed to be close to somebody.

Megan stared at the television, watching the same loops of news footage over and over again. Everyone seemed to be reacting to the so-called epidemic the same way—chaos. Now it was everywhere, not just on the East Coast. People were calling 911 operators and reporting dead people on their front porches or staggering up the street. The attacks began not long after. The dead would group together and storm a place, battering through windows and doors until they were inside.

There were lots of amateur photographers out there, and each one of them managed to capture a vivid little slice of hell for the good people at CNN.

"It's like in Revelations," Janey said as she stared at the television. Jumpy, hand-held camera footage caught a dozen of the dead, all of them either naked or clad only in flimsy hospital gowns, emerging from the doors of a hospital morgue. "The dead are rising to be judged."

"That's horseshit," Lucy said, taking a swig of vodka before handing the bottle over to Earl. "I agree with Earl. It's terrorists."

Earl tipped the mouth of the bottle to Lucy in a toast. "Damn straight it is."

Megan tuned out the discussion, closing her eyes as she thought about Andy and Hannah. She wondered if her parents had taken them to the storm cellar, like when she was a little girl and the weather forecasted tornado warnings. Mom had done her best to make the cellar a safe place, with toys and puzzles and board games, and

Dad had stocked the place with enough bottled water and canned food to last for a year.

They were in the storm cellar, Megan decided. They had to be. That's why no one was answering the phone. They were safely tucked away in the storm cellar.

God, please let that be, Megan thought and squeezed her eyes tight, the fear and dread building up so intensely for a moment that she thought her heart might explode.

"They're starting to wake up," Bobby said loudly.

Megan took a deep breath and focused again. Nothing she could do about anything outside of these four walls. She had to concentrate on the situation now and let everything else fall into place as it may.

"They're probably hungry," Janey said and stood up. "I'll go fix everybody some soup. Would that be okay, Dr. Edwards?"

"Yes, that would be fine." Megan rubbed at her forehead and gritted her teeth until the worst of the pain ebbed away. "Lucy, would you prepare everyone's meds, please?"

Lucy harrumphed, put-out and pissed off, but stood up and went to the medicine locker anyway.

"Bobby?" Megan had to raise her voice slightly to draw his attention away from the television. He was getting too absorbed in the news; now they were showing unedited footage of clashes between the National Guard and the dead people.

"Uh…yeah, Doc?"

"Would you please check bedpans and diapers and empty the catheter bags?"

Bobby made a face, but went to do as asked. Megan couldn't understand how doing his job was any worse than the things he was seeing on the news. She had seen the same footage of an old man getting his head blown away by a soldier five or six times now.

"Undo the restraints, too," Megan added. She had decided that they would only be restrained when they were sleeping; she didn't relish the thought of one of the residents waking up to find that they couldn't move their arms or legs. That would be too terrifying.

The key was keeping a routine, keeping a schedule even in the face of chaos. The residents needed that kind of security, to know that they would get their meds and eat their meals on schedule, just like always. Megan wondered how much of this they would understand, if any of it.

She wondered if it would be cruel to keep them ignorant of the horrors happening just outside the doors. Or would it be a blessing?

Was it even up to her to decide?

They would want to know about their families, those few who remembered their sons and daughters. The knowledge that people were dying at an alarming rate would send them into a panic. And how could she explain to them about Mr. Henks and Mr. Stoller and Mrs. Mallory? The residents were like children, all but two of them suffering from advanced Alzheimers.

Ignorance would be much kinder.

"Bobby?" Megan went to the aide and drew him aside. "When you're finished, please hook up the VCR and bring in some movies, okay?"

"What about the news?"

"We'll take turns going to the breakroom to watch." Megan looked over his shoulder and caught the eye of Mrs. VanZant. The old woman smiled sweetly, her deeply lined face still beautiful despite the cancer that had ravaged her.

Megan's heart caught. This wasn't fair. These people should not have to go through this, not after everything else. None of them should have to go through it.

"I don't want to scare anyone," Megan said softly. "I don't think they need to know what's happening out there, do you?"

Bobby shook his head. "No, ma'am. I guess not."

"How's your arm?"

"Achy. Feels kinda weird." Bobby glanced down at the square of white bandage and winced. "Like it's hot and cold all at once."

Megan flattened her hand against his forehead. He felt feverish, yet his skin was dotted with sweat.

"You might be getting an infection or—"

"I think it's worse than that."

Megan went silent, seeing the sudden blank dread in Bobby's eyes. "What are you talking about?"

"I saw something on the news earlier." Bobby swallowed hard, his Adam's apple bobbing furiously as he fought to control the fear in his voice. "They said not to let any of those things bite you. They think that's how it spreads."

"But your bite wasn't deep—"

"It doesn't matter." Bobby met her eyes again. "What if I'm infected?"

Megan knew better than to try to comfort him with insincere optimism. There was no comfort to be found anywhere.

"I don't know," she said quietly. "I don't know what to tell you."

"I didn't say nothing about it to Janey," Bobby said, quickly glancing in the direction of the breakroom. "Please don't tell her, okay? I don't want to scare her more than she already is."

"I won't." Megan studied Bobby for a moment, remembering the day he started working at the nursing home. He was wonderful with the residents, always ready with a compliment for the ladies or a baseball story for the guys. Bobby, so tall and lanky and sweetly innocent, had been the perfect substitute for their long-lost grandchildren.

It wasn't fair. None of it.

"Listen…" Bobby hesitated, staring down at his shoes for a moment. It was a habit of his whenever he had to tell her something he wished he didn't have to mention. "If it gets bad, like they say it might…would you…" He looked back up to Megan. "Would you help me?"

Megan knew exactly what he was asking. If it got too bad, he wanted to be put out of his misery. God…how had it come to this?

"Yes," she said softly. "I'll help you."

Neither of them spoke for a moment. Megan wished she could hug him the way she hugged Andy and Hannah when they were afraid. She wondered where Bobby's mother was, if she was feeling the same agony that she felt being away from her kids.

"I'll pick out the movies they like," Bobby said, clearing his throat as he tried to smile. "Be back in a minute."

Megan attempted to return his smile. She couldn't quite do it.

***

Megan didn't like what she was sensing from Earl.

An hour or so after their dinner of canned soup, he had started pacing the length of the sunroom, reminding of Megan of a lion in a cage. Earl was a big guy, well over six feet tall and close to three hundred pounds, and Megan had heard a few stories about the things he liked to do after his shift. He was well known around all the bars in town—not for his ability to drink, but for his habit of starting fights and sending guys to the emergency room.

Now he was walking back and forth from window to window, clenching his huge fists at his sides, looking like he was itching to fight.

And Lucy was right there goading him on.

Megan had heard a few snatches of their whispered conversations. Something about taking the van and heading for town.

From the sound of it, the plan was already a done deal. They were just waiting for full dark to sneak away.

The bitch of it was…they would do it. And they could do it. They could walk away without looking back.

But even that wasn't the highest priority on Megan's list of worries. Mrs. Cavendish was having problems with her heart flutter again, and every time that happened, she nearly panicked herself into a heart attack until Megan could calm her down. This time, she actually had one. It was a mild attack, but Mrs. Cavendish was 90 years old. Even the mild ones were too much.

And then there was the ever-worsening news from the outside. The local channels had stopped broadcasting hours earlier, the last transmission a frightening rooftop shot of the dead shambling through the streets. The studio was located only sixty or so miles away from the nursing home. The epidemic—if that was the word for it—was getting closer and closer.

No, Megan thought, glancing at the door leading down to the basement. It's already here.

The only information now came from CNN, and even that was iffy. The main studios in Atlanta were losing affiliates by the hour. During Megan's half-hour of watching the news, she was amazed by how quickly the epidemic had spread. Usually it would take days for a virus or disease to infect as many people as this seemed to be infecting, not hours. A computer generated map tracked the progression of the reports of reanimated dead—because now everyone had pretty much accepted the impossible—and the entire country was covered in red patches, like open wounds. This was where the most damage was being reported.

All the cities were infested. Europe was a war zone. The Mid-East and China were not responding to any requests for information.

And it had all happened in the space of twenty-four hours.

Megan had felt absolutely numb as she watched the reports. The footage was as shocking as before, but now she watched it with a grim sense of duty. Every religious group was calling into the CNN studios and talking to the alleged experts, each of them claiming that this was the Judgement Day. This was the day the world ended. This was the day God called all his children home and sent the sinners down to the lakes of fire in Hell.

Were Andy and Hannah frightened? Megan couldn't stop thinking of them. Andy had just lost his first baby tooth and was so proud that he'd pulled it himself that he'd decided he wanted to be a dentist. Hannah was just discovering the joy of being a prissy little girl, demanding to wear dresses instead of the jeans she used to love and begging to wear nail polish and earrings.

Megan couldn't imagine how they felt right now. She hoped her parents were keeping the worst of it away from them, the way they were shielding the residents from the truth. She hoped that her babies just thought there was a bad storm coming. Nothing more, nothing less.

She would have prayed for it, but she was terrified that God wasn't listening to prayers right now.

"Megan! C'mere! Hurry!"

Megan jumped out of her chair, reacting instinctively to the sheer panic in Janey's voice. She ran out of the breakroom and saw Janey standing in the hallway, just outside one of the residents' rooms.

"What's wr—"

"Bobby! Something's wrong with Bobby!" Janey pulled Megan into the room and Megan instantly gagged at the stench. She had smelled gangrene all too often over the years, but this was somehow thicker, darker than the usual smell of rot. Bobby lay on one of the beds, drenched with sweat and moaning. His bandaged arm had turned blackish-brown.

Infection, Megan thought. He was right. Oh, Jesus…he was right.

"It's that bite, isn't it?" Janey's voice had calmed to a surprising degree. Her eyes were still wide and twitchy, but she was slowly regaining her nurse's composure. "Mrs. Mallory infected him."

"I don't know," Megan said, gritting her teeth as she slowly peeled the bandage away from Bobby's wound. It was as bad as she'd suspected, if not worse. It reminded her of a patient she'd once treated who had been bitten by a brown recluse spider. In hours, the bite area had gone completely necrotic, with the decay widening its radius all around the wound.

This was just like the spider's bite, but far, far worse. The decay was spreading up his arm, black tendrils of rot eating at his flesh.

And there was nothing she could do.

Bobby opened his eyes, wildly thrashing his head as he clamped his jaws and tried not to scream out loud. Janey choked and tried to hold him, but his convulsions were too severe. He bucked and spasmed, as if his muscles were already stiffening with rigor.

"Bobby…" Megan held Bobby down by the shoulders and spoke as firmly as she could make her unsteady voice sound. Bobby's eyes rolled wildly, a thin grey foam frothing at the corners of his mouth. "Bobby…can you hear me?"

Bobby's gaze touched hers for just an instant. He's still in there, Megan thought with a fresh burst of horror. He knows what's happening.

"Bobby…" Megan's mouth went dry, her voice harsh and scratchy. "Do you need me to help you now?"

He nodded slowly, lips curled in a rictus of agony that Megan could never imagine.

She left him then, running to the medicine locker as Janey took her place at his side. Lucy and Earl were anxiously waiting to see what was happening. Fight or flight, Megan thought sourly as she noticed the ring of keys in Earl's hand. The residents were all sleeping, sedated again.

Megan found the bottle she was looking for and hurried back into the room. The blackness now seemed to have etched its way up his entire arm, crawling onto his chest and up his throat.

She quickly tore open a fresh hypodermic and plunged the needle into the bottle. She didn't measure the dosage. She didn't need to.

Then she injected the sedative into the crook of Bobby's uninjured arm, pushing the plunger until the hypo was empty. Bobby immediately calmed, his eyes cloudy and half-closed, but not filled with terror.

The overdose would kill him within minutes, but it would be a peaceful death. He would just fade away to sleep.

Janey stared at Megan, slowly understanding what she had done.

"It's better this way," Megan said softly, feeling idiotic even as she spoke the words. How was it better? Bobby was still dying.

"Can I stay with him?" Janey whispered.

"Yes…" Megan felt tears trickling over her cheeks, her chest tightening so severely that she was unable to catch her breath for a moment. She took a deep breath and forced the numbness to return. "But just for a few minutes."

The rest was left unsaid. Janey nodded and collapsed beside Bobby on the bed, sobbing now with every ounce of strength. Bobby's breathing was growing shallower, fading with each exhalation.

Megan walked out of the room and hurled the empty sedative bottle against the wall, taking grim satisfaction in the sound of shattering glass.

***

"So what do we do with him?" Lucy asked, keeping her voice low as she glanced over Earl's shoulder to the closed door of Bobby's room. It had been a half-hour since he died. Janey sat in front of the door, her legs drawn up to her chest, rocking back and forth as she wept.

The lights had flickered, a warning of the blackout to come. Megan glanced at her watch. Two-thirty in the morning. She felt as if she'd been awake forever.

"I don't know." Megan went to Mrs. Cavendish, listening to her heartbeat for a moment, feeling the thready beat of her pulse. She'd had another heart attack, this one not as mild as the others. Megan had given her nitro and a sedative to calm her down, but it wouldn't take much more to put Mrs. Cavendish out of the game.

Earl pounded the wall. "We have to do something—"

"Then fucking *do* it and shut up!" Megan recoiled at her own outburst, instantly regretting it. She closed her eyes and forced herself to take a deep breath, ignoring the constant throb of her migraine as she willed herself to be calm.

"Mrs. Cavendish is going to die," she said quietly, opening her eyes again. Earl and Lucy stared at her like she was a freak, startled and annoyed by her anger. Janey continued to weep into her hands. "She's had two heart attacks this evening and they're getting stronger. One more will kill her."

"So?" Lucy sneered, and Megan had the sudden urge to punch her. She'd never liked Lucy. Now she understood why.

"We gotta get out of here," Earl said, subtly stepping between Lucy and Megan. "We gotta get to one of them stations, like on the news."

"What about the patients?" Megan asked, even though she knew exactly what Earl's answer would be. "Are you saying that we should just leave them here to die?"

"They're gonna die anyway."

Megan laughed, a sharp, brittle sound. "How compassionate of you, Earl."

"I'm just saying that we can't screw around out here much longer." Earl sat on the arm of the couch, dangling the car keys between his knees. "What'll we do if those things sniff us out? What'll we do if they start coming around here like we saw on TV? We can't defend ourselves here."

"So what are you suggesting? The four of us cut out and leave everybody else restrained in their beds?" Megan shook her head and walked away. "No. I'm not doing that."

"What about your kids?"

Megan stopped at the doorway to the break room. She didn't dare turn around. Not until she managed to control her reaction.

"You know they're out there somewhere," Earl continued. "Question is, do you think you can find them before all them dead things do."

"Leave her be," Lucy said abruptly. Megan half-turned, saw Lucy rising from the couch. "She don't want to come along, leave her here. I don't give a shit either way, long as we get to go."

Megan looked back to Earl. He watched her with something like desperation in his eyes. She knew he was just as afraid as the rest of them. Maybe he thought having a doctor around would be a magic talisman to help keep them safe on the road.

The van was big enough to seat the four of them, but there was no way they'd be able to get the patients loaded up. And even then, what would they do with them when they reached one of the rescue stations? She could pack a bag of their medications, but those would run out within days. And this situation—whatever it was—looked like it wouldn't be over for a long time.

"We need to wrap Bobby up," she said abruptly. "Take him to the cold room before he…before he can come back."

"We're leaving, Meg—"

"I don't care what you do," Megan snapped, glaring at Earl. "But you are going to help me wrap Bobby and carry him downstairs before you go. Do you hear me?"

Earl nodded faintly and glanced over to Lucy, who shrugged.

"Ten more minutes ain't gonna hurt," she said and looked to Megan. "But then we're leaving. Do *you* hear *me*?"

"Loud and clear," Megan muttered, grabbing a sheet off one of the beds.

***

"Pull the ends up over him." Megan folded her side of the sheet up and over Bobby's body and reached for the roll of duct tape. Earl did as told, grimacing as he stared at Bobby's wound. Janey stood in the doorway, completely useless as she cried into the cup of her hand. The constant tears were wearing on Megan's nerves.

"Do you think he'll…you know?" Earl watched Bobby closely, waiting for the first twitch, the first sign that something was wrong.

"Probably," Megan said and ripped off a length of silver tape. She wound it around his feet, hobbling him.

"Shouldn't we do something for him?"

Megan stopped and stared at Earl. "Like what? Last rites?"

"No…it's just…I mean…" Earl shook his head. "It just seems wrong to let him come back like that."

"I know," Megan said softly, wrapping more tape around Bobby's knees. "Put his hands together on his chest."

"I don't want to touch him—"

"Just do it, Earl."

Earl made a face and gingerly lifted Bobby's hands to his chest. Bobby's infected arm was bloated and black. Earl wiped his hands on the seat of his pants after touching it.

"For God's sake…" Megan muttered, taping Bobby's hands together in a praying position. She tore off the tape and tugged the sheet over Bobby's chest. "Lift him up so I can tape his arms down."

"I don't—"

"God damn it, Earl! Either help me or get the fuck out of here!"

Earl looked at her for a few moments, then walked out of the room.

"Damn it…" Megan pinched the bridge of her nose, squeezing her eyes shut. She waited for the worst of the headache to recede, then followed Earl to the sunroom.

He and Lucy were already at the front door.

"You can't go now."

Earl smiled coldly. "Watch us."

Megan noticed the boxes of canned food stacked beside the door. "You're not taking that."

"The hell we ain't." Lucy stepped in front of the pile. "We're gonna need it more than them." She jerked her head in the direction of the sedated patients. "Now if you're gonna come with us, then come. If not, then step off."

For just a moment, Megan considered it. For just that one moment, she could walk away and leave six people strapped to their beds, alone and hungry and terrified.

She wanted to get to Hannah and Andy. She wanted to see her parents. She needed to know that they were alive and unhurt.

She could walk away from these people and let them die.

For that one moment, she could.

"No…" she said, taking a few steps away from them. "I'm not leaving."

Earl laughed and shook his head. "Idiot."

"Whatever." Lucy grabbed one of the heavy boxes, lifting it easily. "Let's go, Earl."

She disappeared into the darkness. Megan could hear the familiar sound of the van door sliding open. Crickets chirped. Frogs called to each other. The night sounded just as it always did.

But there was a smell to it now. Barely perceptible, but there, just beneath the breeze. Megan knew it instantly.

It was the smell of decay.

She wondered if it would be everywhere now.

"You sure?" Earl asked as he hefted a box.

"Yeah…yes…" Megan nodded, backing away from the open door. It was too dark out there. "I can't go."

"Suit yourself." Earl shrugged and started to walk away.

"Wait!" Megan forced herself to follow him to the porch. The smell was so much stronger out here. It made the air feel thick. "What about Janey?"

"She's gone," Lucy said as she slammed the van doors shut. "She's no good for nobody. She'd slow us down."

There was sudden movement in the trees a hundred yards away from the nursing home's porch. Even in the darkness, Megan could see the paleness of the thing's face as it stepped into the clearing.

They found us, she thought.

"Good luck," Earl said as he climbed into the van. Lucy snorted, spat into the dirt, and got into the passenger side. He started the engine, flipped on the headlights.

And Megan suddenly understood why the smell of rot was so strong.

At least twenty of the things were coming towards the nursing home, either drawn by the lights or by the promise of food inside. They looked just as awful as they had appeared on TV. Worse. They were real.

Megan backed into the nursing home, afraid to make any sudden movements in case they hadn't noticed her yet. She closed the door and locked it, even though a small part of her mind knew that the locks would be no good if they all decided to gang up on the door at once.

The van roared through the crowd of dead things, running over them easily. Even inside the nursing home, Megan could hear Earl and Lucy's war whoops.

I made the wrong choice, she realized, leaning against the door as her knees suddenly went watery.

"Bobby! No!" Janey's scream seemed even more piercing in the sudden silence. "Bob—"

It ended abruptly, cut off with a wet gurgle.

Megan ran for the room, skidding to a stop at the open doorway. The bed was empty. A spray of blood fanned across the wall.

Janey huddled in the corner, bleeding heavily from the throat but somehow still conscious, making herself small.

Like a snake, Bobby writhed towards her, pulling himself forward with his bound hands, his feet and knees wrapped and taped in the sheet. Janey's blood dripped from his chin.

He'd bitten her. She'd die of blood loss within minutes. There was nothing to be done for her.

"I'm sorry, Janey…"

Janey raised her head, trying to scream but making only wet wheezing sounds in her ruined throat and saw Megan closing the door. Heard the lock turn.

And then Bobby was on her, and she could see or hear nothing more.

***

Mrs. Cavendish died a few hours later.

Heart attack. In her sleep. Peaceful. Quiet.

Megan tightened the restraints around the old woman's hands and feet, then wound several layers of duct tape around her head.

Of the remaining five patients, Megan doubted if three of them would last until dawn. They were all awake now. They saw what had happened to Mrs. Cavendish. They could hear the scratching just outside the doors and windows. One man, Mr. Norstrom, thought it was his old hound dog begging to come inside.

Megan didn't tell him any differently. He was too happy to hear that ol' Bess had finally come home. She let him tell his stories about the dog, let him fill up the silence while she sat beside Mrs. Cavendish's bed and waited.

A half-hour after she died, Mrs. Cavendish came back.

Megan rolled her bed down the long hallway to the service elevator. Mrs. Cavendish fought the restraints, her thin arms and legs suddenly strong enough to make the heavy leather pull loose. By the time Megan got the bed to the service elevator, the old woman had freed one of her arms.

The ride down to the basement took forever.

Mrs. Cavendish clawed at the tape on her face, pulling it away from her eyes, her mouth. Once she saw Megan, she reached for her with gnarled, arthritic fingers. Megan stayed in the corner of the elevator, holding her breath until they reached the basement.

The doors opened. At the end of the hallway was the door to the cold room.

She could hear something pounding on the other side of it.

Megan's nerve broke. She pushed the bed into the hallway before the doors could close, bouncing it off a far wall. Mrs. Cavendish thrashed wildly. Now her other arm was free.

The elevator doors closed before Megan could see any more.

***

By five-thirty that morning, the only one left was Mrs. VanZant.

The others must have sensed the tension even through their sedated states and allowed themselves to just slip away. Or maybe whatever was bringing the dead back had affected the elderly, so near death anyway.

Megan didn't know. And the fact that she would never know gnawed at her.

"I'm the last one, aren't I?" Mrs. VanZant asked quietly. She had refused the sedatives, choosing to remain awake and aware. She was one of the few patients who hadn't been touched by Alzheimer's.

"Yes, you are." Megan slumped in a chair beside Mrs. VanZant's bed, rubbing at her temples. Her entire face seemed to throb with the force of her migraine. Speaking was almost torture.

"I always seem to be the last one." Mrs. VanZant smiled faintly. "I outlived my husband and all three of my children."

Megan looked at her, thinking of Hannah and Andy. Now that she knew what was really happening out there, she couldn't imagine that they were still alive.

"How did you stand it?" she asked softly.

"I don't know. I just did." Mrs. VanZant shrugged, shook her head. "Every day I wish I'd been the first to go. Let them mourn me instead of…instead of the other way around."

Megan leaned forward and took the old woman's hand. Her skin felt like soft paper. The knuckles were swollen and misshapen from years of arthritis. She still wore her wedding ring on her left hand, and a mother's ring set with the birthstones of her children on the right.

"We're not going to be here much longer, are we?" Mrs. VanZant asked.

Megan listened to the sounds surrounding them. The pounding from the bedroom, where Bobby and Janey remained. The scratches on the window from the dead things outside. The muffled moans and choked screams from the basement.

"No," Megan said softly. "I don't think we are."

"No one's going to help us?"

Megan absently reached for the cell phone in her jacket pocket. The battery had died hours ago. She had never gotten through.

"I don't imagine they will," she said and met Mrs. VanZant's steady gaze. To her surprise, the old woman slowly smiled.

"I always thought the cancer would get me," she said, shaking her head. She gave Megan's hand a squeeze. "Just goes to show that you never know, do you?"

Megan almost smiled back. "Nope. I guess you don't."

"I saw you giving the others something to help them sleep." Mrs. VanZant reached out and brushed a strand of hair away from Megan's cheek. The touch reminded Megan of her mother, the way she would always fuss about Megan's hair being too long and wild, but then brag to her friends about her daughter's beautiful head of hair.

"Sedatives," Megan said softly, almost giving in to the temptation to cry.

"Maybe you should give us some," Mrs. VanZant said, keeping her hand at Megan's cheek. "You look tired. Maybe we should just…go to sleep."

Somewhere in the nursing home, a window shattered.

"Okay," Megan whispered, grabbing a hypodermic needle and a vial of sedative. She wiped at her eyes and pushed Mrs. VanZant's bed into the only room without windows. The break room.

Then she shoved the couch, end tables, bookshelves, anything she could find in front of the door. It wouldn't keep them out, but it would give her a little more time.

She didn't bother to measure the dosage. She filled the hypo and found one of Mrs. VanZant's collapsed veins with her first try. The old woman sighed deeply, but said nothing more.

Megan's hands shook as she tried to fill the hypo again. There was an explosion of wood on the other side of the door. The front door. Now she could hear them moving around out there.

And the smell. They brought the stench inside with them.

Megan jabbed the needle into the crook of her arm, not caring if she hit a vein or not, and closed her eyes as she pushed the plunger. The sedative burned slightly, but her headache began to instantly ease. She felt suddenly light-headed.

I did it, she thought as the hypodermic slipped out of her hand. God help me…

"Come sit with me," Mrs. VanZant whispered, her voice slightly slurred, and held out her arms. "I don't want to be by myself."

Megan crawled into the bed and allowed the old woman to hold her in her arms. She closed her eyes and took a deep breath. Mrs. VanZant smelled of rosewater and lavender. And she was so warm.

"Think of all the things you loved," Mrs. VanZant whispered, stroking Megan's hair with her paper-soft hands. "Don't be afraid. Just go to sleep and dream of them. Remember the way things used to be."

Megan shut out the sounds of breaking glass, the pounding of fists against the door, the moans of hunger. She thought of Hannah and Andy when they were babies. She thought of her parents taking her to the state fair every summer. She thought of her wedding night, of how much she had loved Frank, how she'd never stopped loving him.

She felt Mrs. VanZant's hand slip away from her head, felt the old woman's chest rise and then be still.

The door to the breakroom smashed open, the haphazard pile of furniture crashing to the floor as the dead things fell into the room.

Megan quietly slipped away.

And dreamed.

Family Value

~ 1 ~

"Bitch..."

The word, as muffled and mumbled as it was, was sufficiently loud enough to set Lucy's teeth on edge. She glanced into the rearview mirror and saw her stepdaughter glowering at her with all the rage a fifteen-year-old could muster. And in Jennifer's case, that was quite a bit.

"Care to repeat that?" Lucy asked quietly, meeting Jennifer's eyes in the mirror.

"No."

"You called me a bitch."

"Yeah, so...what are you going to do?" Jennifer sneered. "Tell Henry?"

Jennifer had begun the irritating habit of referring to her father in the third person, acting like he was more of a boyfriend than a father. Lucy knew from a few of her community college psychology classes that Jennifer was attempting to show dominance, marking her territory in overt and obvious ways, but it still bothered her to see Jennifer traipsing about in a tiny nightgown and crawling over Henry's lap for goodnight kisses. Even worse was the fact that Henry was such a goddamn idiot that he refused to see what was going on.

Lucy clamped her jaw shut, refusing to rise to the bait. All she needed was to get into a shouting match with Jennifer, which would immediately be turned into a great melodrama by the time Henry heard about it. Jennifer had been opposed to the marriage from the beginning and had never been shy about voicing her opinion. Even though Henry had been widowed five years before meeting Lucy, she would always be cast in the role of the "other woman" in Jennifer's eyes. The girl had grown used to having her daddy all to herself, and now she had to share him not only with another woman, but with two other kids besides. Coupled with the usual teenage pissiness and Jennifer's natural bitchiness, the result was a horror show that Lucy had to endure on a daily basis.

She didn't want to know what Jennifer's reaction would be when she found out that she was about to have another brother or sister. Lucy hadn't told anyone yet, but she knew beyond a doubt that she was pregnant. And at thirty, with an eight-year-old and a five-year old to deal with, another baby was the last thing she wanted or needed in her life. Hell, she hadn't even really wanted the first two. That particular confrontation with Jennifer was something she wished she could just avoid.

"Are we almost there, Mommy?" Gracie, her youngest, crawled onto her knees in the front seat. Lucy absently reached over and roughly tugged her down.

"Fasten your seatbelt," she said grimly and stared at the road, flicking her gaze to the mirror every once in a while.

"Better watch out," Jennifer sneered, "or the boogyman's gonna get you."

Gracie's eyes went wide. "Mommy..."

Lucy glanced into the rearview mirror and saw Jennifer's smirk. "Jennifer, shut up."

"Yeah, Gracie," Jennifer continued. "The boogyman'll crawl out from underneath your bed and--"

"Damn it, Jennifer! I said shut up!"

"Jennifer's hogging the seat!" Justin yelled. He squirmed and then yelped loudly as Jennifer's sharp elbow dug into his ribs. At eight, he was as gawky and thin as a scarecrow. He usually bore the brunt of Jennifer's rage.

"Quiet down!" Lucy shouted. "All of you...cut it out!"

Jennifer screwed up her face sarcastically and mimicked her words, sending a rush of pure rage through Lucy. Then, just because she could, Jennifer elbowed Justin a second time, catching him in the face. Justin screamed and a spout of blood erupted from his nose. Jennifer just smiled with satisfaction.

"Oh, for Christ's sake..." Lucy muttered, catching sight of the blood in the mirror. There goes the new upholstery. She swerved off the main road and onto the shoulder, trying to will herself to calm down before she opened the Bronco's side door. Even before Jennifer came into her life, Lucy had always been quick to anger and even quicker to act on that anger. Now she felt like as though her temper was on constant red alert, ready to explode at every little thing.

"What the hell is going on?" she yelled, slamming open the side door. Justin held both hands to his bloody nose while Jennifer smirked.

"She hit me in the nose!" Justin lowered his hands as he worked himself into a righteous fury.

Jennifer gave Justin's narrow shoulders a vicious push. "Shut up, you little shithead."

Lucy balled her fists so tightly she could feel her fingernails digging into her palms. Forcing herself to speak slowly and calmly, she said, "Jennifer...get out of the car now."

"What are you gonna do? Make me walk the rest of the way? We're ten miles from home!"

Lucy ignored her and leaned into the van. "Gracie, get in the back with your brother. And Justin, don't you dare get blood on these seats. Do you hear me?"

Gracie did as told, clambering into the back seat as Justin held the collar of his shirt up to his nose, and Lucy slid the side door shut again. She turned to see Jennifer staring at her, one hip cocked and her arms folded over her stomach, a smirk twisting her lips.

"Get in the car," Lucy said quietly, swallowing bile.

"Fuck you."

"I said, get in the car."

Jennifer's smile slanted. "And I said, fuck you. You want me to walk, I'll fuckin' walk!"

Lucy stared hard at the girl for a few long seconds, seeing nothing but pure, unadulterated hate in her eyes. There was no use in pretending they would ever have anything even remotely resembling a normal relationship. No use in trying to make friends with each other for Henry's sake.

"Fine," Lucy said, rounding the hood. "Have it your way."

With that, Lucy climbed into the van and slammed the door. Jennifer still smirked at her from the side of the road, so blonde and slim and pretty. She was at the age when she thought she was entitled to everything, including the unqualified respect of her father's wife. She wanted so badly to break up their relationship, but Henry would not see it. His little girl could never do something like that.

Lucy waited for Jennifer to open the door and get in the van. Jennifer just stood there, mocking her, challenging her.

"Fine," Lucy said to herself and started the engine. Let the little bitch walk.

She pulled onto the road and left Jennifer standing in the dust.

~ 2 ~

"What were you thinking?" Henry's voice echoed through the mostly empty farmhouse, loud enough to carry to the children's bedrooms on the third floor. "How could you have gone off and left her-"

"She wouldn't get in the car," Lucy said quietly, straining to keep her composure. She sat on the edge of the couch while Henry paced in front of the fireplace. The sun had set hours ago. "She's just doing this to-"

"To what? Get back at you for being a bitch to her?"

Lucy's jaw dropped. "I have never been a bitch to her!"

"Bullshit."

"She's the one who's the bitch, Henry. And the sooner you get that through your goddamn head, the better. She's trying to break us up. Can't you see that? Or maybe you'd like it better if I left and you could just fuck Jennifer!"

Henry said nothing for a moment, eyes darkening with rage…and something else. Guilt.

Lucy suddenly remembered the times Jennifer would brag about sleeping with her daddy after her mother died, cuddling up against him in the bed just like mommy used to, keeping him company so he wouldn't be lonely. She thought about the way Jennifer would hurl herself onto Henry's lap, coiling her lithe body around his while they watched television. It had never seemed entirely right to Lucy, but she'd kept her opinions to herself. After all, Henry was saving her from a lifetime of welfare checks and minimum wage jobs and food stamps. Marrying him was the smartest thing she'd ever done; his job paid good money, and for the first time in her life she had financial security. And being Mrs. Henry MacMillan, being the wife of a well-known and successful lawyer, brought her more respect than she'd ever had before. Before Henry, she had been condemned to weekends of trolling the bars for potential husbands, and she wasn't about to go back to scrimping and saving.

"Tell me you haven't done that," Lucy finally said, backing Henry down until he looked away from her.

"You've been jealous of Jennifer from the beginning," Henry said softly. He swallowed hard, still keeping his gaze averted. "She's the only one who ever really loved me."

"This is ridiculous," Lucy muttered, standing abruptly. Suddenly she craved a drink the way drowning lungs craved air. "And you're a goddamn pervert."

"I will never forgive you if something happens to her."

Lucy smirked despite herself. "That's a little melodramatic, don't you think?"

"You left a 15 year old girl alone by the side of the road!"

"So fucking what? She can walk, can't she? She probably caught a ride with one of her stupid friends--"

"You heard about those murders in town last week. What if—"

"Oh please..." Lucy rolled her eyes and poured whiskey over ice. Henry watched too much television; just because some freak decided to knife a couple of women a few counties away didn't mean he was lying in wait in their front yard. But it was just like Henry to overreact and jump to the most melodramatic conclusion. "There was no traffic on that road...I didn't even see a car pass."

"I'm calling the police..."

"It won't do any good," Lucy said wearily. "They'll say she's a runaway and won't do anything for 24 hours..."

"Jennifer would not run away from home!"

"Unfortunately," Lucy muttered into the glass as she took another drink. Henry either didn't hear her or chose to ignore her. He kept staring at the phone, as if expecting it to ring.

His fear annoyed her for some reason. Maybe because in her secret heart of hearts, she knew she wouldn't feel that way if he had been one of her kids. She wouldn't be on edge waiting for the phone to ring, imagining endless horrible fates for them. She made sure they had what they needed, but she didn't feel particularly motherly towards them. She was stupid and got knocked up, and by the time she realized what was happening to her life, it was too late to get an abortion. She knew, though, that without the kids, she wouldn't feel so shackled to her life, so hopeless and bored and trapped...

Lucy abruptly realized what she was thinking, but couldn't bring herself to feel guilty. Yes, she was Justin and Gracie's mother, but she'd never wanted to have kids. Her first husband had insisted that she go through with the pregnancies, then left when he decided that he didn't want to be a full-time father. And then she was stuck with them.

"I'm calling the police anyway," Henry said and grabbed the phone. "Jennifer's too responsible. She knows how I worry about her...she would have called by now."

Lucy rolled her eyes and silenced the remark fluttering on the tip of her tongue by taking another drink of her whiskey. Suddenly exhausted, she tucked herself into the corner of the couch while Henry paced with the phone, his anxious voice becoming nothing but a background drone. She was asleep in seconds.

And it was the first truly peaceful sleep she'd had in days.

~ 3 ~

The call came in the early hours of the morning, as such calls always do.

Lucy woke up instantly, stiff from lying in the same position on the couch for so many hours. Henry, sitting in his easy chair with the phone on his lap, answered before the first ring had ended. Lucy unfurled herself slowly, unable to take her eyes away from Henry's face as he listened silently to the voice on the other end of the phone. His entire appearance changed, aging years in just a few moments. Suddenly his thinning blond hair seemed sparser, the shadow of his beard hollowing his cheeks, the circles beneath his eyes deepening and darkening in seconds. He opened his mouth to speak, but nothing came out. The phone slid from his hand as he stared into nothingness, his jaw working as if he was silently screaming.

Lucy picked up the phone just as it went dead.

"She's..." Henry's voice faded into a raw whisper. "They found Jennifer..."

Lucy didn't speak. Couldn't speak. For all her fantasizing of a life without the girl, for all her dislike of her...she couldn't believe this was really happening...

Or that it was all her fault.

"I have to...identify...her..." Henry choked and involuntarily gagged. "Oh God...I can't do this again..."

"I'll go," Lucy said softly, crouching down in front of Henry, taking his hands.

"No..."

"Yes, Henry." Lucy tried to sound as grief-stricken, as horrified. "Stay with the kids. You're in no condition to drive."

Henry's entire body seemed to collapse inward, grief crushing him from the inside out. His face twisted monstrously, frozen in that horrible moment of mourning so fierce that nothing-no tears, no wails, nothing-could possibly relieve the pain. Lucy gathered him in her arms, feeling like she was following the script of some bad soap opera. Now she was the heroine comforting the hero, strong in the face in adversity and all that crap.

The truth was, she was scared. As soon as the first aftershocks of grief passed, Henry would begin blaming her for Jennifer's death. And then their marriage, only a year old, would end. And the way of life she'd grown so accustomed to so quickly--the new car, the big house, the expensive dinners and free-flowing bank account--would end as well. She'd be back on food stamps and welfare checks, back to the bars and the one night stands...

The tears came unexpectedly, and Henry clutched her closer to him, mistakenly believing that her grief for Jennifer had finally erupted into the bone deep sobs that now shook her.

$$\sim 4 \sim$$

"She's in here..."

Lucy leaned against the cold tile of the hospital corridor's wall, still feeling vaguely dreamy, as though reality hadn't yet kicked in. She didn't want to identify Jennifer's body. She didn't want to do anything but run.

"What happened to her?" Lucy couldn't quite make eye contact with the police officer that stood at her elbow, afraid that if she looked at him, he would know just how little remorse she felt at Jennifer's death. "Where did you find her?"

The officer answered, but Lucy was only able to comprehend bits and pieces of his explanation. Jennifer had been found ten feet from the road. Her throat had been ripped and slashed over and over. And yes, they thought it was the same guy who'd killed those other women. Jennifer had probably bled to death while Lucy and Henry argued about calling the police to look for her.

And still...Lucy felt no guilt. No grief. No regrets. Nothing.

She remained silent as the police officer led her into the hospital's morgue. At that time of night, the place was nearly deserted, lights dimmed with atmospheric accuracy to create small pools of sickly yellow over each sheet-covered body. Lucy imagined she could smell the beginnings of their decay beneath the bleach and antiseptic scent of the hospital. Bare feet stuck out from the bottoms of the sheets, and Lucy was vaguely fascinated by how many people had died with gnarly, overgrown toenails.

And then they reached Jennifer, and the dream-like quality of the entire evening became crashingly real. The edge of the sheet ended just at Jennifer's hairline, revealing blonde hair matted with brownish blood. Jennifer's bare feet peeked out of the other end, her toenails painted sparkly silver, a small gold ring encircling her middle toe. That alone would have been enough to identify her, but Lucy felt an almost morbid need to see Jennifer's face, to see that eternally arrogant smirk reduced to the blankness of death.

The attending pathologist slowly lowered the sheet and Lucy caught herself holding her breath as Jennifer's face was revealed. The girl had not died easily, the agony reflected in her staring eyes, her grimacing mouth. She barely looked like Jennifer. The arrogance was gone, replaced by an expression of fear so awful that Lucy knew her dreams would be haunted for years to come. Even in death, Jennifer's eyes angrily accused Lucy.

It never would have happened if she hadn't left her alone by the road. Lucy had murdered her just as surely as the man who'd wielded the knife.

"That's her..." Lucy finally managed to whisper, her gaze drawn to the ruined flesh of Jennifer's throat. The wound looked oddly bloodless, almost fake. "That's Jennifer..."

The police officer nodded at the pathologist, who pulled the sheet over Jennifer's face again. Lucy felt an almost tangible relief as Jennifer's bulging eyes were finally covered, hidden from view. It was over now. The worst was over.

Now all that remained was burying the dead.

~ 5 ~

The day of the funeral seemed to be trapped somewhere between twilight and darkfall. Rain misted, then fell in fat droplets as they stood around the muddy hole in the cemetery just beyond the farmhouse. Henry wanted to be close to Jennifer, so he chose to bury her in the backyard—or so it seemed to Lucy. By the time they actually lowered the coffin in the ground she was so goddamn tired of hearing cliches like "She's with her mother now" and "Jennifer's in a better place" that she wanted to scream. The girl was dead and gone and that was the end of it. Lucy couldn't wait until the last spadeful of dirt was packed on top of the ridiculously expensive casket Henry had insisted upon. Maybe then she'd get some peace.

In the three days since Jennifer's death, Lucy's life had been a whirlpool of grieving and crying and police interviews and all the other pains in the ass that the murder of a young girl could possibly produce. She wanted to say something to all those people who wanted to promote Jennifer to sainthood, wanted to tell them that the girl was a bitch who wouldn't be missed. Instead, she had to hold her tongue and look appropriately bereaved. Poor Jennifer was gone. Too bad. Yes, she was an angel. Sure, I'll miss her loads and loads.

Meanwhile, whenever she was alone, Lucy felt almost giddy with relief. No more bitch fits if Jennifer didn't get her way. No more fights with Henry over the way he treated Jennifer. No more arguments or shrill threats. No more wondering if Henry was really working late, or if he was sneaking into his daughter's bed. God had done Lucy the favor of a lifetime by taking Jennifer out. If she ever saw that serial killer, she'd shake his hand and buy him a beer.

Now, as Lucy stood at the lip of Jennifer's grave, she felt an almost overwhelming sense of freedom. How had she allowed a fifteen-year-old girl to make her life such hell? Henry stood beside her, his shoulders perpetually slumped, weeping silently to himself. He hadn't stopped crying since the morning Jennifer had been discovered, and while Lucy tried to empathize and be patient with him, the nonstop waterworks were getting all over her damned nerves. Henry couldn't see what he had left, didn't want to realize that he still had a wife. No...all he goddamn cared about was that little bitch.

Lucy caught herself and bit her lower lip, forcing the anger back. She focused on the gaudy headstone Henry had chosen for Jennifer's grave: a huge piece of marble carved in the shape of the letter 'J', with Jennifer's last school photo imbedded in the center. Below the picture were the obligatory dates and the words "Daddy's Angel Always." Gag me, Lucy thought and looked away. The pink coffin was now completely in the hole, covered with a blanket of roses and baby's breath. It was hard to believe that inside that box was the girl who had made her life so miserable, that now it was over.

Lucy smiled, quickly hiding it behind her hand. A little drama club acting combined with the falling rain would make her look just as grief-stricken as Henry. A few more days of gloom and doom and then she could bravely lead Henry and the children towards a brighter tomorrow...or some such crap.

But for right now Lucy planned on enjoying the sight of the pall-bearers tossing shovel after shovel of dirt onto the pristine pink coffin, covering the expensive roses Henry had ordered, spattering the smooth, perfect finish. Ashes to ashes, dust to dust...

She just had to try to stop smiling so much.

~ 6 ~

Three nights after the funeral, the scratching woke Gracie up.

She huddled beneath her blankets, clutching her teddy bear for protection, staring so hard into the darkness that she almost couldn't keep her eyes focused. She wasn't a baby, so she didn't have a nightlight or even a closet light, so she couldn't see what was making the sound. She could just hear the faint scratching...

Something bumped the bottom of her bed. Something underneath her bed.

Gracie squeezed her eyes shut, ducking beneath the covers. Another bump, hard enough to lift the bed frame off the ground and knock her teddy bear out of her grasp. She wanted to yell for Mommy, but couldn't make a sound. If she made a noise, the thing under her bed would know exactly where she was.

The scratching began again, followed by soft giggles. And then, like the wind whispering outside her window, Gracie heard someone say her name.

Not just someone. Jennifer.

For a minute, she forgot that Jennifer was dead, that some bad man had hurt her. She was so relieved that it wasn't the boogyman that she threw back the covers and turned on the bedside lamp. Jennifer was mean, but she was better than the boogyman.

But the room was empty.

"Jennifer...?"

Gracie's voice sounded very loud in the sudden quiet. She sat up and looked around the room, seeing her stuffed animals, her dolls, her books and crayons...but that was all. No one else was in the room with her.

The bed suddenly jolted, nearly knocking Gracie to the floor, and she held on tightly to the headboard, trying to scream even though she couldn't make a sound. Her bedside lamp flickered, dimmed to brown, throwing shadows across the room that made her stuffed animals look like monsters. Gracie began to cry, trying to wake up because she knew this was a bad dream, had to be a bad dream...

An arm stretched out from beneath her bed, claw-like fingernails digging deep into the wood of the floor, carving furrows as something pulled itself slowly into the light.

Gracie screamed.

Another arm crept out, the skin grayish and covered with patches of rot. Then the head emerged, long blond hair tangled and dirty, hanging in clumps. A smell filled the room that made Gracie think of the dogs and cats that got hit by cars and were left in the sun for a long time.

But then the thing turned its head and smiled at Gracie with long, pointed teeth and pinprick black eyes and she was beyond thinking about anything. She screamed as the thing lunged, its mouth gaping and teeth protruding.

And then it was over.

For that night.

~ 7 ~

As Lucy had expected, it only took a few weeks for things to get back to some semblance of normal. Well, for *her* at least. Henry, of course, moped around and sighed a lot, and he went out to the cemetery to sit by Jennifer's grave every evening, but even he was showing some signs of improvement. He hadn't gotten around to formally blaming Lucy for Jennifer's death, but that would only be a matter of time. Right now, he needed someone to make sure he changed clothes on a semi-daily basis and to take care of him. And if it meant keeping their marriage together just one more day, then Lucy was resigned to being that someone. No way she wanted to be single and trying to support two—soon to be three—kids on a minimum wage job. That kind of a life was a death in and of itself.

But life was actually rather peaceful now. Everything was so much better without Jennifer around.

Except for the thing with the kids.

Something wasn't right with them. Gracie clung to Lucy, afraid to let her out of her sight. And she was so shaken, so pale. The least little thing made her jump in surprise, and she would burst into tears with no provocation. Worst of all, she was silent so often now, almost mute as she cowered by Lucy's side. And Justin wasn't acting like himself. He slept most of the day, even during school, and kept to himself. While Lucy enjoyed the peace and quiet, she realized that it wasn't normal for an eight-year-old boy to be so withdrawn.

"Mommy...?" Gracie said the word so softly that Lucy almost didn't hear her speak. They were in the kitchen, Gracie sitting at the table drawing while Lucy prepared a dinner that would more than likely go uneaten. No one but her seemed to have much of an appetite lately.

"What?" Lucy snapped, turning down the fire under the pot of stew

"Why is Jennifer coming back?"

Lucy sat down at the table and studied her daughter for a moment, noticing for the first time the dark circles beneath Gracie's blue eyes. "We talked about this. Jennifer's not coming back."

"But..."

"But nothing. She's dead. The dead stay dead." Lucy straightened in her chair, involuntarily pulling away from Gracie. "Now I don't want to hear anything else about it."

"But I can hear her at night..." Gracie turned her attention back to the drawing, choosing a black crayon. "She's real mad about being put in the ground. She says she wants out."

"Gracie..." Lucy fought to control her rising anger. "Cut it out".

"She comes to my room," Gracie said softly, drawing streaks of black over the stick figure of a little girl. "She's really mad. She hurts me."

Gracie held out her arm, pulling the sleeve back to expose dozens of small scabby wounds, almost like bug bites. Her inner elbow was covered with a purple-green bruise that looked bone-deep.

Lucy stared at Gracie's arm, frown tightening. "What did you do to yourself?"

"Jennifer bites me." Gracie pulled her arm away, not looking up from the paper. She forced the crayon across the page with wider, harder strokes. "She comes to my room at night and even though I tell her not to hurt me, she does anyway..."

"Gracie--"

"And you won't come even when I yell for you." Gracie grip tightened around the crayon. The little girl in the drawing was now totally obliterated. "Why won't you come?"

Unnerved, Lucy quickly placed her hand over Gracie's, unable to take another moment of her mindless scribbling. "Damn it, Gracie...stop!"

Gracie blinked, as if coming out of a trance, and abruptly burst into tears at the sharpness of Lucy's tone. Before Lucy could stop her, Gracie jumped down from her chair and ran out of the kitchen, sobbing uncontrollably.

"Jesus..." Lucy whispered, covering her face with her hands for a moment. Why couldn't things go back to normal? Why couldn't Jennifer just be dead and forgotten?

Why couldn't she just run away from this life and be somebody else?

A gust of wind shook the rafters of the old farmhouse, howling through the eaves like a banshee's wail. An instant later, lightning flashed and thunder rumbled low in the sky, heralding the arrival of yet another storm. Lucy wearily stood and went to the sink, gazing at the dark reflection of herself in the small window. She looked so old now, so tired. Bags hung beneath her eyes, and deep lines bracketed her mouth, giving her a perpetual scowl. She looked fifty instead of thirty, and for a moment she had to actually remind herself that she was so young. She'd led a hard life, and every second of it showed in her face.

Lightning flashed again, igniting the darkness outside the window for a moment, obliterating Lucy's reflection just long enough for her to see the cemetery just beyond the fence surrounding the backyard. Henry was still at Jennifer's grave, despite the rain and the mud and the lightning. She could see him bent over beside the headstone, head down as he wept.

This is going to end, Lucy thought and gritted her teeth, turning away from the window.

~ 8 ~

It was just before dawn when Henry finally came back to the house. Lucy sat at the kitchen table, staring at the cream clotting in her coffee, waiting for him to stumble through the back door. Her nerves were stretched about as far as they could go. Henry had never stayed out all night before. As bad as his grief had been after Jennifer's death, he hadn't felt the need to spend the night at her grave...until now.

She'd gone down to the kitchen, desperate for coffee and a smoke, after waking up to find that Henry had never come to bed. And then she'd stood at the sink, coffee in hand and cigarette between her lips, and watched Henry rise from Jennifer's grave and turn back to the house.

Idiot, she thought in disgust, turning away from the window to settle herself at the table. Only three months along, not even showing yet, but she felt huge and unwieldy. And so tired all the time. It was standard operating procedure for her to be fatigued during pregnancy—God knows, she'd been through the drill enough times to know how her body reacted—but damn...she'd never felt so exhausted before.

She lit another cigarette and inhaled deeply, watching the back door. This constant grieving was going to stop. Henry paid more attention to Jennifer now that she was dead than he had when she was alive—something she hadn't thought possible. She was not going to put up with this freakish behavior another minute. Henry had to remember who held the reins in their relationship.

Henry opened the door and Lucy opened her mouth to begin the tirade...until she saw the mud smeared over his shirt and jeans, clotted in his hair and speckling his glasses, and the blood on his shirt collar and sleeves. His hands, curled into claws, were caked with mud and grass and blood. Rotted rose petals dotted the front of his shirt.

Pink rose petals.

And Lucy suddenly knew what he'd been doing all night.

"Oh, God...Henry..."

"I had to see her..." Henry whispered. He looked at Lucy, but his eyes were distant, almost dead. "She's so cold...she needs her daddy to keep her warm."

He took a step towards Lucy, hands extended, and she quickly skittered away. The thought of him touching her...

"I had to check on her," he said, voice choking as fresh tears tracked through the drying mud on his cheeks. "That's all I did...she's still so pretty...she misses us so much..."

Henry dropped to his knees, head bowed as sobs ripped through him. "I wanted to kiss her goodnight. That's all...she wanted me to kiss her goodnight..."

"Oh my God..." Lucy whispered, glancing up to the sink window to the cemetery beyond the far gate. Unwanted images flashed through her mind: Henry holding Jennifer's corpse, kissing her lips, stroking her hair, holding her dead body close as he curled up in the corner of the grave and rocked her...and...

Her stomach suddenly lurched and she barely made it to the sink before the first wave of morning sickness hit her. At least, that's what she told herself it was.

~ 9 ~

As she cleaned the grave dirt and blood from Henry and bandaged his torn hands and wrists, Lucy had a flash of sudden certainty that he would never be the same again. She'd tried to rationalize his behavior, telling herself that it was just grief, that it would pass sooner or later...but she knew now that it wouldn't. His obsession with Jennifer would never end. He'd dug up her body for Christ's sake...dug it up and...

Lucy closed her eyes and sighed heavily, perching on the edge of the bed with her head in her hands. God...Jennifer's body. If she called anyone about it, they'd end up taking Henry away. Wasn't it against the law to dig up a grave? Could they arrest him? Could she lose everything?

"Shit..." Lucy whispered. She'd have to put the bitch back herself. Jennifer had been dead a month now...and Lucy didn't want to think about what a month underground would do to a body. Especially one as torn up as Jennifer's. She was sorely tempted to just leave the little slut out to rot.

But she couldn't. She had to go out there and rebury her and tell no one-absolutely no one what had happened. And she had to do it before the kids woke up. She didn't want them running around town telling everyone that their stepfather dug up dead bodies in his spare time.

She looked at Henry again, at his weak chin and beady eyes and receding hairline, and knew—with that same certainty that she had known he would never be the same—that she didn't love him. He would stay married to her, no question; he'd never be able to live on his own again. But their relationship as husband and wife was over. Irrevocably, finally over.

Lucy took a deep breath and flattened a hand over her stomach. Thank God she'd never told him about the baby. Maybe it wasn't too late to repair at least one mistake.

But first...first she had to bury the bitch all over again.

~ 10 ~

No way, Lucy thought as she saw the mess Henry had made. No way I can fix this.

Using only his hands--which explained all the cuts and slices and punctures on his hands and wrists--Henry had dug all the way down to the casket, mounding the grave dirt on either side of the hole. Lucy edged her way to the lip of the grave, dreading what she'd find inside it. She tried to steel herself for what she would see, tried to imagine Jennifer's condition so it wouldn't come as such a nasty shock. Henry had chosen a long white nightgown to bury Jennifer in, a gown with a high neck and puffy sleeves that would hide the damage done to her body. He'd said it made her look like an angel...

Lucy peeked over the edge of the hole.

Jennifer didn't look so much like an angel anymore.

Her body sprawled atop the pink coffin, rag doll limp in her once white gown, propped against the wall of the grave in a half-sitting position. Her head hung slack, mud-clotted blonde hair obscuring her face. Her hands lay limply in her lap, palms up, smeared with Henry's blood.

Oh my God, Lucy thought, covering her mouth, fighting the urge to vomit. He'd really done it. Until this moment, she could've almost believed that he'd imagined it all, that he'd only fantasized about digging up his daughter because no one sane would do such a thing.

But here she was.

Lucy gritted her teeth and carefully crawled down into the grave, holding onto the clods of grass surrounding the edge to keep her balance on the slippery casket. She wished she'd worn gloves. The thought of touching Jennifer's dead skin made her stomach do greasy flip-flops. She glanced up to the sky and saw more storm clouds scudding in, obscuring the weak winter sun.

Oh, perfect...

Taking a deep breath, Lucy propped the shovel into the corner of the grave and stood over Jennifer's body. Okay...first thing's first. Move the body.

She bent and grasped Jennifer's ankles, cringing at the feel of clammy skin, and moved backward. Jennifer slid along with her, almost bonelessly limp, until she lay flat atop the casket top. Her hands fell away from her lap, slapping wetly against the casket.

Lucy stopped, keeping her head down, eyes focused on Jennifer's bare feet. She didn't want to look at the girl's face, didn't want to think about this any more than she had to. There was no way she was going to be able to manhandle Jennifer enough to get her back into the coffin. She'd have to bury her as is and hope that no one found out about it. Six feet was deep enough to keep the animals away...and there were no water tables running through the area that she knew of...

I can't do this, she thought, suddenly too tired to move. In that instant, nothing made sense anymore. The world had gone crazy. She was standing in her step-daughter's grave, about to re-bury her. Crazy.

"Just get it over with," she muttered. She closed her eyes for a moment and took a long, deep breath. She was going to have to look at Jennifer's face. Just get it over with.

Lucy opened her eyes again and allowed her gaze to travel the length of Jennifer's corpse. The white gown had pulled up to her waist, exposing long legs that bore no signs of decay. The girl's hands, splayed across the coffin lid, were as pink and soft as they'd been when she was alive. And her face...

"Oh, Christ..." Lucy whispered.

Once sealed eyes were open now, the mortician's gum washed away by the night's rain. Jennifer stared at Lucy, her blue eyes clouded by a gray film, sunken deep into the sockets. Her mouth gaped, little threads dangling from her upper and lower lips. It took Lucy a moment to realize that the mortician had sewed Jennifer's mouth shut…and that Henry must have cut the threads so he could kiss his little girl…

A mist of rain began to fall, instantly chilling Lucy to the bone. She couldn't look away from Jennifer's face. She remembered how Jennifer had been at the morgue, the gray pallor of her skin, the terror etched into the girl's features. She'd looked truly dead then.

She didn't look that way now.

Jennifer's cheeks were rosy, her complexion as pink and flawless as it had been in life. Her lips were full and red, not the flattened blue they had been at the morgue. And even though there was no mistaking the deadness in her eyes, there seemed to be something going on behind them. And her mouth…the corners of it were quirked upward in something like a smile…

"No," Lucy said aloud. "You're dead."

Jennifer's corpse just looked up at Lucy, her open eyes and curled up mouth mocking her. No movement. No breath. No words. Dead.

Unable to bear another moment of it, Lucy reached up with the shovel and pulled down a spadeful of mud, dumping it squarely on Jennifer's face. The dirt speckled over her open eyes, spilled into her mouth, blotted out the smugness on her face.

It was enough to break the spell. Lucy clumsily climbed out of the grave and sat for a moment amid the mounds of dirt, ignoring the steadily falling rain. Jennifer was dead. The funeral home had just done a better job with the make-up than expected. That was all. They'd had a closed casket funeral because of the injuries. She hadn't seen Jennifer since that night at the morgue, so who knew what they had done to fix her up.

Lucy stood and stared into the grave again. Jennifer was just as she'd left her, sprawled on her back with a clot of mud on her face. She hadn't moved. Hadn't cleared her eyes. Hadn't spit dirt from her mouth. Because she was dead.

Taking a deep breath, Lucy began shoveling the dirt back into the grave, covering Jennifer's body one spadeful at a time.

~ 11 ~

Rain turned to snow, and in a matter of hours the cemetery was blanketed by white. Lucy stood at the kitchen window and watched the raw wound of Jennifer's grave disappear beneath the drifts. Thank God, she thought, exhaling a stream of cigarette smoke before lifting her drink to her lips. Since making her decision about what to do about the baby, she had no problem downing a couple of double shots of whiskey. And if it helped her calm down, then to hell with the rest of it.

"Jesus..." she breathed, leaning her forehead against the slick coldness of the window. Now what was she going to do? The thought of packing up her clothes and running away—leaving Henry and the kids and the house and the fucking farmhouse that she'd never wanted anyway—was seductively appealing. Her ex would get the kids and Henry could spend the rest of his days at Jennifer's grave and everybody would be just hunky-dory.

"Mommy..." Gracie's plaintive whine sliced through what remained of Lucy's calm. She tossed back the rest of her drink and turned away from the window. She didn't know what she'd expected to see at the cemetery anyway.

"What, Gracie?" She stubbed out her cigarette and stomped through the house. Dammit...what now? "Where the hell are you?"

She found Gracie in Henry's study, sprawled on the floor with her ever-present pad of paper. Justin sat beside Gracie, head down and shoulders hunched as he slumped over a piece of paper. He didn't look up as Lucy entered the room.

"Mommy..." Gracie whispered. "Look..."

Lucy glanced at the drawing on Justin's pad and felt the whiskey burning its way back up her throat. In thick black strokes, he had drawn a picture of a child asleep on a bed. And floating beside the bed, with a sharp-toothed smile and red eyes, was the figure of a woman with long blond hair and a flowing white dress.

"I told you she was coming back for us," Gracie whispered.

~ 12 ~

Whoever killed Jennifer had found new hunting ground; news reports virtually slobbered over the newest murders in an adjoining county. Lucy couldn't care less. The guy had done her a favor, but now things were going to hell and she didn't like thinking about what could be happening, mainly because the only reasons she could think of were so bizarre, so crazy, that even entertaining the notion made her doubt her sanity.

But...

But what? There was no good, logical explanation for what was happening to the kids. Or Henry. All she knew was that when she went to sleep at night, she slept like the dead. Nothing woke her. And in the mornings she felt like she hadn't gotten any rest at all.

Lucy stared out the window as she popped a couple of No-Doz and washed them down with the strongest coffee she could brew. From her bedroom, she could see the cemetery, the snow almost glowing in the moonlight. Jennifer's ostentatious marble marker stood out amid the simpler headstones, and Lucy found her gaze drawn back to it again and again. The snow had covered the exhumation of last week, and by the time everything melted no one would know what Henry had done.

She glanced over to the bed. Henry's chest barely moved as he slept, the sound of his breathing only a whisper. Once upon a time he'd snored so fiercely that she'd had to buy earplugs. Now it was like sleeping with a dead man. And he slept all the time now. He wouldn't even wake up to eat, refusing even the weak broth she brought for him. In his sleep he dug at the bandages around his wrists, reopening the unhealed wounds, bloodying the sheets.

Lucy had taken to sleeping downstairs on the couch, sickened by the constant smell of blood and piss and other things. She'd tried to keep Henry clean, tried to keep a bedpan under him, but now it didn't seem like it was any use. The thought that he might be dying crossed her mind and kept on going. She wasn't going to allow him to die, because she was not going to be single and raising three kids. She knew exactly how much insurance he had on his life, and knew that it wouldn't even begin to pay off all the debt they had piled up over the past year. She was not going to be so broke and desperate ever again.

But she couldn't take him to the hospital yet, either. Not until those wounds on his wrists and hands healed. She didn't want to explain to the doctor that her husband had dug up his dead daughter by hand, that he'd shredded his fingertips clawing at her casket lid. The truth was, she didn't feel like doing anything. She went through each day in a dozy stupor. The kids were home because of the snow anyway, and they wanted to sleep the day through just like she did, so she didn't have to worry about getting them up and ready and...

Lucy's head nodded as she drifted off, waking only when her chin hit her chest. She blinked, shifting in her chair, and rubbed at her eyes. She didn't know why she was trying to stay awake anyway. If Henry and the kids could sleep the day away, then...

"Mommy...!"

Lucy sat up, groggy. Justin's reedy voice sounded so far away...

Almost like he was outside.

She turned to the window, to the full moon and the ghostly glow of the new fallen snow...to the fresh, open wound of Jennifer's grave in the cemetery...

To the sight of Jennifer gliding over the crust of the snow, the hem of her dirty nightgown trailing limply behind her...

As she held Justin and Gracie's hands and led them towards the cemetery.

"Oh Jesus..." For a moment, Lucy couldn't move, couldn't catch her breath. She could only watch as her children were pulled through the snow, screaming.

Then the paralysis broke, and Lucy stumbled backwards, away from the window, from what she knew could not be happening. I'm dreaming, she thought, the realization bringing an almost giddy relief. I'm asleep and I'm dreaming and this is not happening!

Lucy began to laugh, crumpling onto the bed, curling up beside Henry. She touched his chest and felt the horrible coolness of his skin. His mouth gaped, lips bluish-white, his eyes fixed on some faraway sight. His chest rose, held for what felt like an eternity, and fell, his breath fading in a rattling wheeze.

And on his chest, just below his throat, two marks glistened with clotting blood.

Suddenly Lucy knew. Jennifer had been there. She had come in while Lucy was asleep and...

Lucy scrabbled out of bed, falling into the bedside table, desperate to get away from Henry's stillness. Righting herself, she stumbled away from the bed, glancing to the window again. Jennifer was still there in the snow, but now she had turned back to the house and Lucy could see the impossibly wide smile splitting her face, could see the glint of moonlight on all those teeth...

And she could see the challenge in the little bitch's eyes. Come and get them.

Lucy welcomed the warm flood of rage that washed over her. The anger took away the fear, made the situation somehow controllable. She ran out of the bedroom, stumbling down the stairs, barefoot and careless in her rush to get to Jennifer. She wanted to make that smug smile disappear forever, wanted to wrap her hands around her throat and squeeze until she'd never be able to laugh at her again.

She opened the front door and ran into the howling wind, into the blustering snow, and didn't stop even when she stepped into the shin-high drifts. She couldn't feel the cold. Didn't care. She could hear Gracie and Justin screaming for her but even their cries faded into the background, drowned out by the roar of her own heartbeat in her ears.

Jennifer began to glide over the snow again, easily tugging Justin and Gracie along with her, her grip tight around their arms even as they struggled and reached for Lucy. They were at the grave in seconds. Lucy felt as if she were moving in slow motion, fighting the wind and the deep drifts for every step.

Jennifer paused at the open grave, making sure that Lucy was watching. Then she hurled Justin headfirst into the ground. Gracie was next, her scream following her into the grave.

Lucy felt herself screaming, but heard nothing but the rush-roar of her blood in her ears. Jennifer simply kept smiling, her teeth long and white and sharp, her lips stained rust-red. Her eyes seemed to glow from deep within black hollows, glittering like a cat's.

Before Lucy could get to the grave, Jennifer had descended into it. With the children.

And over the howl of the wind, the sound of wetness, of feeding, drifted into the night.

~ 13 ~

At first she thought it was the wind howling.

Lucy climbed out of sleep reluctantly, clutching the bottle of Jim Beam to her chest, her neck cramped and angled uncomfortably. She vaguely remembered coming back to the house, collapsing onto the couch, losing herself in whiskey and sleep. Her stomach twinged, pain shooting through it before she was fully awake. Probably something with the baby, she thought and sat up, unable to work up enough concern to care.

She heard the sound again, but this time she was awake enough to realize that it wasn't the wind. The wind didn't laugh.

A thud just above her head, hard enough to make dust sprinkle down from the rafters. More laughter. Girlish. High-pitched.

Jennifer's.

Lucy rubbed her eyes as she wobbled to her feet, tossing the empty bottle of whiskey onto the couch. She moved over to the bottom of the stairs, peering up to the darkness. Something white flashed across the landing.

Footsteps moving down the upstairs hallway.

"I know it's you, bitch..." Lucy's voice trembled with hate and fear. She took the first step, clutching the handrail. With each step she could feel something deep inside slipping away from her. She held her lower belly with one hand, gritting her teeth against the waves of cramps.

She disappeared into the darkness shrouding the stairs. At the landing, she could see nothing but the pale glow of moonlight from the upstairs' window. She struggled to adjust to the dimness as she peered down the long hallway to the open door of her own bedroom.

Something moved, a soft whisper of fabric brushing against itself, a creaking of the floorboards.

Lucy took another step forward. "Goddamn it Jennifer...show yourself..."

Silence. Then a soft giggle.

From her bedroom.

Lucy slowly made her way down the hallway, passing the open door of Justin's bedroom. A small nightlight glowed beside his bed and she glanced into the yellow-tinged dimness. Nothing moved.

A gust of cold wind blasted through the hall and Lucy saw the curtains of her bedroom window billowing like dancing ghosts. The bedsprings creaked and groaned almost imperceptibly, the way they used to when she and Henry tried to keep the kids from hearing them at night.

She stepped into the bedroom. Reality fell away.

Jennifer crouched on the bed beside Henry, her white gown pulled up over her widespread knees as she buried her head in the hollow of his throat. She sensed Lucy and raised her head, Henry's blood shiny-black on her chin as she smiled. Her eyes caught the moonlight and shone like diamonds, sparkling within darkened sockets.

Henry's face was frozen in a smile, his throat splayed wide.

Before Lucy could speak or scream or react, Jennifer was jumping away from Henry's body, remaining in that spider-like crouch as she smiled up at Lucy. Her pupils seemed to be pinpricks of light within the deeper hollows of her eyes, half-hidden by the chunks of muddy blond hair that fell over her face.

She scuttled forward, crablike, her smile stretching almost painfully wide over teeth so sharp that her lower lip hung in shreds. Blood dripped from her chin in long, ropy strands.

Lucy backed away, unable to grasp the reality of the moment. She moved in a slow half-circle as Jennifer skittered forward...

And then Jennifer straightened, the hem of the nightgown falling over her knees, past her toes as she gradually floated above the floor, hovering, bobbing slowly in midair as she looked down at Lucy, her smile fading.

"You did this to me..." she whispered.

"No..." Lucy backed into the door, the knob digging painfully into her lower back. Another searing pain ripped through her stomach as hot wetness spread down her inner thighs.

Jennifer's lips twitched as she caught the scent of fresh blood.

She floated forward, the tip of her tongue darting out, as if tasting the air. She took Lucy's head in her hands, and Lucy shuddered at the cold slickness of her touch, unable to look away from the glitter of moonlight on Jennifer's teeth.

"This isn't real...it isn't real..." Lucy heard herself speak, couldn't believe it was her own voice. "You're dead...I buried you..."

Jennifer laughed. "I'm not going to make it so easy for *you*..."

And in the next second slammed Lucy's head against the door.

~ 14 ~

Lucy woke up smelling her own blood.

She touched her throat, found only smooth unbroken skin. Her fingertips wandered to the back of her head and felt slickness, the scalp pulpy and tender to the touch. Her stomach still cramped. She could feel her body expelling the baby she'd carried only a few months. Good riddance, she thought, grimacing.

But then she remembered. Everything. And realized it wasn't a nightmare, wasn't a bad dream.

Dizzy, Lucy crawled onto her hands and knees, then--clutching the door for support--got to her feet. She looked towards the bed. Henry was gone.

And she remembered the kids. The nightmare she'd had about Jennifer leading them away.

She stumbled down the hallway, leaving a smear of blood wherever her hand or head touched, a trail of dark drips leaking down her leg to the floor. Justin's door was open, and Lucy hesitated a moment before reaching in and turning on the lights.

No use. They were gone. Henry was gone. The baby was gone. Jennifer had taken them all.

And Lucy was finally free.

The sudden exhilaration that followed that realization startled her. But it was true. Everything that had bound her to this life was gone now. She could start over again now. She could clean herself up, change her name, take Henry's money and run. No one would have to know. No one would believe her if she told them what had happened anyway. They'd all think she did it.

So she had to run, didn't she? She had no other choice, right?

Tears burned Lucy's eyes as she realized she could finally walk away and never have to come back. The kids were gone. She had no responsibilities except for herself.

Laughing, she staggered down the hallway, almost out of her mind with the pure joy of freedom. She would leave now. Disappear. People would think that whatever had killed Henry and the children had killed her too...and she'd left enough blood on the floor to substantiate that story. She had two hundred bucks in her pocketbook, and she could stop by the bank in the morning to withdraw the money they had in savings. Then she could be gone. Forever.

Lucy grabbed her pocketbook and the car keys, leaving her coat on the rack. She wouldn't feel the cold, not when she'd have hundreds of thousands of dollars to keep her warm. Grinning, she flung open the front door and ran onto the porch...

And there they were.

Gracie and Justin stood barefoot in the snow, holding hands. Their eyes glittered as they stared at her, grim-faced and pale. Justin's head lolled limply to the side, drool hanging from his open mouth. The front of Gracie's nightgown was splotchy with blood. Henry stood behind them, naked except for his boxer shorts, his throat ripped apart so deeply that Lucy could see the yellowish glint of his spine.

Lucy glanced away from them for a moment to the Bronco. Could she make it? If she ran, if she didn't fall, could she make it?

"What do you want?" she asked, edging closer to the porch steps. It would be close, but she could get past them. She knew she could.

"We want you to stay," Gracie whispered. Henry nodded, reaching out to her.

Lucy shook her head, mad laughter caught in her throat. "No...no way...no..."

"We...belong...together..." Henry wheezed, each word sounding as if it were bubbling up from his chest. "We're...family..."

"Fuck you!" Lucy screamed, making a break for it. She skittered past their outreached hands, feeling the coldness of their fingertips against her arm, and then she was at the SUV, her hands fumbling with the handle. They were getting closer, not walking through the snow but skimming over it.

The sight made Lucy falter, the keys falling from her hand. With a sob, she dropped to her knees, blindly searching through the snow for the keys. This wasn't going to happen. It couldn't happen...

Her hand closed around the key ring. She shot to her feet and fumbled with the lock, afraid to look behind her, afraid not to look. She finally fit the key in the lock just as Henry's hand closed around her shoulder. Jerking away from him, she opened the door...

...And hands shot out from beneath the Bronco, catching her ankles and pulling hard. Lucy screamed as she felt herself falling backward, as she looked up and saw Henry and the children grinning down at her, as she raised her head and saw Jennifer dragging herself up the length of Lucy's body, that impossibly wide smile dripping blood and drool...

And then, after one last scream, she didn't want to see anything anymore. The world went black, and everything finally went away.

~ 15~

Lucy shivered, opened her eyes. She couldn't understand why she wasn't dead.

She was on her back. Snow drifted lazily onto her face, the skies above dark with clouds. The moon was full, hiding behind the drifts.

For a moment, she couldn't remember anything. Then she felt the cold keys in her hand, remembered how desperately she'd needed them, remembered scrabbling for them in the snow as Henry and the children...

Suddenly awake, Lucy tried to sit up...but couldn't. She felt too weak, too tired to move. She looked around and saw the walls of a grave surrounding her, saw her world reduced to a narrow rectangle far, far away.

And there, towering over her, she saw Jennifer smiling down, joined by Henry and Justin and Gracie. Jennifer held a clod of dirt in her hand.

"No, please..." Lucy whispered, tears burning her eyes, tracking down over her temples. Exhaustion felt like a hundred pounds pressing down, paralyzing her. "Please, no..."

Jennifer held her arm out over the grave, letting the dirt sift through her hands, sprinkling over Lucy's face, into her open eyes and mouth. Lucy screamed, choking, spitting, gasping for breath. She opened her eyes to see Henry floating into the grave, holding Justin and Gracie's hands. The three of them smiled at her, eyes like silver coins, teeth like daggers.

"*We're* family again..." Jennifer said and grinned, gliding into the grave to stand at Lucy's feet. "But don't worry...we're not going to make you join us."

Jennifer flashed a horrible smile as Henry slipped one arm around her shoulders and gathered the children closer to him with the other.

"This is *my* family now."

Lucy managed one last, desperate scream.

Then they were all on her at once...and the last thing Lucy heard over the sucking, tearing, rending sounds of their feeding was the whistle of the wind passing over the open mouth of the grave.

Trailer Park of the Damned

"I told you, Jimmy Ray…I don't like that thing in here." Jolene slammed down a can of beans to make her point, turning to scowl at Jimmy Ray. "Them things is evil and I don't like 'em."

Jimmy Ray grinned and tapped ash into the Elvis at the Gates of Heaven ashtray. Bastard knew that it was Jolene's favorite. "It ain't hurtin' nothin, Jo. Look at it. It's too dumb to know it's even here."

Jolene reluctantly turned around. Jimmy Ray had caught the thing the last time he and the boys went out hunting. Damn if it weren't the ugliest thing she'd ever seen. Hard to believe it had ever been a woman.

"I don't want it in the trailer with me," she said, trying to make her voice sound less shaky. "What if it breaks loose?"

"It ain't gonna do nothin', Jo. Jesus Christ…" Jimmy Ray sighed and ran a hand through his greasy hair. "I thought I could have some fun with it, is all."

Jolene rolled her eyes. "I told you I don't like you doin' that."

"Well what the hell else is there to do around here? Man's got to have some fun, don't he?"

Jolene couldn't look at Jimmy Ray as he grinned at her, disgusted by the man she'd had the bad luck to end up with. She remembered the time that dead kid had gotten through the blockade and stumbled into the trailer park. Jimmy Ray and his fellas had strung the boy up and had a good old time with him, using him for target practice with their bows and guns. Even some of the women had got in on the action, but some of the things they did to the kid were worse than anything the men could dream up.

It was just like Jimmy Ray said: nothin' else to do since them dead folks started getting up and walkin around pretty as you please. TV didn't show diddly-shit anymore, and once they'd gotten the trailers into formation and arranged the guard watches and got all the details taken care of, there just wasn't nothing to do. You couldn't even go to the Sav-Mart anymore…not that that was such a big loss.

Things were so much better back in the old days, when you could kill a person and by God they stayed dead.

But that was a long time ago, so long that Jolene had stopped keeping track of the days. Now every day was the same: wake up, kill dead folks, eat some godawful crap out of a can, kill more dead folk, and go to bed when the sun went down because there was nothing else to do. Most of the time she was bored stupid.

"Look at her," Jimmy Ray said, lighting another cigarette as he nodded toward the zombie chained in the corner. "Figure she knows what's goin' on?"

Some almost lost bit of intelligence shone in the woman's eyes as her mouth opened in a slanted, painful grimace and she moaned. Her skin was as glossy and slick as a snail's, her stomach a hollow hole beneath her tattered baby-doll t-shirt. She was a fresh dead, not as stinky as most of 'em, and if you looked real hard you could tell she used to be pretty once. Jolene didn't feel like looking that closely.

"Go get me them pliers," Jimmy Ray said and crushed the cigarette out in Elvis's face. "And the tin-snips. Ain't used them in a long while…"

Jolene sighed, glancing one more time to the heap of moaning flesh in the corner, and went to do as Jimmy Ray commanded. Wasn't much else she could do.

***

"Why the hell do I have to clean this up?" Jolene yelled for Jimmy Ray's benefit as he lolled around in bed. In the morning sun, the mess seemed even worst than it had before they'd gone to bed. Chunks of moldy flesh were everywhere, twitching independently of each other as the zombie's head sat on the kitchen table and watched with hungry eyes. "And why the hell didn't you do her head like you said you was? Damn it, Jimmy Ray…you know I hate when they look at me."

Jimmy Ray rolled onto his back, one skinny tattooed arm flung over his eyes. "Jolene, just clean the shit up and shut up, would ya? I'm tryin' to get some sleep."

"What about me?"

"What *about* you?" Jimmy Ray cracked open an eye and stared at her. "Listen, bitch…I'm trying to get some sleep. I'm the one got to go on the goddam Sav-Mart run in the morning."

"Nobody's makin' you go," Jolene muttered just loud enough for him to hear. Then, louder, "More like you're goin' to go screw around with that Naomi bitch."

"You just leave Naomi out of it."

Hit a nerve, Jolene thought with an almost perverse pleasure. So it was true, what all the gossip hens had clucked about. Jimmy Ray really was floozing around with that little bimbo three trailers down.

Jolene wasn't sure if she was relieved or crushed by his betrayal. Once, a long time ago, she'd actually thought she loved him. Now she couldn't imagine loving someone like Jimmy Ray Baisden. The reasons she stayed with him were practical, not romantic.

"Hell, if you wanna take my place when they go to Sav-Mart in the mornin'," Jimmy Ray said, interrupting himself with a ferocious yawn, "then fine by me. I'll tell Bill that I ain't going. Hell, I'd *like* to be able to sit around on my ass all day."

"Screw you, Jimmy Ray."

"Maybe later," he said and rolled onto his side again, instantly asleep.

Bastard. Jolene slammed the bedroom door shut and turned back to the mess in the kitchen. Snapping on a pair of pink-tinged rubber gloves, she started gathering up the bigger pieces, tossing them into a Hefty bag. The head on the table kept watching her, snapping every once in a while when Jolene got too close. And that irritated the piss out of Jolene. She grabbed the head by its long blond hair and held it up to eye level. There was something there in its eyes, something remaining deep inside its brain. Jolene could almost believe that it knew exactly what had happened to itself, that even now it realized that all was lost but refused to give up and just die.

"Life's a real bitch, ain't it?" Jolene said and smiled sadly, dropping the head into the Hefty bag. She had to get this cleaned up fast before Jimmy Ray woke up again and started hollering for breakfast.

***

"What's goin' on?" Jolene asked as she tossed the garbage bag onto the constantly smoldering bonfire. Her friend and neighbor, Gerdie, was distracted by a gathering in front of Bill Varney's trailer.

"Somethin' about the Sav-Mart run. Bill heard that the place got broke into." Gerdie craned her neck to see over the crowd. "Jimmy Ray goin?"

"Nah…said I could go in his place if I wanted."

"Are you?"

Jolene shrugged. "Might. Don't know yet. I'm bored as hell up in that trailer."

"Looks like y'all had somethin' to do last night…" Gerdie eyed the garbage bag as the plastic curled and melted away, revealing the zombie girl's head. Damn bitch was still trying to take a bite out of something. "Ned brought one home a few days ago, just to play around with. You ain't never seen such a mess."

"Tell me about it. They don't care about messin' up the linoleum or nothin." Jolene wrapped her arms around herself and shivered. "Whoo…gonna be winter 'fore too long."

"Heard we might have snow for Halloween. Prob'ly why Bill's wanting to do the Sav-Mart run sooner instead of later. Food supply's gettin' low…" Gerdie sniffed, then spat onto the burning pile. "Hell…might have to end up eatin' *them* things if we ain't careful."

Jolene made a face, could feel her stomach churn at the very thought of eating one of the dead folk. "I'd just as soon starve, thank you."

Gerdie flashed her a grin that wasn't entirely friendly. "We'd have to just eat *you*, then, wouldn't we?"

A chill trickled down Jolene's spine, but she forced herself to return the smile and keep acting friendly. Nowadays, it didn't pay to piss anybody off. You never knew when they might decide to cry zombie and blow your head off. Nobody was giving too much of a damn who got killed lately anyway.

"I'd best go talk to Bill about the run," Jolene said and smiled again, making her exit. Gerdie barely noticed she was gone; the older woman was busy staring at the flames as they licked and ate the pieces of zombies who'd had the bad luck to cross into the perimeter last night. Jolene had heard the gunshots, but ignored them; after a while, you just didn't pay attention to it.

Jolene made her way across the commons area of the trailer park, remembering the way it used to be. Right after the dead folk started coming back, Bill Varney had gotten everyone together and proposed his idea of doing a wagon-train number with the trailers, circling them to keep the zombies out. He'd been real smart to do it before the dead folk found their way out into the boonies. By the time the first zombies popped up, the outer perimeter of empty trailers was in place and everybody was armed to the teeth, just waiting to kick some dead ass. Luckily, they were so far out of the way that they didn't have to worry about huge bands of zombies stumbling onto them. Nobody knew they were out there.

There were only fifteen trailers in the inner circle. Most folks up and ran once they heard what was going on, thought it'd be better to be out on the road and take their chances. Jolene couldn't understand their thinking. Surely it was better to have one safe place, with lots of guns and men and protection, than to be out there on your own.

Things weren't really so different now than they were back in the olden days, when a gun and a man were all a woman really needed. Jolene liked the fact that she had one of the biggest, meanest, son-of-a-bitches in the trailer park as her man, and she liked the status that gave her among the other women. They envied her because of Jimmy Ray, and Jolene never forgot it, even when he pulled stunts like he had last night. She knew that despite it all, she was lucky, and she knew that it wouldn't take too awful much to change that luck.

Especially when a guttersnipe like Naomi White waited in the wings to take her place.

"Hey, Bill...?" She caught herself sweetening her accent, softening her voice, because she knew all too well how Bill Varney felt about women. He liked them quiet, stupid, and obedient, and woe be unto any smart-mouthed bitch who tried to stand up to him. Jolene had felt the backside of his hand many a time. Bill simply would not abide a mouthy woman.

Bill turned around, hands stuffed into the pockets of a corduroy jacket that was at least two sizes too small for his huge belly. His face puckered with irritated distaste when he saw her. "What do you want, Jolene?"

Jolene smiled and lowered her head, keeping her eyes downcast. She knew how to play him now: be polite and sweet and maybe let him take her back to his trailer for an hour or two. She'd been with him before, back when all the men were deciding what woman they wanted, and knew exactly what she needed to do to get her way.

"Bill...I was just wonderin' if maybe I could go with y'all..." She shyly glanced up at him. "On the Sav-Mart run."

Bill snorted. "Hell, no."

She knew he was going to say that. "Well, okay...but Jimmy Ray's not feelin' real good and he said if I wanted I could go and take his place and—"

"And since when is Jimmy Ray Baisden the boss of this place?" Bill glared at Jolene, his jowls wobbling as his cheeks darkened. She'd never seen him look so mad before, not even the time she'd mouthed off to his wife about how bad he was in bed. "Lord God almighty," he muttered. "I swear I ought to just feed some of you to the zombies and be done with you."

"I'm sorry, Bill..." Jolene took a chance and moved closer to him, being sure to push out her chest and keep her expression as sorrowful as possible. "I didn't mean to get you all upset..."

Bill didn't say anything, but Jolene could read the look in his eye. He wanted to see how far she'd go to try to get her way. She'd expected that, too.

"Well...hell..." He hawked up a gob of phlegm and spat into the dirt. "I don't like the position you're puttin' me in, Jolene. You know I ain't able to spare nobody on one of these runs."

"I know, Bill..."

Bill stared at her for a minute, narrow eyes squinting even more as he sized her up. "You show up in the morning with Jimmy Ray's shotgun and all the ammo you can carry. And I want you to know that I won't hesitate to put a round between your eyes if you so much as get scratched by one of 'em fuckers. You got me?"

Jolene smiled. "I got you."

Bill nodded, then grabbed hold of Jolene's butt, never changing expressions as he glared off into the distance. "Now get your ass up to my trailer so we can work out the rest of the deal."

Jolene's smile faltered, but she managed to catch herself before the disgust showed. "Sure thing, Bill..."

He gave her another squeeze, then walked away, not even bothering to look at her again. But that was to be expected. That was the way things were now.

Jolene went to his trailer and waited.

***

A half-hour later, it was mercifully over. A hundred extra pounds and a gut full of stale beer made Bill less than a stallion, and he'd taken out his frustration on her with his fists. The beating wasn't any worse than she'd experienced at the hands of Jimmy Ray—or even her daddy, for that matter—so she'd closed her eyes and waited for him to tire himself out. Luckily, a couple of jabs to her belly and an open-handed slap to her cheek were all Bill could muster.

At least this time the bruises wouldn't show.

Jolene took her time as she walked back to her trailer, enjoying the feel of the cold air on her burning skin. The scent of smoke from the bonfire still hung heavy in the air. She tried to tell herself that all she smelled was burning leaves, tried not to think about the other things that had been thrown onto the bonfire.

But it was there. The smell of roasting flesh, the smell that was so like the scent of baked ham that it could almost make your mouth water if you didn't know what you were smelling.

The thought, as well as the memory of Bill's fumbling, violent hands on her body, made Jolene's stomach lurch. She doubled over at the corner of her trailer, bracing herself with one hand against the rusted metal, gagging up nothing but phlegm as she gave in to the nausea. She stood like that for a few moments, her head hanging low, gulping in foul-tasting air as she fought to settle her raging stomach.

And that's when she noticed that the trailer was rocking. Not much, just a little. Just enough.

And she heard the sound of Jimmy Ray doing what Jimmy Ray only thought he did best.

Jolene went cold. Not because of what Jimmy Ray was doing, but because of what that now meant. She had been deposed as his woman. Her tenuous power was now struck down completely. Because he had taken up with someone else—most likely that Naomi bitch—Jolene was now at the mercy of the rest of the trailer court. She no longer had a man to protect her.

But that didn't mean she had to let them know how much the thought of being alone terrified her. They'd be on her like a pack of rabid dogs if they had any idea how vulnerable she was.

Jolene spat into the dirt once more, clearing her mouth of the last of the bile-flavored phlegm, and marched into the trailer, slamming the door behind her, stomping through the hallway to the bedroom. Jimmy Ray jumped a foot when she pushed through the bedroom door, and Naomi let out a surprised scream, but Jolene didn't even look at them. She grabbed a battered knapsack that had once belonged to her brother and started shoving her things into it, so blinded by rage and fear that she barely knew what she was picking up.

Jimmy Ray and Naomi made gobbling sounds of indignation that Jolene completely ignored. She stuffed blouses, jeans, underwear, socks into the bag, leaving the dresser drawers open, rattling hangers in the closet. What she couldn't fit in the bag she just clutched close in her arms.

And when she was through, she walked right out of the bedroom without even a glance at Jimmy Ray. Naomi, holding the threadbare blanket up to her scrawny chest, gaped at Jolene with wide eyes, as if she expected her to explode.

Jolene just kept walking. There was nothing left for her here.

***

One of the trailers on the outer perimeter was empty, so Jolene dumped her stuff in there. It'd be good enough for a few days, until she could sweet talk her way into the bed of one of the men. A few of them had taken to keeping several 'wives', so it wouldn't take long for Jolene to move in on one of them. She saw the way they looked at her, the way they watched her when she was with Jimmy Ray.

And even though she wasn't crazy about the thought of some new goon taking up where Jimmy Ray left off, she'd resigned herself to it. That was just the way things were now. The way they had to be.

The trailer was fairly secure, so she wasn't afraid to be there alone. Hell, it'd been so long since she'd actually been by herself that the feeling was almost intoxicating. No picking up Jimmy Ray's shit-streaked underwear. No cooking only the foods he liked. No jumping up to do as he commanded every time he wanted a beer or a quick roll in bed.

She didn't know what to do with herself.

Whoever had owned the trailer before the dead folks rose up had taken pretty good care of the place—hell, compared to Jimmy Ray's trailer, this was a palace. The furniture was dusty but nice, and the bed was king-sized. The first thing Jolene did—after checking the strength of the boards on the windows and making sure that the door was double-locked and dead-bolted—was rummage around the linen closet for clean sheets. Then she made up the bed, crawling into it fully-clothed, sprawling with her arms and legs spread to take up every inch of room, wallowing in the fact that she could have the whole bed to herself instead of the sliver on the edge that Jimmy Ray had always allowed her.

It felt so good to be alone that for a few moments, she forgot about the fact that dead people walked around just outside their trailer camp. She forgot about the fact that now that she didn't have a man to protect her, she'd be at the whim of every guy in the camp. She forgot about all that as she drifted into a sound, dreamless sleep.

Because it felt good to be by herself. Better than she'd ever imagined it might feel.

***

"Okay, people…here's how it's gonna go." Bill slung his shotgun over his shoulder as he looked out at the group. He met Jolene's stare for a half-second before his gaze slithered away. "Stay in a group once we get out of the van. Keep your ammo close. No safeties on the guns. I don't want a bunch of them assholes coming at us and catching us with empty chambers. You watch everybody else's back and they'll watch yours."

In the pre-dawn chill, Jolene shivered even though she wore two sweaters beneath an old camo jacket she'd found in her new trailer. In a sling over her shoulder, the shotgun that Bill had given her felt unusually heavy, and the bag of shells hanging at her waist seemed to weigh a hundred pounds. She just hoped she'd be able to run if it came to that.

"Like I said," Bill continued, "we're gonna get out of the van and form a circle, guns out. Shoot any fucker that gets close. Once we get into the store, we separate into two groups of three. Everybody knows their partners, and you know what area of the store to hit. Follow your lists and don't get anything that ain't on it. I want one person to gather the goods while the other two watch their back…"

Jolene's throat felt like it was closing up, her tongue thick and woolly in her mouth. Bill had led these Sav-Mart runs a half-dozen times and had only lost a couple of guys, but all of a sudden she didn't trust his so-called leadership. She had no real reason to feel that way, but…she did.

"You got twenty minutes to get your shit and get out." Bill hitched his pants up and adjusted the wide buckle of his belt beneath the overhanging shelf of his stomach. "We meet at the front of the store. Unless a window blew in or a door got opened, there shouldn't be too many of 'em waiting for us inside. Everybody ready? Let's move out."

The four guys around Jolene ran to the van, acting like they were getting ready to go squirrel hunting for the weekend. She knew all of them: Buddy Vance, just barely out of his late teens but whose face was still swollen with yellow-headed pimples; Ray Howser, who went to junior high with Jimmy Ray and always tried to touch Jolene when nobody was watching; Ned Gordon, Gerdie's husband and a world-class asshole alcoholic; and old Carl Yancy, one of Jolene's daddy's best friends and a lecher through and through. Why anyone trusted these four, along with Bill, to bring back supplies for the camp was beyond her. She was amazed they managed to get through a raid without shooting themselves.

Jolene glanced back to the camp, to the women who watched her with narrow eyes, and knew what their opinion of her was. She was getting too uppity, daring to think that she could hold her own with the men. That kind of thing just wasn't done anymore. For a second, she wanted to go to Bill and tell him to just nevermind, that she didn't want to go after all.

But that wasn't gonna happen. She'd put up with too much shit from Jimmy Ray and Bill and Gerdie and every other jerkwad in the camp for way too long. Getting to go on the raid wasn't much, but damn if it wasn't more than she'd had. And now that she was on her own, she needed to prove that she could take care of herself. It might make a big difference in how she was treated when they returned.

Jolene climbed into the van and laid her shotgun across her knees, closing her eyes for a second as the side door slammed shut. She hadn't been out of the camp since the day the dead folk started coming back, and she didn't know what to expect once the trailers were moved and they went back to the outside world again.

If the world was still there.

***

They hit the first pocket of dead folk about a mile outside the camp, just as the sun was beginning to make its way over the mountaintops. There were about ten of them, all dirty and grungy and half-naked, shuffling down the middle of the highway, doing that stupid deadhead walk that made them look almost comical. The sight of them both thrilled and frightened Jolene. It was her first conflict. Her first test. She gripped the shotgun tightly, ready for the zombies to attack the van.

"You fellas ready for some action?" Bill shouted as he drove. All the guys around Jolene roared their approval. Jolene licked her lips and tried to calm down. She could shoot straight and run. That was all a person needed to know how to do.

They were almost on the zombies now. Soon they'd be swarming over the van, slamming filthy hands against the windows, pressing their open mouths to the glass as they tried to chew their way through. Then they'd have to fight and—

And Bill plowed through them like bowling pins. Never even slowed down.

As the men whoo-hooed and whistled, Jolene twisted in her seat and watched the decaying rubble of the zombies smack the pavement like wet confetti. They were much more fragile than she'd expected. She knew the ones Jimmy Ray brought home were fairly easy to mess with, but…but somehow she'd expected the zombies in the wild to be tougher. Smarter, maybe.

But they weren't. They were just dumb old bags of meat.

For the first time since deciding to make the Sav-Mart run, Jolene relaxed. Maybe this was gonna be easy.

***

"This is it, boys…" Bill weaved the van through the skeletons of abandoned cars, cresting the hill that overlooked the Sav-Mart. "Ain't seen this place in a while, have we?"

Buddy Vance grinned and spat a gob of chaw into a paper cup. "They got any porno up in there?"

"Naw, not here." Bill sounded almost disappointed. "Got beer though, and cigs." He looked into the rearview mirror and caught Jolene's gaze. "'Sides…what do we need porno for when we got us a prime piece sitting right here with us?"

Jolene felt her stomach drop and her bile rise all at the same time. She didn't much like the tone of Bill's voice, and she definitely didn't like the way the other fellas were looking at her now. It was like he'd flipped a switch in their heads.

She cradled the shotgun close and kept her mouth shut. Maybe he was joking. The man had no sense of humor, but…maybe he was just joking anyway.

"Old Jimmy Ray won't like anybody messing with his woman," Roy said. Roy had blond hair and a billy-goat beard, and when he leaned in too close to Jolene she caught a whiff of rotted teeth and stale beer.

"She ain't Jimmy Ray's woman no more," Bill said as he drove into the Sav-Mart parking lot. "Ain't that right, sweetheart?"

Zombies were everywhere—crawling out of abandoned cars, stumbling through the parking lot aisles, throwing themselves against the closed glass doors of the store, but Jolene was only barely aware of them now, more afraid of the men around her than the monsters outside.

"Me and Jimmy Ray had us a little talk last night." Bill's piggish eyes met hers in the mirror again. "He's done with ol' Jolene. Said she was getting too mouthy, too smart-ass, so he went and got him some fresh meat. Said we could do whatever we wanted to do with this little lady."

Jolene saw the smile on Bill's face, the leers on the faces of the four men around her, and suddenly understood why Bill had allowed her to come along on the raid. Easier to take care of the problem. They could do whatever they wanted to her, then go back to the camp and say that she got herself killed because she was just a stupid woman who was out of her league. And nobody would care. Sorry ass bastards…

"Yep…real shame Jimmy Ray didn't feel like makin' it this morning," Bill said, backing the van up to the open doors. He pulled in at an angle, pinning a female zombie against the concrete wall and crushing her. The zombie flailed her arms, still baring her teeth and trying to scrabble her way free, but nobody was paying much attention to what was going on outside the van.

Jolene tasted metal, felt her spit flow until it flooded her mouth and gagged her.

"So this is how it's gonna go down," Bill said, smiling as he turned in his seat and stared at Jolene head on. "We are gonna march your skinny ass inside and find us a nice office with a good lock on the door. Then me and the boys are gonna do our thing and then, well…then the dead folk are gonna get whatever's left." Bill's smile turned even meaner. "But don't worry, Jolene. Somebody'll put a bullet 'tween those pretty little eyes before you come back. Promise."

Jolene could only stare at him. Her entire body felt hollow, icy. She felt the stares of the men around her, knew what they were thinking, what they were planning, and wondered how many shots she could get off before they overwhelmed her. Part of her couldn't begin to understand why they were doing this to her now. She knew these guys, had lived with them in the trailer park for years, had grown up with some of them. She looked them each in the eye, silently begging them to realize what they were doing.

And nothing changed.

"Come on," Bill said gruffly. "We're wastin' daylight. Let's go."

Before Jolene knew what was happening, Buddy was sliding open the van door, heedless of the rush of rotted arms that suddenly filled the van. The men easily held them off with well-placed shots, laughing as they nudged the zombies away with the barrels of their guns. As goat-bearded Roy grabbed her arm, Jolene felt one of the dead folk brush her free hand; she cried out at its touch—so cold and vaguely slimy—as she recoiled backwards, right into Roy's lap. He laughed in her face, blasting her with that dead meat smell, and Jolene could instantly imagine him on top of her, forcing himself in her…

In a panic, she launched herself off Roy and into the grasping mass of arms. She went into them without hesitation, turning off her mind as she raised the shotgun and blasted whatever stood in front of her. A zombie in a flannel shirt went down, followed by a woman with curlers in her hair and fuzzy slippers on her feet. The other zombies backed off, something like comprehension dawning in their glazed eyes.

She was only dimly aware of the men's cheated shouts from the van, only vaguely aware of the hungry moans of the zombies as they tried to catch up with her. Instead she sprinted across the parking lot, heading for the second set of doors that led into the supermarket area of the store. There were only a few zombies between her and those doors, and she'd damn sure rather have their dead hands on her than Roy's.

Bullets whined past her and she knew that the fellas weren't aiming for zombies. She zig-zagged through the dead folks, her heartbeat pounding in her ears, her breath ragged and almost painful. As she got closer to the second set of doors, she could see that vandals had broken through them, opening the place up to the zombies as well as themselves. Didn't matter. Inside the store there'd be places to hide.

Jolene squeezed through the broken glass, hoping there wouldn't be something waiting on the other side.

***

So far so good.

The place was so quiet she could hear the quiet buzz of flies, the soft scuff of zombie footsteps somewhere in the distance. Every few seconds one of them moaned and sent a shiver down her back. They sounded so damn hungry…

Jolene shifted the shotgun in her arms and edged along the wall, waiting for her eyes to adjust to the darkness. If a zombie came up on her now she'd be in a world of hurt; the place stank so bad she wouldn't even be able to smell one sneaking up on her. And that smell…so rank that Jolene had to clench her teeth and keep swallowing rapidly so she wouldn't puke all over the place. The zombies had risen during Sav-Mart's peak shopping hours, which meant that half-chewed carcasses had been left to rot in the aisles. The ones that hadn't been too badly mauled rose up again, of course…but there was still plenty enough left to raise a stink.

The darkness grayed until she could finally make out faint shapes. To her right was the abandoned deli counter. To her left, the shopping buggy area. Nothing seemed to be moving in her immediate vicinity, although she could hear the faint shouts of the guys. They'd be inside the store in just a few minutes.

She moved slowly, feeling ahead of her with each step. If she remembered the layout of the store, she could keep to the right and get to an exit. Maybe she could find an office to hide in for a while. Grab some canned food and a couple of bottles of water, hole up in a locked room, wait this whole thing out. Those idiots were more than likely to give up looking for her after a while anyway. They'd go back to the trailer park and she would…

She'd what? Where'd she have to go now? Jimmy Ray had sold her out to those yahoos, so he obviously didn't want her back…not that there was much to go back to, anyway. Problem was, she didn't have much in the way of ammo, so she couldn't stay on the run indefinitely. Her only hope was to stay in one piece long enough to find some more survivors—bikers, maybe—and get herself another man to take care of her. Then she'd be okay.

She just had to get through this first.

Glass shattered from the front of the store, and Jolene knew that Bill and his lapdogs had lost their patience with the game. They'd ruined the place—now it would be picked clean by any survivors wandering through—but there wasn't much left in the way of supplies, anyway. All the frozen food had long since gone over, and most of the canned stuff was gone. Jolene passed the bread section and caught a whiff of the green scent of mold.

Just keep on going, she told herself, scanning all around her as she kept her back to the wall. Keep on going.

Something moved to her left and she automatically pulled the shotgun up, drawing a bead before she could even identify her target.

A little girl stumbled over the hem of her nightgown, her eyes glowing like a cat's in the dimness of the store. Most of the flesh from the girl's throat was gone, so her head bobbed from side to side, front to back, as she walked, her little mouth opening and closing, her little teeth snapping together like a steel trap.

For a moment Jolene couldn't move. She'd never seen a zombie kid before. Until this moment, she hadn't even given much thought to dead kids. In the back of her mind, she guessed she'd somehow thought they were exempt from this whole nightmare. Bad stuff couldn't happen to little kids.

But it did. And it had.

The little girl dragged a blood-splattered teddy bear, her fingers tangled in its ratty bow tie. Her nightgown had Raggedy Ann's face on it.

And she had no throat. The kid had no fucking throat.

Jolene didn't dare fire, even if she could have made herself pull the trigger. Despite everything, she knew she couldn't shoot a kid. Even if the kid was already dead.

Jolene kept moving, keeping an eye on the girl, hoping she'd just lose interest in her. As she inched deeper into the store, she saw more of the zombies stumbling around, each of them lost in their own misery. So far none of them had caught her scent yet...except for the little girl. The smell of all the rotting meat disguised Jolene's own sweaty stink--which was a small blessing she supposed. At least it bought her a little more time.

Gunshots blasted through the store and Jolene froze for a moment, tearing her attention away from the dead girl as she desperately tried to get an idea of where Bill and his guys were. They'd seen her come in through the second set of doors, which meant they probably had a pretty good sense of just about where'd she'd be. She could hear them shouting to each other, laughing as gunfire echoed. They were stirring up the zombies, agitating them into louder moans. The dead folk were coming out of hiding now, appearing almost from nowhere as they stepped out of darkened aisles and rose up from pools of shadows.

Any second now they'd sense her. Then there wouldn't be enough time to do anything but die.

"Jolene!" Bill's shout cut the silence, sounding closer than Jolene liked. "You'd best get your ass out here right now, girl. Ain't nobody playin' with ya now."

The zombies turned toward his voice like flowers turning to the sun. They knew the sound of fresh meat when they heard it.

Except for the little girl. She kept her eyes on the prize, staring at Jolene as she continued to stumble closer.

Jolene started moving again, shuffling sideways as quietly and quickly as she could manage. Sweat burned her eyes, rolled down her sides and back. There was a backroom here somewhere…a loading dock or something. She remembered it was right in the middle of the meat department.

She peered ahead in the gloom, looking for the opening. She saw a wide doorway between the freezers. Two male zombies stood just in front of it, swaying gently. Waiting for her.

Behind her, the little girl gained a few more feet. She was close enough now that Jolene could see straight through her throat to the dull whiteness of her spine.

Jolene slowly turned the shotgun in her hands, gripping the cool barrel with sweaty hands. If she fired, she'd bring Bill and the boys running. Best she could do was take a few swings and hope for a solid hit.

Heart stuttering, then pounding almost painfully, Jolene took a step closer to the little girl. Poor little thing…she looked so sweet…so young…

The girl lunged, all teeth and drool, and Jolene reacted without thinking, swinging the shotgun with all the strength she had. It connected wetly, sinking into the girl's rotted pumpkin of a skull, and the dark light instantly went out of her eyes.

She dropped in a heap, and Jolene nearly joined her. She couldn't do this. Even though the people were dead, even though they were trying to *eat* her, she couldn't do this.

But this was the world now. A world where you had to run and hide and forage and steal and kill if you wanted to survive. You were either dead or alive, and damned either way.

Tears threatened to blur Jolene's vision, but she forced them away. The noise Bill and the others were making was getting too close now. And the zombies were too animated, too alert.

Too hungry.

Jolene felt panic, cold and thick, rising up inside her as she stood helplessly over the body of the dead little girl. She didn't know what to do. There were too many zombies, too many of Bill's men. Either way she ran, she'd more than likely die.

She raised the shotgun. It'd be so easy to just fit that barrel against her forehead and pull the trigger and...

And what? Heaven? Hell? Nothing? Would death be worse than life?

With her luck, it would. Her luck had landed her in the middle of that damned trailer park hell. Her luck had brought Jimmy Ray and his pliers and tin snips and fists into her life. Her luck was shit, and she didn't trust it anymore.

Hell with it...

Jolene ran away from the meat department, away from the swinging doors that led to the offices, away from the sound of Bill's shouts. She kept the gun cocked and ready, held close to her chest as she silently moved through the corpse-strewn aisles. Bill would find the body of that little girl and know that she had put her down; Jolene just hoped that he assumed she'd gone for the obvious safety of the offices.

Her foot squelched into something slippery and she nearly lost her balance, slamming her hip painfully into the metal shelves as she caught herself. In the dimness she could see that she had made it into the sporting goods section—no food smells here, so there weren't as many zombies milling about. She leaned against the shelves for a minute, trying to keep her breathing as quiet and steady as she could, looking at everything except what had caused her to stumble. This area hadn't been as badly looted as the others, probably because it was so deep inside the store. And because there was nothing immediately useful to looters, like food or...

Jolene straightened up as she realized what she had found.

Leaning the shotgun against the shelves, she moved as fast as she could, grabbing a couple of backpacks, a sleeping bag roll, a lantern and oil, boxes of matches, a thick coil of nylon rope. She shoved a folded one-man tent into the backpack, as well as hunting knives and an industrial strength can opener. She took one of the bigger knives and slid it down the front of her jeans, shivering at the feel of the cold leather sheath. Then she pulled on one of the backpacks. It rested high on her back, pulling her shoulders straight, aching the base of her spine, but its weight felt good and comforting. Slinging the other heavy pack over one shoulder, she scooped up the shotgun and an empty backpack. As she made her way down the aisle, she grabbed a baseball bat: a heavy Louisville Slugger that swung like a dream.

Then she hit the aisles, tossing cans of Spam and beans and anything else she could find into the empty backpack. She was reaching for a dented can of tuna when a zombie snuck up behind her, revealing itself only by a hungry moan. Without a second thought, Jolene whirled around and slammed the bat into its skull, knocking the thing to the floor. The only sound was the crunchy crack of the wood against bone, not enough to draw attention.

Jolene smiled to herself. The bat was an excellent idea. Puts 'em down without wasting ammo, quick and quiet.

She finished filling the pack and slung it over her shoulder with the other. The weight slowed her down, but that was okay. Her idea would work. Had to work. And if it didn't, then it didn't matter just how damn heavy the pack was, anyway. All Jolene knew was that she wasn't going to rot away in the middle of goddam Sav-Mart while Bill and those pigs went back to the trailer park and whooped it up. And she wasn't going to sit around waiting for somebody to save her ass, either. For the first time in her life, she understood that there were no princes to carry you over the rainbow and into the happily ever after.

She'd have to carry her own damn ass. And she'd either do it or die trying. Simple as that.

"Jolene! You stupid bitch! Get your ass out here now, goddam it!"

Bill's voice was close enough to make Jolene drop to her haunches behind a display of dog food. She peeked over the edge of the bags and saw Bill moving just ahead of her, heading back to the front of the store. The other four men had split off, but Jolene had the feeling they weren't too far away. Probably closing in on her like a pack of wolves.

Jolene glanced at the baseball bat. She could do this. Easily.

Bill and the others had left the van parked close to the shattered glass doors, only a hundred or so yards from where Jolene stood. A few zombies staggered between her and the van, but their gait was so slow and jerky that she had no doubt she could get past them easily.

She could go now. She could run out those doors and disappear into the hills and Bill and Jimmy Ray would never be able to find her. There were lots of mountains to get lost in, lots of caves and abandoned houses where she could set up camp.

The bright sunlight of dawn poured in through the glass doors. She could go. She could run and go now and leave Bill in a world of shit.

But then she wouldn't have the small pleasure of seeing him die. And that one fact made a whole lot of chances worth taking.

Jolene moved before she could change her mind, zig-zagging through the zombies. One of them, an old woman, stepped right in Jolene's way. The woman's flat eyes glowed, her mouth toothless and gaping.

She went down with one swing of the bat.

Jolene shrugged out of the backpacks and left them leaning against the doors. Three zombies stood between her and the rest of the store. Three raggedy-ass, broke-down bags of bone. Easy. She made sure the shotgun was secure in its shoulder-sling, its weight deeply comforting against her back, and gripped the bat with both hands. Time to go.

One of the zombies, a guy who looked like he'd been a little too well-fed before all the shit came down, stumbled closer to her, his mouth open and drooling as he reached for her with greedy hands. Jolene waited until he was almost able to touch her…and then she swung the bat wide, catching him just above the shoulders and knocking his head almost completely off. It dangled upside down over his back, held fast by a few rotted tendons. Jolene pushed him away with the bat, cringing when her knuckles accidentally brushed against his body. The zombie fell onto its stomach and lay helpless on the floor, still reaching for her.

Jolene fought back a gag and took a shallow breath, calming her nerves before the second of the zombies staggered her way. This one had been a young girl, probably pretty once. Now her long blonde hair hung in tangled clumps, clotted with rusty dried blood, skinned completely away just over her right ear, where mottled gray-black brain matter peeked through. The girl's face had dried like tanned leather, lips peeled back to reveal braces on sharp yellow teeth. One eye was gone, deflated in its socket like a burst balloon.

They just kept getting worse. Jolene swung the bat again, splitting the girl's head with one blow. The girl dropped, and Jolene felt her stomach lurch, bile burning its way up her throat. She spat to clear her mouth, unable to allow herself the luxury of vomiting. The stench of the zombies seemed to get even stronger when they were put down. It reminded Jolene of when she was younger and she and her brother would kill stinkbugs, just to see if they'd smell worse after being squished.

The sudden memory stung. She and Robbie hadn't seen each other for years—not since she'd taken up with Jimmy Ray over her family's objections. The last time she saw Robbie they'd fought over her relationship with Jimmy. Then Robbie moved down to the southern part of the state with his wife and kids and that'd been the last she'd seen of him. It hadn't been a good way to part. Not a good way at all.

She hadn't thought of Robbie in a long time. She wondered if he was still alive…or if he'd turned into one of these things. Knowing Robbie, the way he'd never liked to fight, the way he always tried to reason his way out of a problem, she figured he'd probably died when the first wave of zombies rose up. He probably wouldn't have wanted to believe it was happening until one of the things actually got him.

She just hoped that he wasn't walking around out there somewhere. That would be too much to bear.

The third zombie—an old man with wire-rimmed glasses hanging from what remained of his ears—shuffled towards her with his hands outstretched. It wasn't until after Jolene had swung the bat and put him down that she realized she was weeping.

She allowed herself a moment, swiping at her eyes with the collar of her blouse, wiping the snot from her nose with the back of her hand, forcing herself to take deep breaths and delay the tears for later. And for just an instant, she was struck by how truly ridiculous everything suddenly seemed. There she was, standing in the middle of Sav-Mart with a bloody baseball bat in her hand and dead people walking around, crying her eyes out.

If she had laughed just then, she would have lost her mind.

A burst of gunfire startled her. Closer now. Bill and the guys were making their way back to the front of the store. She figured he planned on leaving her there, dead or alive. She didn't have much longer.

She slipped deeper into the store, following the sound of their footsteps as they crashed through displays. She was in front of them; they'd have to get past her now to get to the doors.

No use in making it easy for them.

Jolene looked around, hackles rising as Bill's footsteps got closer and closer. It would've been nice to have been in the gun aisle, or even close to the propane camping ovens, but no…her shitty luck had held out and she was smack in the middle of the baking aisle. Nothing but flour and cake mixes and oil…

Jolene suddenly smiled. Now here was an idea…

She grabbed an armful of the plastic bottles of cooking oil and began twisting the caps off, watching for Bill to appear at any moment. She squirted oil down the aisle, upturning the bottles right down the middle as she side-stepped to the other end, leaving herself a narrow path along the shelves. Her heart was beating so hard, so fast, that she thought she might black out.

But it was time to finish this goddam mess. Finish it and go home…wherever that would be.

She took a deep breath, closed her eyes for a moment, and began screaming.

The zombies reacted instantly, their moans intensifying as they honed in on her location. Jolene's muscles tensed as she watched them creep closer in the dimness, their arms reaching, fingers twitching to touch her. She screamed again, barely able now to squelch her growing panic.

Slowly, forcing herself to remain calm, Jolene began to inch her way back up the aisle, careful to keep her footing steady as she followed her narrow path. She moved sideways, swinging her gaze from one end of the aisle to the other. Damn it, Bill! Where the hell are you?

"Bill!" she screamed, trying to put the proper amount of cowed fear in her voice. "Help me! Please! I'll do anything you want...just don't let them get me!"

It wasn't Bill who showed up. It was goat-bearded Roy.

Good enough.

"Get over here, you stupid bitch!" Roy motioned with his gun, hands trembling as he stared wide-eyed at the group of zombies amassing at the other end of the aisle. A few of them had ventured closer, sliding ungracefully on the oil and collapsing into messy heaps. There were maybe twenty of them now.

"I can't, Roy!" Jolene sobbed, flattening herself against the shelves as she covered her face and pretended to cry. "I'm too scared!"

"Jesus Christ..." he muttered. "Bill is gonna beat your ass, you know."

Jolene kept faking her tears. She knew that Roy was much weaker-willed than Bill, that he wouldn't be able to just leave her there. She also knew that he was afraid of coming after her because the zombies on the other end of the aisle were just too damn close.

She peeked through her fingers and saw him looking nervously over his shoulder for Bill, unsure of what to do. If he didn't do something quick, it wouldn't matter anyway. The zombies were slowly picking their way down the aisle, sliding on the oil, but holding onto the shelves for balance. Bastards learned quick.

"Roy!" she screamed. "Please!"

"Aw, godamn it!" Roy shook his head, stamped his foot, and made his decision.

About five strides into his run, he hit the oil.

And kept right on going.

As he whizzed past her, Jolene could see an almost comical look of confusion on his face as he slipped and slid down the aisle. The confusion cleared up real quick when he saw the wall of dead folk waiting for him at the end of the aisle. That's when he started screaming.

He plowed into them like a bowling ball. And they were on him in a heartbeat. Jolene stuck around long enough to see one of the zombies wrench away a chunk of Roy's throat in its teeth, and then she tip-toed down to the other end of the aisle, careful not to slip or make a sound. Roy's garbled screams faded into bubbly gurgles, and then to thick silence. After that, there was nothing but the wet sounds of feeding.

Jolene barely noticed. By her count, she still had four more assholes to take care of...with one particular asshole topping the list.

But first...since she had a little time...

She slowly made her way to the hardware department, avoiding the lone zombie here and there. Most of them were attracted to the sounds of feeding coming from the baking aisle, drawn by the scent of Roy's blood. She couldn't hear where Bill and the others were—and she didn't know if that was a good thing or a bad thing.

Then she was in the relatively unlooted hardware department, surrounded by lamps and lightbulbs and hammers and nails and all sorts of lovely little bits of metal. Years of watching Jimmy Ray's favorite action movies had taught her a few tricks, but until now, she'd never thought she'd have any use for them.

She just hoped she had enough time.

Moving quickly, she shrugged out of her jacket and pulled off one of her sweaters, tying the arms together to make a makeshift bag. She grabbed handfuls of nuts and bolts and nails from the open bins, dropping them into the sweater even as she looked ahead for the next thing on her mental shopping list. She didn't know exactly what she was making until she saw the canisters of kerosene.

Jolene smiled despite herself. That could work.

She grabbed three canisters of kerosene and a roll of black electrical tape, keeping one eye on the end of the aisle and both ears open for the sound of scuffling footsteps. Using her teeth to rip off a couple of lengths of tape, she shoved the canisters into her sweater, wrapping the tape around it until she was sure that nothing would spill out.

Oh, yeah…that could work.

She shrugged back into her coat, slipping the shotgun back across her shoulders, and gathered up the sweater-bomb and the baseball bat. She scanned the aisle, looking for something, anything, else that might get her out of here in one piece. Somewhere to her right, she could hear Bill yelling for Ned. He sounded close, but not too close. She still had a little time…but only a little.

Her gaze caught on a length of chain used for chandeliers, curled up in its bin like a silver-skinned snake. The sight triggered a memory of one of Jimmy Ray's zombie round-ups; he and some of the other men had used a chain like a whip on a female zombie, laughing every time it wrapped around her arms or legs, cackling like hyenas when the end of the chain—wrapped around a baseball, with nails and knife blades and other sharp things sticking out of it—hit her squarely in the throat and nearly took her head off. It was a nasty weapon, and it had done its job all too well.

Jolene grabbed the chain, doubling the end of it into a loop. She ran to the other side of the aisle, to the selection of padlocks, and grabbed an armful. She quickly opened them, glancing around every few seconds, sensing that her time was running out. Fumbling with the tiny keys, she unlocked each padlock until she had twenty of them open. She used one to fasten the loop of chain, then—after a quick search of the shelves—opened five larger padlocks. Those she attached all along the loop, every ten links or so. And to those larger locks, she added the smaller locks.

Jolene stood and gave the chain a swing. Not too heavy, but she wouldn't want to be on the other end of it.

With a smile that was little more than a baring of her teeth, Jolene grabbed a few more lengths of chain and a couple of extra padlocks.

Time to get this over with.

***

She heard Ned before she saw him.

Not known for his gentlemanly manners, Ned was notorious around the camp for blasting the most ferociously eye-watering farts known to mankind. His stomach couldn't handle anything but the blandest foods—which was fortunate for him, given their diet of canned food and boiled water—but whenever he was stressed, his bowels would make their unhappiness known in loud and fragrant ways.

And he was tooting the old butt-trumpet in grand style now.

Jolene edged around an aisle, peeking around a display of spider-webbed pocketbooks, and saw Ned at the jewelry counter, filling a white plastic Sav-Mart bag with gaudy fake diamond rings and sparkly necklaces. What he would need a bag of cheap costume jewelry for was beyond Jolene's guess; she figured he thought that if he had a few trinkets to spread around to the younger women, he might have a better chance of getting some non-Gerdie nookie. At five-four and about three hundred pounds, he needed all the help he could get.

Ned looked around anxiously, and Jolene had the feeling that he was more nervous about being caught by Bill than by the zombies. There were a few of them wandering in the nearby toy aisles. One zombie, a young boy, was particularly fascinated by a rack of stuffed animals. Even with his throat torn out and one arm wrenched out of his socket, it was easy to see that once upon a time the boy had been a cute kid.

Jolene looked away. No time to think about stuff like that. Not now, not ever.

Ned kept his head down, greedy as he scooped armfuls of jewelry into the bag, blissfully unaware of Jolene's presence as she silently stepped up behind him. She held the chain tightly, hands cramping as she squeezed the links. All she had to do was swing the chain. That's all. Ned was just as bad as the others. She'd been on the receiving end of his anger more than once, and God only knew what he did to Gerdie when they were alone.

Ned stiffened slightly and Jolene froze, sure that she'd been caught. Instead, Ned grunted with the force of another eye-watering fart, chuckled to himself, and went back to work.

Jolene hesitated only a moment.

"Ned," she said softly.

He half-turned, still bent over the glass case, and she swung the chain. All twenty-five padlocks found their target and Ned's nose exploded in a spray of blood as chips of yellow-black teeth flew through the air. He didn't scream; he just kept making a thick whuffing sound as he tried desperately to understand what had just happened to his face. His eyes, starkly white against the mask of blood, met Jolene's and silently begged for mercy.

Jolene swung the chain again, this time bringing it down across the back of his head, slamming him face-first into the glass jewelry case. He stopped moving.

She stepped closer to him, grimacing as she checked for a pulse, hoping that he was dead. Instead, there was a faint, thready heartbeat. Blood kept pulsing from his nose and mouth. Bastard didn't have the good sense to die…and Jolene was fast learning that she didn't have the stomach for killing living men.

Jolene took a deep breath and released it, nervously watching the area for approaching zombies. They'd be attracted by the rich stink of blood; it wouldn't take very long for a crowd to gather.

But she had to take care of Ned. She couldn't let him walk out of this place alive.

She quickly weighed her choices. She could keep slamming the locks into his head and crush his skull, but that would destroy his brain and keep him from coming back…and she dearly wanted these assholes to exist in a world of pain for as long as inhumanly possible. She could slit his throat, but she didn't think her queasy stomach could handle the sensation of actually sinking the knife blade into his flesh.

Shooting him was out of the question, because it would alert the others to her position…

She could hear the zombies shuffling closer, moaning hungrily. Not much time. She should just leave him there…

Jolene almost smiled. Good enough.

She quickly tugged Ned free of the display case, grimacing at the state of his face. Splinters of glass peppered his forehead and cheeks, even his eyelids. He was a big man, so getting him over to the support beam just beside the jewelry section was a backbreaking chore. But she managed, and she didn't bother to stand him up on his feet as she leaned him back against the beam. As he slumped there, breathing slowly but deeply, she wound the length of chain around his beer belly, under his arms, locking it around the back of the beam. Nothing fancy, but it would hold. Even when he came back from the dead and decided he was hungry.

Ned grunted, head snapping up as he opened his eyes and blearily focused on Jolene. "…the fuck…?" he muttered.

The first of the zombies stepped out of the aisles, a young, naked woman with wild, frizzy hair and a grayish-blue tinge to her skin. Her breasts were gone, and her gashed stomach flapped open to reveal an empty hollow. She turned in the direction of Ned and Jolene and stumbled forward, teeth clicking together loudly as her mouth opened and closed hungrily.

More followed her. All of them were aware of Ned now, aware of the thick scent of his blood.

Ned, unable to look away from the group of zombies gathering, grabbed at Jolene's arm. "Jolene…don't do this…" His voice choked with tears, rising with panic. "Oh God…please don't…"

Jolene jerked her arm away from him, backing away slowly, glancing over her shoulder to make sure there were no nasty surprises creeping up behind her. The naked zombie got to Ned first, straddling his lap to go for the soft meat of his throat, ending his girlish scream in a wet gurgle.

Jolene finally turned around. That was all she needed to see.

***

The other two were surprisingly easy to find.

Jolene followed the sound of their voices into the toy area, moving very slowly, because she had a bad idea of what she would find when she found Buddy and Carl. She knew all too well what kind of activity would inspire their whispers and giggles. It was the kind of thing that was frowned upon at the camp, but only on the surface. Jolene knew for a fact that some of the guys made a practice of taking the prettier zombies, the ones who weren't too bloated with rot, and 'adjusting' them—knocking out their teeth, cutting off their fingers—until they were suitable sex toys. When the dead women began to fall apart, they were just thrown out of the circle of camp and left to the sun and wind.

So she knew what she would see when she finally found Buddy and Carl. They must have found themselves a pretty one.

Jolene slowed, hesitating at the end of an aisle, leaning against a display of yellow and orange waterguns. She held the sweater bomb loosely in the crook of her arm as she carefully unsheathed her shotgun.

"Damn it, Buddy…Bill ain't gonna let us bring one back with us!"

"He will if we do her teeth and hands here. Gimme the hammer. Hold her down."

A sickening crack, followed by the hollow sound of the zombie's moan. Jolene closed her eyes for a moment and willed her gorge to settle down. Do it quick, do it fast, and then get the hell out of this place. She didn't know how much more she could stand.

She stepped into the aisle, unnoticed by either man. As Buddy kneeled on the zombie girl's upstretched arms, Carl straddled her stomach, slamming the hammer into her teeth as he laughed at her struggles.

Jesus Christ, Jolene thought, stunned into inaction. Maybe we deserved this. If this is the best we can do...

Buddy noticed her first, sweat dripping off his pimply cheeks as he snapped his head up and met her eyes. Jolene could see the sudden, shocked guilt in them.

"Oh, shit...Carl!"

Carl, hunched over the girl, half-turned toward Jolene. His smile widened as he straightened up.

"Well, looky who joined the party..." Carl glanced over at Buddy. "Bill would definitely let us take *her* back with us."

Jolene thought of that hammer coming down on her mouth, thought of their dirty hands on her body, and tossed the sweater bomb into the middle of the aisle. It skidded and slid, coming to a rest right beside Carl's knee. Both men looked at it, then back to Jolene.

She already had the shotgun in her hands.

And one shot did the job.

Jolene ducked back behind the display of waterguns as the kerosene blew, catching a few bits of shrapnel in her back but ignoring the pain as she gloried in the screams of Carl and Buddy. That bomb was crotch level with both of them.

She peeked around the edge of the display. The toy aisle now looked as if a red paint bomb had exploded; blood dripped from the shelves, pooled on the floor, covered the three lumps of flesh lying in the middle of the aisle. Jolene eased into the aisle, needing to see, to know.

Both of them were still alive, but barely. Buddy's face had taken the brunt of the explosion; it looked like a pile of bloody ground beef with a neck. His breath rattled from the hole that had been his mouth. Jolene was pleased to note that his teeth had been broken and chipped by the flying metal.

Carl, still half-atop the zombie girl, had been wounded even more horribly than Buddy. Everything above his left knee was gone...crotch included. He clutched at the emptiness between his legs, hands sinking wrist deep into the bloody mess.

Jolene knew she had to hurry now, that the blast would bring Bill running, but she wanted to stay just a moment longer, to savor the moment even as it disgusted her. She had never thought she could be capable of doing this, never thought she would ever have to find out what her limits truly were.

But now she knew. For better or for worst, she knew.

God help her.

***

She ran back full throttle for the front doors, keeping her head low and shoulders hunched, just in case Bill was tracking her with his riflescope. She wanted to finish things near the front door, so she could make a quick get-away and—

Something slammed into her stomach, taking her breath away as she collapsed. Jolene rolled away, scrambling for footing, half-expecting to feel teeth sinking into her flesh at any moment.

Instead, she saw Bill standing over her, a smirk on his face and his rifle in his hands. He'd used it as a club. Apparently he'd learned the same lesson that she'd learned: don't waste ammo.

And from the look on his face, Jolene had the feeling that he wanted to keep her alive a little longer.

"Bitch..." Bill kicked at her, catching her in mid-thigh. Jolene clenched her jaw and jerked away, tightening her grip on the baseball bat. Bill noticed. "Naw...don't even think about it..."

He lifted one foot and slowly lowered it onto her hand, grinding. Jolene released the bat.

"Now...get your ass on up."

Jolene slowly rose, cradling her hand to her chest. So far most of the zombies were occupied with the Ned buffet over in the jewelry department, but she knew that distraction wouldn't last for long. Not when there was fresh meat to be had.

Bill grinned at her, and Jolene could see that whatever he'd called humanity was now totally gone.

"I hate an uppity bitch," he said with a smile, grabbing a handful of her hair before she could even react. He yanked her close to him, her face right up to his. The stink of his breath—a combination of rotting teeth and stale beer—made her gag. "You messed up bigtime, girlie."

Jolene gritted her teeth and forced herself to keep her eyes on Bill's. The zombies were beginning to take notice of them now, pulling away from the cooling bodies of the others in search of a warmer meal. She could hear them moving around in the darkness, scuttling like roaches.

"I'm gonna do you slow," Bill whispered, pulling Jolene so close that his lips brushed her cheek. She flinched away but he held her tightly. "I'm gonna leave you out here for these fuckers, and then I'm gonna watch them tear your ass apart."

Jolene's hand slid to her stomach, beneath her blouse. The handle of the hunting knife felt warm beneath her palm.

"And then you're gonna come back," Bill said, his voice rising slightly, growing almost hysterical. "And I'm gonna let you."

It would be so easy to slide the knife into Bill's fat gut. One quick movement, one quick jerk upward, and his guts would be on the floor and he'd be dead. Easy. But it'd be too easy. There were other ways.

Jolene slowly smiled.

And then she slashed.

The first swing of the hunting knife caught Bill's left thigh, high near the groin, slicing deeply into the artery. His eyes bugged almost comically with shock as the first gout of blood splashed out, steaming hot and stinking of copper. He released Jolene's hair and looked down at himself, taking a staggering step backwards, sending a fresh spray across the floor.

Jolene followed him and slashed again, the knife tearing across his belly, putting enough force behind the blow to cut deeply into his gut. Bill stared at his stomach, straightening up slightly as the first ropy curls of intestine began to slip out of his body. The stench of blood and bile seemed to thicken the air.

It drew the zombies like moths to a flame.

Bill collapsed to his knees, one hand feebly trying to hold his belly together, the other reaching out to Jolene, as if he actually expected her to do something. His eyes shone with horrible understanding. He knew what was happening. What was going to happen.

"Please..." he whispered. Fat tears rolled down his cheeks. His lower lip actually trembled. "Please, Jolene...don't leave me..."

The zombies were closer now, coming in from all sides. In less than a minute, there'd be too many to get through, even with the shotgun.

Bill wailed like a newborn.

Jolene moved swiftly behind Bill, grabbing him beneath his arms. She pulled at him, dragging him towards the front doors, trying not to notice that the gash in his belly widened and spurted out more gore with every step. A few of the zombies fell to the floor, lapping at the puddle of blood and bile Bill had left behind. The rest of them followed, shuffling along with renewed speed.

"I knew you wouldn't leave me..." Bill's voice rose, words slurring and running together as he rolled his head back to look up at Jolene. "I knew you wasn't gonna do it...don't have it in you...fuckin stupid bitch..."

Jolene said nothing, keeping her eyes on the advancing crowd, trying to keep an eye on the area behind her. The van's doors were open, just a few feet away. If she let go of Bill, she could make it...but then that would ruin everything.

She found a reserve of strength and manhandled him the last few feet to the van, dropping him heavily to the floor. She rooted through one of the backpacks, digging out the coil of rope, then threw the packs into the back of the van. Bill looked expectantly up at her, raising his arms like a child waiting to be lifted.

Jolene slammed the van doors.

Then she reached down to Bill's jeans, snagging the van keys off the cheap plastic keychain that hung from his beltstrap.

"You're riding on the outside, Billy-boy," she said and grinned, wrapping the rope beneath Bill's arms, looping it around his chest, hitching it with a tight knot. Too weak to argue, too stupid to understand, he just stared at her with glassy eyes.

Until she tied the other end of the rope to the rear fender. Then he got wise real quick.

"Don't..." he murmured. "Please..."

Jolene ignored him. She'd watched him and the other yahoos pull this trick a dozen times, sometimes using live people as their toys instead of the zombies. Jimmy Ray and the others had always gotten a big kick out of seeing what being dragged over asphalt and gravel could do to a human body.

"Don't worry about it, Bill," she said as she tightened the knots and glanced back into the store. The zombies were closer, their whines and moans drawing the attention of the dead folk in the parking lot. "By the time they get to you, you'll probably already be dead."

Jolene crouched down beside him, taking a precious extra moment to look into his eyes. "And when you come back—and Bill, you will come back—I'm gonna let you."

There was no remorse, no grief in Bill's eyes. Just that same, dumb hatred. That was all Jolene needed to see.

She jogged around to the driver's side of the van and clambered in, stowing her shotgun securely beside her as she started the engine. She revved it a few times, nice and loud, a dinner bell for all those hungry dead folk out there. In the seldom-used tape deck, she found an old Lynyrd Skynyrd cassette. She cranked it up as loud as she could stand, smiling as the twangy opening notes of "Freebird" filled the silence.

"Come and get it, fellas," she said, grinning as she slowly pulled away from the doors of Sav-Mart. Bill's screams cut through the music; she couldn't tell if they were caused by the zombies or by the movement of the van. Either way, she didn't give a particular shit.

Jolene glanced into the rearview mirror and smiled, seeing nothing but dead folk stumbling along behind her as she rolled slowly along. Looked like she had just enough gasoline left for one last visit to the trailer park.

She hoped Jimmy Ray didn't mind a few unexpected guests.

Jolene's story continues…
An excerpt from the upcoming novel
Blessed Are the Dead

She still heard their screams.

Sleeping came hard for Jolene, but when her body finally gave up and she was forced to fall into an exhausted doze, she could still hear the people at the trailer park screaming. She knew she was responsible for their deaths, and for everything that came after, but they'd deserved it. All of them. She knew their dirty little secrets. She knew who was diddling his little girl in the middle of the night and who was beating his wife half to death once a month and who was doing nasty things to the dead folk when they thought nobody was watching.

She'd watched from the van as the dead broke through the defenses. They'd flowed past her like she was a stone in the creek, flooding the park, taking down anyone in their way.

And it was her fault. She'd led them there.

She hadn't realized the extent of what she had done until it was all over and the final screams had finally faded away. From where she sat in the van, she could see silhouettes against the fire, bodies being torn to pieces, the freshly dead rising to join the others. The quiet was almost worse than the screaming, because it was the silence of the dead. It was the silence of the people she had known, had once considered friends.

She drove away, blind in the night, and didn't look back. She knew they would follow her.

***

Jolene spat out a mouthful of gas and quickly stuck the tube into the empty gas can, keeping her back to the van as she scanned the horizon. The Trans Am had gone into a ditch, both doors yawning wide open, keys still in the ignition. For a fast, stupid moment, she considered trading the van for the Trans Am. She'd wanted one ever since she learned how to drive.

But the windows were shattered, the seats were stained burgundy with dried blood, and the windshield was spiderwebbed with cracks from the impact of someone's head, judging from the blood splatter. No protection. No security.

No way in hell.

Movement caught her attention and she stiffened, turning towards a copse of trees a few hundred yards away from the Trans Am. Two of them stirred in the shadows of the trees, which meant that there were probably at least a dozen more in the vicinity. She had known they were there when she pulled over, but she had to take the risk. She was finding fewer cars along the road, and she didn't like the thought of running out of gas in the middle of nowhere.

Every nerve in her body twitched, every hair stood on end, but she forced herself to breath slowly, to move deliberately, to keep her eyes on the trees even as she withdrew the rubber tube and stuffed it into the pocket of her jacket. Wasted gas dribbled out of the Trans Am engine, but she knew the difference between taking a chance and being an idiot. It was time to get gone.

She kept her back against the van as she slid around the rear doors, slowly ticking her gaze across the trees. Three more of them stepped into the sunlight. She could smell them now. They were fairly fresh. Still wet. Most of the older dead had dried up into husks.

Jolene watched them shambling her way, trying to gauge how long it would take them to rush the van. One thing she had learned since being on the road was that those things could move fast when they wanted. They could come out of nowhere and before you knew what was happening, they had you surrounded. It had happened to her once, and she dreaded the next time she was caught so off guard.

She opened the driver's side door carefully, making as little sound as possible. The day was so still, so silent, that every noise seemed to boom and echo throughout the valley.

They heard it anyway. A few more of them came out of a ramshackle house across the road.

Jolene's stomach heaved but she managed to climb into the front seat and slam the door. No use being quiet now. They knew she was here. She didn't know if they could communicate with each other or not, but somehow they would know how to stalk her, how to attack.

She turned the key in the ignition, whispering a prayer as the engine rumbled and turned over.

And as she drove away, she watched them in the rearview mirror, stumbling along the middle of the road, following her.

***

Nights were the worst.

The hills of West Virginia used to be scary enough back when things were normal, back when you could drive along dark dirt roads and at least see electric lights in the houses you passed. Now that everything had changed, the nights were long and dark and terrible. Jolene used that time to drive, comforted by the illumination of her headlights. She slept—when she could force herself to sleep—in the middle of the day. She knew in the back of her mind that she could be overpowered just as quickly in the daytime as the night, but she couldn't make herself park at night and close her eyes. Not when there were so many shadows moving in the darkness.

Ever since leaving the trailer park, she'd stayed on the road, driving blindly up and down the hollows and back roads. She didn't expect to find anyone alive, and part of her wasn't even sure she wanted to find any survivors. What if they turned out to be just as bad as the bunch she'd escaped?

But company would be nice. Especially at night.

So she drove, slowly inching her way mile by mile, watching for glimpses of lantern lights or fires. She usually saw nothing but the dead things aimlessly moving along the roads. Always walking. Always searching for life, just as she was. Sometimes she wondered if she had become one of them while she'd been sleeping, if she were just as dead inside.

Jolene usually forced herself to stop thinking about stuff like that. She knew she had Bill's pistol under the driver's seat, and that she'd used all the ammo for it but one bullet that still sat chambered in the barrel. That one was hers, saved for the day when she either couldn't take another minute, or the choice was taken away from her by those things. One bite, one overwhelming attack, and the barrel of that gun would fit just perfect in her mouth. Angle it upward, make sure she hit the brain, and everything would be over.

Some days she was more than ready for it to be over. But then she'd feel a flutter in her belly, a reminder of Jimmy Ray's last night with her, and she knew she'd be sticking around a little longer.

Now that she was going to be somebody's momma, she had no choice.

Jolene's eyes burned as she stared at the twin cones of light stretching in front of the van. She figured it to be close to three in the morning. Still too long before dawn. She hadn't seen any of the dead for the last few hours, so she guessed most of them had moved on or fallen apart. In the three months since the day at Sav-Mart, she'd seen bodies that were little more than scraps of meat on skeletons, still moving, still walking, as long as the tendons and muscles held together.

A few miles back she'd seen a sign for the End Times Church—exactly the kind of place she would have been scared to death of before the dead rose. Her mother had dragged her to churches like that, where the only thing they loved more than talking about all the horrible and bloody ways the world was going to end was just how much all the terrible sinners would suffer in the pits of hellfire.

Momma had believed it all, and she made sure to send Jolene up for every altar call to save her wayward daughter's soul.

Jolene let them baptize her, let them pray over her, let them put their hands on her head to drive out the demons that were making her such a rotten daughter, but she never believed any of it. She always figured she was going through enough hell on earth with Momma and whatever boyfriend she was sleeping with for that week. Between Momma's drinking and the men's drunken pawing of her when she tried to sleep, she didn't believe in much of anything the church had to say.

But now a church meant the possibility of people, and people meant that she might find some decent food for the baby, or get a good night's sleep for once. And finding people meant that six months down the road, she might not have to deliver her baby alone in the back of that filthy van.

So she'd turned the van in the direction of the church signs and prayed, even though she wasn't sure anyone was listening.

She passed a few hand-lettered signs, urging people to come to the special revival that would deal with what the church was calling the "Days of Lazarus." The date of the revival was back when the dead first rose, when nobody knew that shooting them in the head would put them down permanently and that a bite from one of them was a guaranteed death sentence.

Jolene turned off the paved road, still following the signs, and maneuvered the van along a dirt path. There were no lights in the part of the hollow, and the hills came right down to the edges of the road. The trees were thick, in full bloom of summer, and canopied overhead, blocking out the faint moonlight. Jolene had the uncomfortable feeling of driving into a giant's stomach. Like Jonah and the whale.

But she couldn't turn around and get out. Not yet, anyway. She had to drive all the way to the church and hope they had a parking lot. And hope that her stupid decision wasn't the one that would get her killed. She had to watch herself closely now. She wanted to find someone so badly that it was starting to affect her better thinking. She couldn't afford to make such dumb mistakes.

Jolene kept one hand on the wheel and touched her gently rounded belly with the other. Hard enough to keep herself alive. She didn't know what she would do now.

The dead folk began to come out of the woods, attracted by the sound of the van's engine. One of them was a skinny older man who still wore a mean look, even though half of his face was torn away. A woman, not much younger than the man, followed in his footsteps. Her throat was gone. Two younger girls walked behind her. They'd been pretty once.

Jolene wondered if they had been a family once, if that was what kept them wandering the earth together, even after death.

They had watched her rumble by in the van, their flat eyes glowing like cat's pupils. They made no attempt to even reach for her.

Jolene saw the silhouette of a shack further up on the hill, the kind of ramshackle old place that looked like it would blow down in a hard wind. She knew by looking at it that there would be no running water inside, that there was an outhouse in the backyard and no electricity. Sheets still hung in the side yard, ghostly pale in the dark. It was the kind of house she'd grown up in, before Momma moved to the trailer park.

She was so distracted by the shack that she almost didn't see the dead girl walking along the middle of the road. Jolene stomped on her brakes, but the girl didn't react. She was covered with dirt and mud, blending into the shadows except for the white glow of her eyes. She didn't look up, didn't even notice the van. Her attention was focused on the thing she held in her arms.

Jolene didn't want to look. Didn't want to know.

But as the girl walked placidly by the driver's side of the van, Jolene could see what she was carrying so tenderly. Thank God she couldn't see if the baby was still moviing or not. She didn't think she could bear that.

Tears burned her eyes and she wiped at them with the hem of her shirt. She watched the girl walk into the red glow of the tail-lights and then disappear back into the darkness.

Jolene turned around at the End Times church, where the doors were open wide and the smell of rot was so strong that she caught a whiff of it even with the windows up. She hoped whoever had died in that church, whoever that family was that she'd passed on the road, had died still believing in a better life after this one.

She passed the family again on the way out as they made their way down to the main road. This time she didn't slow down.

***

The days were getting warmer. Sleeping in the van was nearly impossible now, so she cat-napped whenever she grew too exhausted to drive. She didn't dare open the windows, so she sweltered in the mid-day heat, dozing uncomfortably in the small bed she'd made of couch pillows she'd found in an abandoned house. When she did sleep, she had fever dreams of the last days in the trailer park. She'd wake up to the sound of screams in her head.

She passed the time by reading whatever books she could find, everything from romance novels to science fiction stories. She'd never been allowed to read before—Momma always thought she was trying to show off and make everybody else look bad, and Jimmy Ray believed she shouldn't be interested in anything but him. She had always loved reading, and now that she had nothing but time, she would spend hours poring over her books, keeping a dictionary close by in case she found a word she didn't know. There were a few times when she was so fascinated by a book that she hadn't even noticed dead folks gathering at the front of the van, peering in at her through the windshield.

She didn't let that happen very often. Since then, she'd gotten very good at keeping one eye on her book and one eye on her surroundings. If she attracted too much attention, she'd start driving again, until she'd left the dead far behind her.

Supplies were getting low, and she dreaded the day she'd have to start scrounging again. She felt like such a thief breaking into peoples' houses, taking whatever they'd left behind. It felt wrong.

The pictures were the worst. The photographs they left behind. The memories of their lives before the world ended. Jolene couldn't look at their smiles without imagining what they probably looked like now, with their teeth bared for entirely different reasons. At first, she had been fascinated with the different ways people had lived. The ways they decorated their houses. The things they valued and the trash they threw away.

That's when she felt most like a thief. She would walk into their homes and take whatever she wanted. Food, blankets, books, clothes. She'd try not to look at the photos, try not to imagine what had happened to create the puddles of blood drying sticky black on the floor.

It always seemed like such a shame, all those beautiful houses standing empty now. She'd dreamed of owning a little house of her own, a place where she could have a flower garden and a front porch and all the room she'd ever need. Her entire life, except for the years she and her Momma lived in the shack, was spent in the trailer parks, moving from one tin can to another, all of them blending together over the years. Jimmy Ray had always laughed at her when she talked about her little house.

Now she'd never have a home. Nobody had a home anymore.

Lunch was a can of Spam choked down with a few swallows of warm, flat Pepsi. She did a quick inventory of her food supplies as she ate. Five more cans of Spam. Three cans of mixed vegetables. A half dozen liter bottles of Coke and Pepsi. A few candy bars left over from a stop at an abandoned gas station, where she'd been caught off guard and had to waste a few precious bullets on a dead man with a gut full of maggots.

She knew it wasn't healthy enough for her now. She needed vitamins. Good food. Sleep. She needed to find a place to wait out the rest of the pregnancy, where she wouldn't have to worry about living from day to day, hand to mouth. She needed a doctor to keep an eye on the baby's development, and a nice, clean hospital room to have the baby in, and a nursery with a crib and a rocking chair and all the things she used to imagine she'd have if she ever had a baby.

Instead she had a van that smelled like canned meat, and pillows stolen from the homes of dead people, and a gun under the front seat that was the only bit of hope she had left.

She just couldn't understand where everybody was. Surely she wasn't the only person left alive. That just couldn't be.

She curled up on the pillows again, suddenly too tired to even try to read. She would sleep and then drive, and maybe she would find a few houses along the way. And maybe, just maybe, she would find someone alive in them for once.

...to be continued

Rebecca Brock—mild-mannered librarian by day, mild-mannered horror writer by night—has had stories included in *History Is Dead, Love, Damned Love, Decadence of the Dead, Brainchild: A Collection of Artifacts, Cold Flesh*, and *The Book of More Flesh*. She provided research for over a dozen DVD commentaries for Joe Bob Briggs, as well as Briggs's books *Profoundly Disturbing* and *Profoundly Erotic*. She's written book reviews for Bookgasm.com and contributes a regular column on writing to *Ology* magazine (www.ologymagazine.com). She's currently working on adding to her collection of rejection slips by writing more horror stories and novels, as well as the occasional script. Visit her futile attempt at being cool on MySpace at www.myspace.com/pb_writer and at www.thehorrorhack.com

www.ingramcontent.com/pod-product-compliance
Lightning Source LLC
Chambersburg PA
CBHW020831260626
47169CB00003B/926